'In this engaging and accessible book, Michael K. Glenday has painted a lively and vividly living portrait of F. Scott Fitzgerald as the gifted artist.' — **Stephanie Ann Smith**, *Professor of English, University of Florida, USA*

first novel, *This Side of Paradise*, which brought him a blaze ıful fame, to his last, unfinished novel, *The Last Tycoon*, Fitzgerald's appeal as one of America's most quintessential ıas continued to maintain its hold on twenty-first-century

eader-friendly study of Fitzgerald's major fiction, Michael day:

new readings of the author's canonical works, including *The Gatsby* and *Tender is the Night*

s on the very latest research in his reassessment of the ideas ignificance of Fitzgerald's major novels

res the core themes of the novels, as well as their consider contribution to the spirit and complexity of modern-day ican culture.

ng no prior knowledge, this book is ideal for those seeking a formed introduction to Fitzgerald's fiction, as well as those for fresh and original insights into his extraordinary work.

K. Glenday was appointed Research Affiliate in the ent of Literature at the Open University, UK, in 2005. He is g co-editor of the *F. Scott Fitzgerald Review* and his previous ns include *Saul Bellow and the Decline of Humanism, Norman* d the co-edited volume *American Mythologies: Essays on ary Literature.*

ALL

The University

Other books by the author

Saul Bellow and the Decline of Humanism

Norman Mailer

American Mythologies: Essays on Contemporary Literature (co-edited with William Blazek)

F. Scott Fitzgerald

Michael K. Glenday

palgrave
macmillan

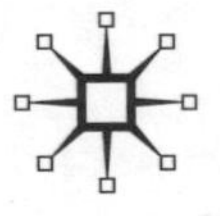

First published 2012 by
PALGRAVE MACMILLAN

Palgrave Macmillan in the UK is an imprint of Macmillan Publishers Limited, registered in England, company number 785998, of Houndmills, Basingstoke, Hampshire RG21 6XS.

Palgrave Macmillan in the US is a division of St Martin's Press LLC, 175 Fifth Avenue, New York, NY 10010.

Palgrave Macmillan is the global academic imprint of the above companies and has companies and representatives throughout the world.

Palgrave® and Macmillan® are registered trademarks in the United States, the United Kingdom, Europe and other countries.

ISBN 978–0–333–66899–3 hardback
ISBN 978–0–333–66900–6 paperback

This book is printed on paper suitable for recycling and made from fully managed and sustained forest sources. Logging, pulping and manufacturing processes are expected to conform to the environmental regulations of the country of origin.

A catalogue record for this book is available from the British Library.

A catalog record for this book is available from the Library of Congress.

10 9 8 7 6 5 4 3 2 1
21 20 19 18 17 16 15 14 13 12

Printed and bound in China

For Elina: rakkaani, kiitos, aina!

And for David my brother, with love always

'He was our darling, our genius, our fool . . . he was Gatsby, a greater Gatsby.' (Glenway Wescott on F. Scott Fitzgerald, 1941).

Contents

Acknowledgements

This book could not have been completed without the tolerance and understanding of Sonya Barker, Commissioning Editor at Palgrave Macmillan. For that support I will always be in debt. To Jenni Burnell, Felicity Noble and Juanita Bullough I am also very grateful.

I am grateful to the Open University, which allowed me a period of study leave to complete the book and provided a number of travel grants to present conference papers on F. Scott Fitzgerald.

Much appreciation is due to my colleagues on the Board of the *F. Scott Fitzgerald Review,* as well as to the wider community of scholars whose work in the field of Fitzgerald studies has been inspirational.

There are others who have given support over the years: Dr Hilda Spear, who first nourished my interest in Fitzgerald; Dr Angus Calder, my dear friend whose kindness and lively intellect were so uplifting; Dr William Blazek; Dr Steve Perrin; and the many students whose insights have enriched my experience of Scott Fitzgerald's work.

Many thanks for permissions are due to Craig Tenney and Phyllis Westberg at Harold Ober Associates.

Special thanks are due to Jackson R. Bryer, whose work as a Fitzgerald scholar has greatly assisted this study, as it has assuredly those of many others over the years. His timely mediation to support the publication of this book in the United States is very much appreciated.

Finally and most especially I am indebted to the estate of F. Scott Fitzgerald, and to Eleanor Lanahan, whose swift and sympathetic intervention ensured this book's publication in F. Scott Fitzgerald's homeland. For that I will always be grateful.

Part of Chapter 5 had its first publication in the essay collection *Twenty-First-Century Readings of* Tender is the Night (Liverpool: Liverpool University Press, 2007), edited by William Blazek and Laura Rattray.

The author and publishers wish to thank the following for permission to use copyright material:

Extracts from *THE GREAT GATSBY* reprinted with the permission of Scribner, a division of Simon & Schuster, Inc., from *THE GREAT*

GATSBY (Authorized Text) by F. Scott Fitzgerald. Copyright © 1925 by Charles Scribner's Sons. Copyright renewed © 1953 by Frances Scott Fitzgerald Lanahan. All rights reserved.

Extracts from *TENDER IS THE NIGHT* reprinted with the permission of Scribner, a division of Simon & Schuster, Inc., from *TENDER IS THE NIGHT* by F. Scott Fitzgerald. Copyright © 1933, 1934 by Charles Scribner's Sons. Copyright renewed © 1961, 1962 by Frances Scott Fitzgerald Lanahan. All rights reserved.

Extracts from *THE LAST TYCOON* reprinted with the permission of Scribner, a division of Simon & Schuster, Inc., from *THE LAST TYCOON* by F. Scott Fitzgerald. Copyright © 1941 by Charles Scribner's Sons. Copyright renewed. Copyright © 1993 by Eleanor Lanahan, Matthew J. Bruccoli and Samuel J. Lanahan as Trustees under agreement dated July 3, 1975 created by Frances Scott Fitzgerald Smith. All rights reserved.

Every effort has been made to trace the copyright holders but if any have been inadvertently overlooked the publishers will be pleased to make the necessary arrangement at the first opportunity.

1
Introduction

A few months before he died aged 44 in December 1940, F. Scott Fitzgerald wrote what now seems an astonishing, deeply ironical letter to his old friend and editor Maxwell Perkins at the press of Charles Scribner's Sons in New York. It tells of how completely he felt he had been forgotten by his readership in that final year of his life, and also shows him taking the measure of his place in American letters. The tone is strangely valedictory, and yet amidst the sad recognition that his public appreciation has dwindled away to nothing, there is a residual defiance, a refusal to allow his reputation to be extinguished:

> I wish I was in print ... Would the 25 cent press keep Gatsby in the public eye—or is the book unpopular. Has it had its chance? Would a popular reissue ... make it a favorite with class rooms, profs, lovers of English prose—anybody. But to die, so completely and unjustly after having given so much. Even now there is little published in American fiction that doesn't slightly bear my stamp in a small way I was an original ... I have not lost faith. (*Life in Letters* 445–6)

To this, those who love his fiction, and perhaps especially *The Great Gatsby*, will want to shout in protest against these understandable fears, enjoin with Fitzgerald's intuition of the ineradicable originality of his art, and above all cheer the triumphant quicksilver of his writing, which could never be contained by a temporary decline in public appreciation. As his life ended, we want him not to have felt, as he did, 'My God I am a forgotten man' (Bryer and Barks 331). For there was never to be one chance for such a novel as *Gatsby*; it was never to be boxed in by such reductive measures as the time and place of its first publication. Instead it has sold in millions and been translated into many languages, long ago becoming required reading in 'class rooms', and favoured by 'profs, lovers of English prose—anybody' who wants to be introduced to, or reminded of, what the rush, glide, and profundity of first-class fiction should be. In the largest way, Fitzgerald is indeed an original.

Francis Scott Key Fitzgerald grew up in the long shadow of the Great War, and died as the Second World War began. Though his sometime friend and contemporary Ernest Hemingway is more often remembered as the writer who often took war as his subject, as James H. Meredith notes, 'one of the main regrets of [Fitzgerald's] life was that he did not get over to France' as a combatant and the loss 'seemed to have haunted him' (152) for the rest of his life. When he was working for MGM in Hollywood in the last years of that life, his secretary, Frances Kroll, recalled the meetings he had on set with David Niven, 'who was very charming to Fitzgerald'. Fitzgerald 'was envious of Niven, but not because he was a star. He was envious because of Niven's adventure. Niven was going off to war. Ever since he missed World War I, Fitzgerald had been something of a thwarted soldier' (Latham 233–4). Even in a letter of 1937 before the outbreak of the Second World War, and just before he left for Hollywood, Fitzgerald is making very explicit parallels between his experience as a writer and the chaos of a war-torn sensibility, telling Pauline Brownell that he'd

> had a strange two months trying to pull together the fragments of a lost year and I wonder if life will ever again make much sense. Being sober and comparatively ascetic should do it but it hasn't. I am still unhappy and worried—the very worst condition for writing—and can understand how Europeans felt after years of war that left them accidently [*sic*] alive. (DeVinney 195)

Writing meant commitment and the courage to sustain that in adverse conditions, sometimes self-imposed. Soldiering, and soldiering on, seemed to him apt metaphors for the life of creative dedication. As he wrote in his 'Introduction' to the 1934 edition of *Gatsby*, 'I have a pride akin to a soldier going into battle; without knowing whether there will be anybody there, to distribute medals or even to record it' (Bruccoli and Bryer 157).

At the start of his career as a writer, however, Fitzgerald saw himself not as the sequestered artist but as the literary spokesman for his generation. Indeed from 1917, the earliest manuscript records of his first novel in progress show his awareness of this as he wrote, 'I'm trying to set down the story part of my generation in America and put myself in the middle as a sort of observer and conscious factor … I'm writing almost desperately' (*Epic* 84). Published in 1920 when he was just 24, *This Side of Paradise* was itself drafted against a background of war and from an associated context of threatened mortality, as he acknowledged the possibility of dying in the war along with the rest of his generation (he was a commissioned officer, a second lieutenant in the infantry and, 'like all infantry lieutenants at the time, Fitzgerald expected to be killed in battle' [*Epic* 84]), as well as a precocious urge towards immortality, telling his mentor Edmund Wilson, 'I want to be one of the greatest writers who ever lived, don't you?' As a young man writing his first novel, Fitzgerald tried his best to make living and writing highly bounded fields, so much so that while an undergraduate at Princeton University, he 'worked hard at writing and wasted little time on his studies' (Bruccoli and Bryer xiii), though just a few weeks after the publication of *Paradise* there was already an emerging tendency to pander to the rhetoric of the bohemian stereotype, as in a 'Self-Interview' he described writing the novel as 'sort of a substitute form of dissipation' (Bruccoli and Bryer 162). In his *Ledger*, however, and taking the measure of his Princeton years, there was his honest appraisal—'outwardly failure with moments of anger but the foundation of my literary life' (171).

Fitzgerald was always a Princetonian. One of his earliest publications was the prizewinning football song, 'A Cheer for Princeton' ('Raise your voices, loud and free / Strong and steady / Ever ready / For defeat or victory' [Deffaa 38]), and even in the last seconds of his life, before he was struck down by a fatal coronary seizure, he was reading an article about the Princeton football team in *The Princeton Alumni Weekly*. In her *Portrait of Hemingway*, Lillian Ross recalled the day when Hemingway, in typically reductive style,

> showed me where he once walked across Fifth Avenue with Scott Fitzgerald. 'Scott wasn't at Princeton any more, but he was still talking football,' he said, without animation. 'The ambition of Scott's life was to be on the football team. I said, "Scott, why don't you cut out this football?" I said, "Come on, boy." He said, "You're crazy." That's the end of that story".' (65–6).

Within *This Side of Paradise*, Princeton is certainly the map upon which the state of the larger American union is charted, the spine and fundament of Fitzgerald's rendering of *homo Americanus* as it faced its prospects in the immediate aftermath of the war. His first novel brought him sudden exaltation and exposure to the eddies of fame as its voice and vision seemed to express *le force d'âge*, its portrait of unencumbered 'youth in the saddle' judged by some reviewers to be 'the only adequate study that we have had of the contemporary American in adolescence and young manhood ' (Rascoe 305). It gave readers what Fitzgerald called 'a fresh picture of life in America', selling more than 20,000 copies in its first week, when sales for first novels were normally a fraction of that ('Early Success' 59). The novel's virtues were also its faults, faults forgiven because they were an integral part of its author's own youthful nerve. *Paradise* was praised for its playfulness of form, and its willingness to replace predictable coherence with an apparent spontaneity of utterance, so that prose is interrupted by poem, poem by one-act play, narrative flow by episodic diversion, giving the novel an air of risk-taking vitality; being compared as it was to another formally experimental and semi-autobiographical contemporary picture of youth, James Joyce's *Portrait of the Artist as a Young Man* (1916), also did Fitzgerald's literary début no harm on the world stage. Kirk Curnutt's essay on Fitzgerald and youth culture argues that he 'owed his early success to the fact that adolescent and post-adolescent readers were ripe for fiction that substantiated the newfound confusion and complexity associated with teenage life' (*Cambridge Companion to F. Scott Fitzgerald* 32). While the swagger of Fitzgerald's young hero, Amory Blaine ('Amory thought that he was exceedingly handsome. He was.' [*This Side of Paradise*. Ed. James L.W. West III. Cambridge: Cambridge University Press, 1995. 25. All further references are to this edition]), flattered also those readers who identified with the pose, just beneath the 'code to live by, which, as near as it can be named, was a sort of aristocratic egotism' [24], the murmurs of Fitzgerald's own fears are also clear in Amory's self-appraisal—'capable of recklessness and audacity, he possessed neither courage, perseverance nor self-respect' (25).

Self-harm was a more likely prospect as Fitzgerald acknowledged that 'with its publication I had reached a stage of manic-depressive insanity' ('Early Success' 60). The young man who wrote *Paradise* was fast becoming a burden to himself, while to others, including his friends and acquaintances, he was a draw but also sometimes a risk to know. Memoirs of Fitzgerald include two by Anita Loos and Lillian Hellman, both of which partly involve his behaviour as a driver of motor cars. Loos remembers knowing Fitzgerald 'in his great days in the twenties' just between the publication of *Paradise* and his next novel, *The Beautiful and Damned* (1922). Walking along Fifth Avenue, she made the mistake of getting into Fitzgerald's car when he drove up beside her: 'I didn't know that he was tight. We had a wild ride to Great Neck; I thought that he was going to kill us both' (Latham 5). According to Loos, later that evening Fitzgerald, in a drunken rage, indeed did try to kill both Loos and his wife Zelda. They both had to be rescued by the Fitzgeralds' butler. Fifteen years later it was Lillian Hellman who was Fitzgerald's passenger. Now on the other coast of America, driving with him was still dangerous, but for quite an opposite reason:

> I was surprised and pleased when he asked if I would ride with him … . My admiration for Fitzgerald's work was very great, and I looked forward to talking to him alone. But we didn't talk: he was occupied with driving at ten or twelve miles an hour down Sunset Boulevard, a dangerous speed in most places, certainly in Beverly Hills. Fitzgerald crouched over the wheel when cars honked at us … I saw that his hands were trembling on the wheel … By way of explanation, Fitzgerald said, 'You see, I'm on the wagon.' (Latham 19–20)

Whether on or off the wagon, or riding fast or slow, Fitzgerald's lifestyle was certainly one that at times played fast and loose with convention. As the 'Roaring Twenties' began, his marriage to Zelda Sayre seemed to further inflame such tendencies, and perhaps in its first years, at least, justifies Lionel Trilling's judgement that Fitzgerald was 'rather more interested in life than in art' (250). In his biography *Scott Fitzgerald*, Andrew Turnbull also allows that 'the quality of a life can be more impressive than art' (324), but in Fitzgerald's case, although the art he made may have drawn from the life he lived, it was never subordinate to it, and even in the case of *This Side of Paradise, The Beautiful and Damned* and *Tender is the Night*, three novels that are agreed to be autobiographically based to varying extents, the transforming truth of art is what dominates.

In a fascinating late passage in his *Notebooks*, Fitzgerald acknowledged that 'Books are like brothers. I am an only child. Gatsby my imaginary eldest brother, Amory my younger, Anthony my worry. Dick my comparatively good brother but all of them far from home' (158). That he saw Anthony Patch of his second novel, *The Beautiful and Damned*, as 'my worry' is hardly surprising. Of all the major characters in Fitzgerald's novels, Anthony is the most broken morally, the most exhausted mentally and the least likely to recover from his slump and isolation. Madness has overwhelmed his dreams of the easy wealth he hoped he would inherit from his tycoon grandfather, and in the end even the refuge that madness offered fails him as 'a thick, impenetrable darkness came down upon him and blotted out thought, rage and madness together—with almost a tangible snapping sound the face of the world changed before his eyes' (*The Beautiful and Damned*. Harmondsworth: Penguin, 1972. 361. All further references are to this edition). The novel is Fitzgerald's fable of an American *folie à deux* (Zelda, who spent many years undergoing psychiatric treatment in various psychiatric clinics, was in 1932 admitted to the Henry Phipps Psychiatric Clinic in Baltimore. The clinic's director, Dr Adolf Meyer, diagnosed Zelda as presenting with a shared psychotic disorder—*folie à deux*—and his plan was to treat both Scott and Zelda together), of personal integrity unravelling, and Anthony and Gloria Patch's eventually gilded state is given to the reader as the bitterly ironic finale to their lives of tawdry dissipation. As noted by Kirk Curnutt, their 'descent into decadence seems an effort to squander their youth before time can claim it' (*Cambridge Companion* 45). If, on the cusp of the postwar decade, *This Side of Paradise* gave us its picture of American youth aflame with energy, however directionless, in his second novel Fitzgerald shows us gilded youth burnt out, exhausted by the self-consuming waste of that energy. The sparkle of *Paradise* has been extinguished by the dread seriousness of *The Beautiful and Damned,* a novel in which any more substantial meanings are all but overwhelmed by its own detailed observance of drunken decline. The detail is indeed almost photographic in its presentation of Jazz-Age New York, with its movers, shakers and takers, a city fit for the damned of the novel's title, a gathering of meretricious sort that would have resonated all too clearly with those undergoing purgation in Dante's model of human folly. The picture is a memorable one, however; as noted in one of the novel's most perceptive reviews, 'what a crew they are—these loafers, drunkards, climbers, and rich wastrels of a great metropolis ... the picture of the time is there; a really amazing picture. It represents no mean achievement' (Beston 337).

'Life becomes complex with marriage, money or something and when it gets really complex, it is absolutely insoluble except in the simplicity of the grave', Fitzgerald wrote to himself towards the end of his life (*Notebooks* 326). Moving to Europe and the South of France in May 1924, however, he found the peace he needed to work, deriving from a less complex lifestyle if not quite a simple life, complicated as it was by Zelda's dalliance with the French aviator Edouard Jozan. Party-going and giving at their home in Great Neck, New York, overlooking Long Island Sound and close to the mansions of the super-rich (but a short imaginative step from there to the lavish parties thrown by Jay Gatsby at his Long Island estate), gave way to a relatively inexpensive sojourn on the French Riviera and a more realistic opportunity to work again, after a nine-month hiatus, on his new novel, *The Great Gatsby,* which he completed in October 1924 at the villa he and Zelda rented by the Mediterranean at St Raphaël. Expatriation was at the core of this success; it was as if the distance between France and his homeland allowed Fitzgerald to gain creative purchase on his novel, allowing his imagination to soar while also providing him with the concentration of mind necessary to structure and draft the narrative. The Fitzgeralds were also able to gain social structure from their friendships while living in France, in particular benefiting from the friendship with Gerald and Sara Murphy, wealthy Americans also living on the Riviera with a villa (which they named 'Villa America') near Antibes. Gerald, the scion and eventual president of the New York luxury-goods store Mark Cross, was also an artist and *bon viveur* whose life offered Fitzgerald a blueprint for the hero of his fourth novel, *Tender is the Night*. The two couples became lasting friends, and Honoria Murphy Donnelly remembered the closeness of that friendship, telling an interviewer that 'my parents were *enormously* fond of the Fitzgeralds, and I remember my father's early letter to them saying that "when the train pulled out there was the sound of tearing in the land." They hated to see them go' (Miller 19).

Fitzgerald looked up to the Murphys, and 'stood in awe of Gerald's unfailing propriety' (Turnbull, *Scott Fitzgerald* 168). His charm, elegance, and thoughtfully stylish use of wealth were qualities that Fitzgerald admired and respected; he was the model of the gentlemanly virtues, the master builder of a an enlightened *salon* that came to have an historic resonance, the home visited by the likes of Picasso, Fernand Léger, the Hemingways, Dorothy Parker and John Dos Passos. Honoria, then a 12-year-old, remembers 'looking down at the terrace from her bedroom window, seeing the flowers and the lovely food and the ladies in their beaded dresses, and thinking "how it all blended in, and how you just wanted it to last forever"' (Tomkins 112). *The Great Gatsby* emerged from this benign background. Its voice is ostensibly that of the narrator Nick Carraway, but Fitzgerald did not efface himself completely, and the reader senses that the deepest, most compelling voice is a poet's – that of Fitzgerald himself. In his discussion of the novel, Lionel Trilling heard in it 'the tenderness toward human desire that modifies a true firmness of moral judgment' (253). Without that tenderness of voice, Gatsby could easily be reduced only to foolish semblance; instead he is in the end held and raised up by its poetry to become a manifestation of all that is archetypally best in human desire, his yearning spirit free of the dust that chokes and overwhelms the dreams of others.

Fitzgerald claimed Jay Gatsby's spirit for his own, writing to Max Perkins from Italy, where he and Zelda were wintering in 1924, 'Gatsby sticks in my heart' (*Life in Letters* 91), while in 1925 he wrote from Paris to his friend John Peale Bishop that Gatsby 'started as one man I knew and then changed into myself' (*Life in Letters* 378). His hero possesses 'some heightened sensitivity to the promises of life ... an extraordinary gift for hope, a romantic readiness' (*The Great Gatsby*. Ed. Matthew J. Bruccoli. Cambridge: Cambridge University Press. 6. All further references are to this edition), qualities Nick Carraway presents as unique in his experience, but Fitzgerald himself possessed those qualities, and exhibited them again and again throughout his life. 'I am sure I am far enough ahead to have some small immortality if I can keep well', he confided to his *Notebooks*, even as he was sickening towards the end of his life (336). As Glenway Wescott wrote so memorably a year after Fitzgerald's death in 1941, 'you might say he was Gatsby, a greater Gatsby. Why not? Flaubert said, "*Madame Bovary, c'est moi*!"' (124). If, as some believe, 'like T.S. Eliot's *The Waste Land*, *The Great Gatsby* is a religious work because it has as its source a deeply felt religious emotion' (Piper 111), then its religion is one in which its hero finds salvation through passion. Gatsby is not the exceptional man, but the exceptional spirit, and as Gilbert Seldes wrote, 'his story remains poignant and beautiful' (361). The novel's meaning and at least a significant part of its long-lasting appeal has seemed to derive from its increasing relevance to readers as the decades have passed by. It was not a novel that was appreciated by its times, but is assuredly one that addresses the rampant materialism of our own more cynical age. Fitzgerald complained to Edmund Wilson in 1925 that 'of all the reviews [of Gatsby], even the most enthusiastic, not one had the slightest idea what the book was about' (*Life in Letters* 109). Now, it is to be hoped, we do.

The Fitzgeralds for the most part lived abroad from 1924 to 1931, and apart from the precious seven months which saw the completion of *Gatsby*, this time was later summed up by Fitzgerald as 'seven years of waste and tragedy' (Mizener in Kazin 1951, 33). Though he had begun the first drafts of his next novel during the summer of 1924 at Antibes, it would be a further ten years until the publication of *Tender is the Night* in 1934. Perhaps Trilling's reference above to 'the tenderness toward human desire that modifies a true firmness of moral judgment' in Fitzgerald's art is again helpful, and it is for some readers and critics his most moving and intimate work of art. The novel's title, drawn from John Keats's poem, 'Ode to a Nightingale', goes to the heart of Fitzgerald's concerns. As Philip McGowan contends, 'the Romantic centre to Fitzgerald's own fictional world tallies readily with the wistful yearning of the Keats poem, which seeks perpetual bliss in the face of irrevocable mortality' (204). The poem offers death as an escape from the pain and austerity of life, and by the end of his story, Fitzgerald's hero, Dr. Dick Diver, has experienced a full measure of life's sorrows and travails, some of them self-imposed. The *ménage* that he and Nicole Diver created by the Riviera sands is remembered only as a transient moment of creativity, of human relations elevated to a level of graceful import. It cannot, however, withstand its eclipse by the forces ranged against it, as Dick's idealism and professional code as a physician give way gradually to self-indulgent weakness as he drifts into alcoholism, while he is ineffectual against the powerful and corrupt machinations of the rich and privileged, for whom Dick's ability to heal is but a utility to be bought and sold.

Tender is the Night takes its characters and plot as indicative of the larger disintegrative forces at work in European history between the two world wars; in these ways it is an historical novel which personifies the inevitable march of arrant, totalitarian power ranged against fragile personal ethics. Nicole's bullying sister Baby Warren, for instance, is intended as a personification of the decadent and implacable abuse of power in an era of inter-war fascism. In such terms Dick Diver succumbs as an appeaser of such forces – 'he had been swallowed up like a gigolo, and somehow permitted his arsenal to be locked up in the Warren safety-deposit vaults' (225). Visiting the Somme battlefield of the First World War, he is already prepared to read there the signs of his own defeat, seeing there the death of love and associated humane values—'why, this was a love battle—there was a century of middle-class love spent here' (68). In such scenes the novel discloses its com plex plot as one that mobilises political and historical themes of larger resonance, while at the same time sustaining and implicating such themes within a credible and convincing representation of character. Betrayal of values is very much a core theme of the novel, and at the novel's close, the cruel glare of the Riviera sun highlights Nicole's infidelity with Tommy Barban, his surname surely a contraction of the barbarian impulses he represents. That light contrasts most memorably, however, with the gentle darkness summoned up by Keats's 'Ode to a Nightingale', chosen by Fitzgerald as the novel's epigraph: 'But here there is no light / Save what from heaven is with the breezes blown / Through verdurous glooms and winding mossy ways.'

Fitzgerald was also increasingly conscious of the mediations between his own life and those of a context shadowed by war. He wrote to Zelda in June 1940, six months before his death:

> Twenty years ago *Paradise* was a best seller and we were settled in Westport. Ten years ago Paris was having its last great American season but we had quit the gay parade and you were gone to

> Switzerland. Five years ago I had my first bad stroke of illness and went to Asheville. Cards began falling badly for us much too early. The world has certainly caught up in the last four weeks. I hope the atmosphere ... is tranquil and not too full of war talk. (*Life in Letters* 452)

The letter provides a chronology for the Fitzgeralds' cumulative breakdowns throughout the decade that was ending as another war began in Europe. With Zelda's mental breakdown at the start of the 1930s being accompanied five years later by Fitzgerald's own 'crack-up', the title he chose for a confessional essay he wrote for *Esquire* in 1936, it was extraordinary that somehow he managed to pull himself out of the mess he was undoubtedly in, a combination of nervous collapse, physical infirmity and alcohol dependency, all accompanied by the lukewarm reception and modest sales of *Tender is the Night* when it was published in 1934. In these conditions he turned once again reluctantly to Hollywood as a possible exit from financial ruin, having made previous inconsequential sallies there in 1927 and 1932. In the summer of 1937 it was very much an option of last resort, driven as he was by increasing debts arising from a lifelong inability to manage his financial affairs, and by the need to pay for both Zelda's ongoing treatments in expensive sanatoriums as well as their daughter Scottie's education. With a lucrative contract from the MGM studio, which recognised his potential as a scriptwriter, he would once again find his commitment to what was to be his final, unfinished novel, *The Last Tycoon*, compromised by the urgencies of present-day needs. Of course, his artistic sensibility was never completely in suspension, and his day-to-day experiences as a contracted scriptwriter working in the Hollywood studio system would eventually have creative issue, contributing as they did to his imagination of the Hollywood that appears in *The Last Tycoon*; but concentrated work on this novel did not really begin until the start of 1939, when his contract at MGM was allowed to lapse. Still, there is ample evidence that despite bodily fatigue, Fitzgerald benefited greatly from the more structured working environment of Hollywood. There he found a relative stability, while his close relationship with Sheilah Graham, a society journalist based in Hollywood, also gave him emotional reprieve from the years of anguish arising from Zelda's illness and their enforced separation. 'Schooled by suffering', by the time he arrived in Hollywood, Fitzgerald 'had attained a knowledge of himself and of the human condition that may truly be described as tragic' (Turnbull, *Scott Fitzgerald* 313).

The Last Tycoon shows evidence of a renewed pragmatism in Fitzgerald's approach to his subject, a willingness to exclude the diversions from a robust clarity of plot and theme that he felt had damaged *Tender is the Night*, and a determination to cut through to the essence of what made his tycoon-hero, the Hollywood producer Monroe Stahr, an expression of not only the movie capital's business ethic but also a personification of what Brian Way calls 'the fullest expression of the type of the American artist' (18). Therefore, from the start it was intended to mark a self-conscious return to the most salient virtues that had characterised *The Great Gatsby*, as Fitzgerald wrote Zelda in October 1940, 'I am deep in the novel, living in it, and it makes me happy. It is a constructed novel like Gatsby, with passages of poetic prose when it fits the action, but no ruminations or side-shows like Tender. Everything must contribute to the dramatic movement' (*Life in Letters* 467). Of course his comparisons with *Gatsby* are pertinent (though it seems certain that the novel, had it been completed, would eventually have been much longer, at least twice as long as *Gatsby* was) to this plan, but it may also be that his work as a movie scriptwriter has influenced the stress he gives here to the new novel's highly constructed design. While modelled upon the film producer Irving Thalberg (who had died in 1936), Stahr was to have been a tragic hero whose life and work not only exemplified the classic rags-to-riches myth of the American dream, but also would exhibit the executive virtues Fitzgerald so much admired, possessing undoubted leadership skills while combining all with the sensibility of an artist. Stahr's tragic status derives from the sacrifice of his individualist, visionary ethic to the corporate cynicism that serves the Hollywood studio system. He is the last tycoon because he represents the ultimate in enlightened command, a merchant prince who is lauded by all who work for him.

'I am sure I am far enough ahead to have some small immortality if I can keep well' (*Notebooks* 336). In the end Fitzgerald's purchase upon the 'immortality' of art was already much firmer than he could ever know when he wrote this in 1940. However, as Frances Kroll Ring, his secretary in Hollywood, remembers, his ability to 'keep well' was much less secure:

> He did want to secure his reputation with his peers and his readers and he hoped the new book would do this for him. Yet despite the mood of calm, I have a dark impression that lingers—of a walk we took up the street at one day's end. I was going to my car; he was

going on to Schwab's Drug Store on Sunset Boulevard, just a couple of blocks away. He was wearing a dark topcoat and a grey homburg hat. As we kept pace, I looked over at him and was chilled by his image, like a shadowy figure in an old photograph. His outfit and pallor were alien to the style and warmth of Southern California—as if he were not at home here, had just stopped off and was dressed to leave on the next train. (*Against the Current* 99)

* * *

More than 70 years after Fitzgerald's death, this study of his fiction has been well served by a wealth of scholarship in a new century that has seen his international reputation not only secure, but flourishing. The Selected Bibliography to this book shows much of the record, with essay collections such as *F. Scott Fitzgerald: New Perspectives* (2000), *The Cambridge Companion to F. Scott Fitzgerald* (2002), *F. Scott Fitzgerald in the Twenty-first Century* (2003), *A Historical Guide to F. Scott Fitzgerald* (2004), *Twenty-First-Century Readings of* Tender is the Night (2007) and *F. Scott Fitzgerald in Context* (2011), along with multidisciplinary, comparative and textually incisive scholarship by Ronald Berman; studies by French scholars such as Pascale Antolin, Elisabeth Bouzonvillers and Marie-Agnès Gay (all 2000); introductions to Fitzgerald such as those by Ruth Prigozy, *F. Scott Fitzgerald* (2004) and Kirk Curnutt, *The Cambridge Introduction to F. Scott Fitzgerald* (2007); life study as exemplified in biographies by Kendall Taylor (2001), Andrew Hook (2002) and Edward J. Reilly (2005); and primary-source collections that renew and shape the archive such as *Dear Scott, Dearest Zelda: The Love Letters of F. Scott and Zelda Fitzgerald* (2002), edited by Jackson R. Bryer and Cathy W. Barks. All of this scholarship is buttressed with authority by the ongoing definitive Cambridge edition of the complete works of F. Scott Fitzgerald, with James L.W. West III as General Editor.

Fitzgerald's life ended in Hollywood, and while the movie business and MGM provided him with much-needed work as a screenwriter, his fiction was also involved with its people and possibilities; the relationships between that fiction and the visual arts have seen notable film studies of Fitzgerald, such as those from Somdatta Mandal (2004) and Gautam Kundu (2008). Lively websites such as those of the F. Scott Fitzgerald Society and the F. Scott Fitzgerald Centenary Home Page – from that seedbed of Fitzgerald scholarship, the University of South Carolina – testify to online vitality. The F. Scott Fitzgerald Society publishes annually *The F. Scott Fitzgerald Review* and its *Newsletter* and organises conferences in the United States and Europe.

This study is gratefully informed by such scholarship and hopes to build upon it by providing a gateway which will prove fruitful for readers requiring an intimate witness to Fitzgerald's life and work. The primary focus is upon the novels, with a study of selected short fiction and the important non-fiction, essays and letters, where appropriate. The book is organised around the decades of Fitzgerald's writing life and accepts him as a writer with a deep consciousness of history, an awareness of time's mutations – which is often given a dramatic presence in his fiction – a body of writing that manifests the author's acute sense of the challenges faced by American life and its values as the country tried to recover from the waste of war after 1918.

Fitzgerald's writing shows him as a novelist of responsive integrity, cognisant of life's glittering surfaces and of the snares they present. It is writing that exploits those surface details as the signs of inner voids. He once confided to his *Notebooks* that in 'any given individual life or situation things progress from good toward less good. But life itself never does' (199), while in the same source he acknowledged: 'Zelda's idea: the bad things are the same in everyone; only the good are different' (199). In such terms he comes across as an artist fired by a deeply inquisitive conscience, whose Christian ethic, however backgrounded, is a conditioning undertone. The bacchanalia of Gatsby's parties are only that narrative's most aggregate register of a culture in febrile disarray, though both of Fitzgerald's previous novels had offered explicit examples of an American civilisation encumbered by a similar neurosis.

The collapse of agreed values in the aftermath of war is present with varying degrees of affective force in all of the fiction considered here. The characters are often presented as people dismayed. Their confusion and the sudden rifts of instability that afflict their worlds show us Fitzgerald's willingness to dramatise self-knowledge as contested. Those who emerge as heroic are defined by their ability to stand outside the neighbouring confusion – Dick Diver is 'the man of repose'; Jay Gatsby is, in the end, a model of solitary integrity; Monroe Stahr is 'the Emperor ... the last of the princes' (29). The self is reinvented with strategic purpose for Fitzgerald's heroes; identity is a mechanism finely geared to try for survival in 'this side of paradise'. Within that realm the obstacles to human perfection are many, and they are a large part of Fitzgerald's subject.

But in his art they are not all and do not conquer all. W.B. Yeats's jeremiad

> The blood-dimmed tide is loosed, and everywhere
> The ceremony of innocence is drowned
> The best lack all conviction, while the worst
> Are full of passionate intensity ...
> ('The Second Coming')

was too comprehensively bleak for F. Scott Fitzgerald. That 'blood-dimmed tide' is not Gatsby's ocean. There, buoyancy is still possible for the few, bettered by their heroic will. 'Winnowed from failures',[1] they are given to inspire us, as they 'beat on, boats against the current' (*Gatsby* 141).

2

An Elfin Harlequinade: *This Side of Paradise* (1920)

'The history of my life is the history of the struggle between an overwhelming urge to write and a combination of circumstances bent on keeping me from it' ('Who's Who – and Why', in *Afternoon of an Author* 83). Born in 1896, F. Scott Fitzgerald wrote this in 1920, the year *This Side of Paradise,* his first novel, was published. The statement is uncannily predictive of what would indeed be a writing life impeded by tragic, often self-imposed handicaps. Towards the end of that life Fitzgerald recognised but probably failed to relish the double irony that *This Side of Paradise,* perhaps his weakest novel, yet remained his most popular book in terms of first-edition sales. Its composition was also unusual in being accelerated rather than impeded by his personal circumstances at the time – most specifically the need to publish quickly a winning novel so as to impress his Southern belle, Zelda Sayre, whose commitment to their relationship was on the wane – 'if I stopped working to finish the novel, I lost the girl' ('Early Success', 57).

The novel survives as an important text in the history of twentieth-century American literature, a classic example of that entity which is greater than the sum of its parts. As Fitzgerald later wrote in his memoir 'Early Success', 'the whole golden boom was in the air' (59) of the postwar United States, and participating in it he found that for him it had turned into 'that first wild wind of success' (58). Although it is now difficult to imagine F. Scott Fitzgerald grafting in factory overalls, he tells us that he had, early on, 'taken a job repairing car roofs at the Northern Pacific shops' in Minnesota, though the blue collar would soon be swapped for blue blood as his novel, with what he called its 'fresh picture of life in America' (59), was accepted for publication by the prestigious firm of Charles Scribner's Sons in New York. Fitzgerald quickly became, in Glenway Wescott's phrase, 'a kind of king of our American youth' (116). The American century had begun and the nation itself was hungry for those who could exemplify and express the spirit of the age. Indeed, images of golden kingship are not difficult to associate with contemporary accounts of Fitzgerald's youthful ascendancy, though he himself acknowledged the derivative origins of *This Side of Paradise* from the start, as he made clear in the novel's preface. His editor at Scribner's, Maxwell Perkins, eventually decided not to use the preface in which, with astonishing honesty, its young author had been prepared to tell his readers that his novel had its earliest origins in 'a tedius [*sic*] casserole of a dozen by [Compton] McKenzie, [H.G.] Wells, and Robert Hugh Benson, largely flavored by the great undigested butterball of [Oscar Wilde's] *Dorian Gray*' (393). About the finally published novel, though, the preface says next to nothing: 'I began another novel; whether its hero really "gets anywhere" is for the reader to decide' (395), although in the letter he sent to Max Perkins accompanying the preface, he was careful to finish with his belief that 'I certainly think the hero gets somewhere' (*Life in Letters* 32). Remembering that early success many years later, Fitzgerald told of the lingering feeling of fakery that still hung about him at that time, the knowledge that being an author was itself a pose, 'that one wasn't really an author any more than one had been an army officer, but nobody seemed to guess behind the false face'. As for the novel itself, 'a lot of people thought it was a fake, and perhaps it was' ('Early Success' 60). If anything, the fakery was much less a part of the novel he wrote than it was the life he lived, which was a matter of secondary importance at the time. Fitzgerald's First World War commission was to the infantry as a second lieutenant; he later became aide-de-camp to General J.A. Ryan, although the war ended before his unit was sent overseas. If his commitment to his studentship at Princeton University was abraded by his work on *Paradise*, some flavor of his shaky dedication to army life also appears in his lines: 'The drills, marches and Small Problems for Infantry were a shadowy dream. My whole heart was concentrated upon my book' ('Who's Who – and Why' 85).

The intense relationship between first novel, romance, money and fame was further established as Fitzgerald remembered that 'all in three days I got married and the presses were pounding out *This Side of Paradise* like they pound out extras in the movies' ('Early Success' 60). Marriage and fame were now facts of life for the young author, shaping a new world whose financial coordinates were easily calculated: 'I found that in 1919 I had made $800 by writing [while] in 1920 I had made $18,000' ('Early Success' 61). He affected a certain pragmatism in the face of such facts, for 'one was now a professional – and the new world couldn't possibly be presented without bumping the old out of the way' ('Early Success' 61). A key fact of his biography, recognised by Fitzgerald himself, was derived from his intimate knowledge of both old and new worlds, of living betwixt and between: 'For my point of vantage was the dividing line between the two generations, and there I sat – somewhat self-consciously' ('Early Success' 60). Often regarded as the exponent of the Jazz Age to which he gave its name, this crucial self-assessment shows that from the start of his writing career Fitzgerald also saw himself as apart from the new postwar generation, privy to other insights than were given to those whom he regarded as naïve in their belief that living was a 'reckless, careless business' ('Early Success' 60). Constitutionally, his imagination would propose a completely other reality for his characters and settings, for as critic Sy Kahn noted, Fitzgerald created heroes 'whose sources lie in the moral codes of American life previous to World War I' (Kahn 34). At the same time that 'America was going on the greatest, gaudiest spree in history', at the deepest level of his writerly imagination Fitzgerald was inflamed not by carnival uplift but burdened by something much darker: 'All the stories that came into my head had a touch of disaster in them – the lovely young creatures in my novels went to ruin, the diamond mountains of my short stories blew up, my millionaires were as beautiful and damned as Thomas Hardy's peasants' ('Early Success' 59–60). And looking back from 1917 to 1920, in another key phrase he wrote that although 'in life these things hadn't happened yet', his intuitional nature was at least unwilling to believe that the histrionics of the Jazz Age were built upon any solid foundation. Fitzgerald's life, ironically so linked in cultural history with the American Dream of success, was in his own assessment already bereft of dreams by the mid-1920s when he was only 29 years old – 'I who had no more dreams of my own' ('Early Success' 62).

While noting the 'spurious and imitative side' of *Paradise*, Fitzgerald's shrewdest critics were also willing to acknowledge its most 'memorable feature', namely 'that it announced a change in standards' in postwar American life (*Second Flowering* 23). And this may still be the best reason to attend to the novel – since as an index of the seminal mood swing of the culture, *This Side of Paradise* stands as a bellwether, its importance emanating from its feisty challenge to what Fitzgerald's narrator calls 'the mistakes and half-forgotten dreams of dead statesmen' (*This Side* 260), so that it becomes an acute social document of the Jazz Age, 'a record of the beginnings of a social revolution' (Cross 21–2). The novel's weaknesses were indeed bound up with its strengths, for if, as Edmund Wilson complained, 'it is not really *about* anything', its message was nevertheless determinedly positioned, its final vision that of a powerful 'gesture of indefinite revolt' (*Shores* 28) against the sins of the fathers. Fitzgerald's Amory Blaine, the youthful hero of *This Side of Paradise*, is presented in the novel's coda as nothing if not a confident signatory to this transition of values:

> I simply state that I'm the product of a versatile mind in a restless generation – with every reason to throw my mind and pen in with the radicals.... I and my sort would struggle against tradition; try, at least, to replace old cants with new ones.... One thing I know. If living isn't a seeking for the grail it may be a damned amusing game. (256–7)

Without Max Perkins, his young commissioning editor at Scribner's, it is, however, doubtful that the novel would have been published so soon, if at all, and precisely because it broke the mould of not only American fiction of its time but also of the Scribner list, the house style of which was typified by the conventional 'genteel tradition' of writers – both American and British – such as Henry Adams, Henry James, George Santayana and Edith Wharton. Fitzgerald, however, remained proud of his Scribner's contracts, telling Perkins after the publication of *The Great Gatsby* that he was aware of what he called 'the curious advantage to a rather radical writer in being published by what is now an ultra-conservative house' (Turnbull, *Letters* 203). Even in its earliest drafts Perkins knew he had a hold of something special, and although on first presentation the novel was rejected by the stuffy Scribner board, Perkins encouraged Fitzgerald to redraft it and gave him specific advice accordingly, suggesting most explicitly that he change the narrative voice from the first to the third person, and return it to Scribner's for a further review. Perkins eventually won the day, telling his boss, Charles Scribner II, that 'a publisher's first allegiance is to talent and ... if we're going to turn down the likes of Fitzgerald, I will lose all interest in publishing books' (Berg 16).

The historic acceptance letter Perkins was subsequently able to send to Fitzgerald on 18 September 1919 is worth consideration:

> I am very glad, personally, to be able to write to you that we are all for publishing your book *This Side of Paradise* ... As the first manuscript did, it abounds in energy and life ... The book is so different that it is hard to prophesy how it will sell but we are all for taking a chance and supporting it with vigor. (Berg 16)

Perkins had used very similar terms with which to praise Fitzgerald's early short stories, telling him that their great beauty was to be found in their truth to life – they 'are direct from life it seems to me. This is true also of the language and style; it is that of the day. It is free of the conventions of the past which most writers love' (Berg 17). He shows here that he had found in Fitzgerald's fiction a voice that expressed the coming of the modern, a voice to challenge the tired rhetoric of the past. Perhaps also he recognised the futility of trying to resist this voice – for as he told his fellow editors, if Scribner's refused to publish Fitzgerald then others surely would accept the young author's work. He had a calm and steady intuition that *This Side of Paradise*, for all its faults and perhaps too because of them, was a text to greet the moment, the dawning new days of the 1920s, full of restless energy and life. It had the shock of the new and, indeed, it was that 'the book is so different' which marked out its frank appeal, first to Perkins and then to its audience, a youthful generation also inspired by its freshness. The book indeed seemed to mark the distinct features of a generation, and as Roger Burlingame noted in his 1946 history of the house of Scribner's, it wakened America's 'comfortable parents ... into the consciousness that something definite, terrible and, possibly, final, had happened to their children' (Berg 20).

In this context Perkins's achievement should not be underestimated. After the event, and as *This Side of Paradise* took its place in history, it was all too easy to see that his decision to stand or fall by the novel's publication had a profound logic to it, but at the meeting of Scribner's board in mid-September 1919, and facing across the table the hostile old guard of Scribner himself, his brother Arthur, and the firm's intimidating editor-in-chief William Brownell (at that time a fearsome doyen of literary taste in America), Perkins's resolute support was brave. The new generation, lost to the old, found an authentic version of itself within the pages of Fitzgerald's novel, and resisting its *jeu d'esprit* perhaps in the end no longer seemed worth the odds to old Scribner and his peers. Along with Amory Blaine, American youth would inevitably find its way, out of the mess of war, out of 'that dirty gray turmoil to follow love and pride' (*Paradise* 260), as their right.

Some critics found *This Side of Paradise* easy to mock, less easy to shoot down; and as it began to sell in large numbers and gained in notoriety they found that, in Glenway Wescott's words it 'haunted the decade like a song, popular but perfect, [and] hung over an entire youth-movement like a banner' (119), a song for newly incarnated romantics shaking loose their wartime austerity. And in the pages of the influential New York journal *The Smart Set*, its editor, the uber-arbiter H.L. Mencken, found *Paradise* on publication to be 'a truly amazing first novel – original in structure, extremely sophisticated in manner, and adorned with brilliancy that is … rare in American writing' (Berg 19). For Fitzgerald's own responses to the effects upon him of his first novel's publication, the best source is perhaps contained in his wistful memoir 'My Lost City' (1945), written in 1933 but not published until five years after his death. Although at the end of the memoir New York 'no longer whispers of fantastic success and eternal youth' (31), in the opening paragraph those romantic possibilities are early 'crystallized' for him in two symbols of beguiling promise. As a boy of 10, 'there was first the ferry boat moving softly from the Jersey shore at dawn', and five years later, as a schoolboy visiting Broadway to see musical comedy and its Ziegfield stars such as Ina Claire and Gertrude Bryan, 'I was unable to choose between them – so they blurred into one lovely entity, the girl. She was my second symbol of New York. The ferryboat stood for triumph, the girl for romance. In time I was to achieve some of both' (20). Both triumph and romance came to him as an immediate result of the publication of *Paradise*, an intoxicating blend that saw him represented to the world as 'the archetype of what New York wanted … not only spokesman for the time but the typical product of that same moment (23–4). Inevitable realisation that he 'was unable to play the role' of New York personified (24) eventually followed, but still the emotional matrix that characterised both the place and its romantic possibilities never left him and his first novel, as all of his novels, is infused by such energies. In 1925 he wrote of the 'enormous emotion' that he had put into *Paradise*, adding that although the emotion was 'immature', it nevertheless energised the whole, giving 'every incident a sort of silly "life" ' (*Epic* 122), while in H.L. Mencken's copy he wrote with similar honesty, 'this is a bad book full of good things' (*Correspondence* 55) – amongst the best of which can be counted the emotional energy driving its author's imaginings as he stepped up to the first threshold of his life as a writer.

'I really believe that no one else could have written so searchingly the story of the youth of our generation' (*Life in Letters* 17), Fitzgerald himself wrote to Wilson in 1918 with the characteristic confidence he had in those early years. He had a cocksure belief in his novel's ability to document the only milieu he knew intimately, that of American youth emerging from adolescence into maturity. He knew his readership, too, and was right to predict in the same letter that 'if Scribner's takes it I know I'll wake some morning and find that the debutantes have made me famous overnight' (17). In choosing an age-old literary form, the novel as *Entwicklungsroman* – which deals with the development of the hero from childhood through to maturity – Fitzgerald was also fortunate to encounter that subject at the same time as the United States itself was emerging from its self-forming as a nation, and taking confident possession of its mature status in the world. Thus *Paradise* was both the first twentieth-century novel to re-create in detail the experiences of a privileged Ivy League-educated American youth and also one of the first to reflect the surrounding contemporary cultural matrix. 'Nobody who would know what it was like to be young and privileged and self-centered in that bizarre epoch can afford to neglect it' (188), wrote William Troy of *This Side of Paradise*, acknowledging thereby that the novel's significance derives at least partly from the extent to which it combines within itself both *Entwicklungsroman* subject matter and historical value. Fitzgerald's 'novel defined adolescence as a process of emotional *and* historical accommodation' (Curnutt in Prigozy ed., *Cambridge Companion* 33) 33), so reflecting the larger flux of the American moment. No need to wonder, then, that it sold in such large numbers, for it recognised and to an extent celebrated its readership, mirroring their culture, their dreams and desires. Wilson, for his part, was forthright in Fitzgerald as a being perfectly fitted to the labour of creating such a novel *du rêve d'un enfant*, writing of him in an essay of March 1922 as 'a rather childlike fellow, very much wrapped up in his dream of himself and his projection of it on paper' (*Shores* 31), even going so far as to envision both the author and his characters as 'actors in an elfin harlequinade; they are as nimble, as gay and as lovely – and as hardhearted – as fairies' (*Shores* 32).

Fitzgerald had indeed started young in the realms of nostalgic imagining. As a boy growing up in the capital of Minnesota, the city of St. Paul, 'he went around earnestly telling the neighbors he had been found on the Fitzgerald doorstep one morning wrapped up in a blanket, to which was pinned a piece of paper emblazoned with the name of the royal House of Stuart!' (Piper vii). As Malcolm Cowley noted, Fitzgerald 'regarded himself as a pauper living among millionaires, a Celt among Sassenachs' ('Third Act and Epilogue' 149). He would continue to stress his Celtic roots long into maturity, and they contributed to his romantic and creative history at different levels. For instance, Amory's mentor, Monsignor Darcy, 'between his trips to all parts of the Roman-Catholic world', lives in 'an ancient, rambling structure ... rather like an exiled Stuart king waiting to be called to the rule of his land' (29). On their first meeting, when Darcy and Amory discuss their enthusiasms, slipping 'briskly into an intimacy from which they never recovered' (31), it is perhaps inevitable that Amory's unbridled romanticism would lead him to declare himself as an ally of lost causes: 'I was for Bonnie Prince Charlie ... and for the Southern Confederacy' (31), while at the start of *The Great Gatsby*, Nick Carraway tells us that 'the Carraways are something of a clan, and we have a tradition that we're descended from the Dukes of Buccleuch' (6). In a 1920 letter to Edmund Wilson Fitzgerald even enclosed a spoof 'Family Tree of F. Scott Fitzgerald', in which his Scots–Irish lineage, leading from the likes of 'Duns Scotus, Mary, Queen of Scotts [*sic*], Sir Walter Scott, Duke Fitzgerald (Earl of Leinster)', issues eventually in 'F. Scott Fitzgerald (drunkard)', the final parenthetical offhand designation a chilling self-appraisal even at the age of 24 (*Life in Letters* 43).

The dreams of life in their many forms were indeed always Fitzgerald's subject, the increasingly tragic plots of his novels deriving from his characters' awakening from heroic musings to confrontations with leaden reality. If, as R.P. Blackmur put it, great-spirited art is made 'by heroizing the longing to be freed from reason; the whole human world shares and expresses itself in this longing' (47), in the case of Fitzgerald's novels the most memorable instance of the type, Jay Gatsby, is in the moments before death perhaps saved by death from just such an awakening into reason. At the end of his story, as Nick Carraway waits in the thick gray drizzle by Gatsby's grave in West Egg, and hears one of the few mourners there present murmuring, 'Blessed are the dead that the rain falls on', he 'tried to think about Gatsby then for a moment, but he was already too far away' (136), a blessed distance beyond the constraining nets of reason that could never quite hold him even in life.

Not *Gatsby*, however, but *This Side of Paradise* is in many ways the most metaphysical of all Fitzgerald's texts, manifest most pointedly and strangely in the novel's 'Devil' episodes, and mediated through Fitzgerald's own Roman Catholic upbringing which, in the years prior to the novel's publication, had been an explicit expression of his spirituality. His friendship with Monsignor Sigourney Fay was, along with Princeton University, one of the signal influences upon his ideas as the novel took shape. Fitzgerald first met Fay in 1912 at the Newman School in Hackensack, New Jersey, a Catholic preparatory boarding school for boys which Fitzgerald attended from 1911 to 1913, just prior to attending Princeton University. A convert to Catholicism, whose evident diplomatic and evangelising skills were quickly noticed by both Washington and Rome, Fay was sent to London as Washington's envoy to liaise on American foreign policy with the British Foreign Secretary Lord Balfour, and in Rome met also with Pope Benedict XV on the same errand. Fay was an intelligent man who, by many accounts, exhibited considerable charm and charisma; his influence upon the young Scott Fitzgerald was undoubtedly profound and long-lasting, and Fitzgerald's debts to him were publicly acknowledged in *This Side of Paradise*, which carries the formal dedication: 'To Sigourney Fay'. If *Paradise* can be read as the first revelatory chapter in Fitzgerald's own *libro vitae*, then the name of Sigourney Webster Fay was writ large in its philosophic underpinnings at that time and he appears in the novel as Monsignor Thayer Darcy, Amory Blaine's Catholic conscience. According to one of Fitzgerald's biographers, 'it is easy to understand the huge, eunuch-like priest's fatherly affection for the handsome, blond boy and Fitzgerald's admiration for Fay, who introduced him to his first glass of wine and to a more sophisticated world than he had ever known' (Piper 47), introductions which allowed Fitzgerald's first access to the society and culture of upper-class Catholic intellectuals. Perhaps the most important of all those introductions was to Shane Leslie, a wealthy County Monaghan-born man of letters who was descended from Scots–Irish landed aristocracy (inheriting the family baronetcy as Sir John Randolph Leslie) and was first cousin to Sir Winston Churchill. At the time he met Fitzgerald, Leslie was a recent Roman Catholic convert who became a passionate supporter of Irish Home Rule and had an evangelising commitment to his faith and politics. Leslie's blue-blood education had taken him from Eton College to King's College, Cambridge, from which he graduated in 1907 and where he had became a close friend of fellow student Rupert Brooke, publishing the latter's earliest poems in the Oxford literary magazine he edited. Introduced by Fay to Fitzgerald, Leslie soon saw him as 'an American Rupert Brooke' (Sklar 25), and was also encouraging him 'to believe that he would write the unwritten great Catholic novel … of the United States' (Sklar 11). It was Leslie who, with the highest of recommendations, sent the earliest manuscript of *This Side of Paradise* (at that time Fitzgerald was calling his novel *The Romantic Egotist*) to his own publisher and friend Charles Scribner.

The title *This Side of Paradise* was taken from Rupert Brooke's Edwardian love lyric 'Tiare Tahiti', the final two lines of which Fitzgerald also used as one of the two epigraphs to the novel – ' … Well this side of Paradise! / There's little comfort in the wise'. In the context of the poem's meaning, the lines are a *carpe diem* injunction, as Brooke's speaker sets the here-and-now sensuality of 'time-entangled human love' in a South Seas paradise – 'The palms, and sunlight, and the south' – against love in the heavenly eternal Kingdom:

> When our laughter ends,
> And hearts and bodies, brown as white,
> Are dust about the doors of friends,
> Or scent ablowing down the night,
> Then, oh! then, the wise agree,
> Comes our immortality.

Alas, on this earthly side of that heavenly paradise, there's little comfort to be found in such immortal wisdom, says the poem, and Fitzgerald's novel, however painful Amory Blaine's lovelorn experiences, seems to agree. In this respect, 'Tiare Tahiti' has echoes of Andrew Marvell's 'To His Coy Mistress' ('the grave's a fine and private place / But none I think do there embrace') or perhaps more likely it reminded Fitzgerald of Keats again, on this occasion his 'Ode on a Grecian Urn', where in paradisaical 'dales of Arcady' the human figures depicted upon the urn are, as it were, imprisoned, so that the 'Fair youth … canst not leave thy song' nor the 'Bold Lover , never, never canst thou kiss'. The vision of an eternal 'Heaven's Heaven' in Brooke's poem also predicts 'there's an end, I think, of kissing', and therefore the 'comfort' offered by 'the wise', with its promise of immortal bliss, can do little to lessen the lure of a fully sensual corporeality: 'the whispering scents that stray /

About the idle warm lagoon / ... Limbs that gleam and shadowy hair'. As Amory Blaine realises, 'there were so many places where one might deteriorate pleasantly' (242), including the South Seas, where romantic decline or, as Fitzgerald's narrator puts it, going 'to the devil ... safely and sensuously' (242) would be accompanied by a most compatible *son et lumière*: 'sad, haunting music and many odors, where lust could be a mode and expression of life, where the shades of night skies and sunsets would seem to reflect only moods of passion: the colors of lips and poppies' (242).

After Fay's death in January 1919 Fitzgerald wrote, 'I'll think of the days when I came back to school to join his circle before the fire as the happiest of my life' (Piper 48), and to Leslie he also wrote that 'now my little world made to order has been shattered by the death of one man.... Fay's death has made me nearly sure that I will become a priest' (*Life in Letters* 22). Yet that the particular Brooke poem he should choose to reference was 'Tiare Tahiti', and that he gave its final lines in particular such priority in his novel's title, may, along with the evidence available from his letters, indicate his quickly growing distance from religious matters at that time. In the same context it may also be significant that Fay's death had come just before Fitzgerald's marriage to Zelda Sayre, an Episcopalian, in a Catholic nuptial at St Patrick's Cathedral, New York, on 3 April 1920. The primary love relationship of his life had begun, and in many ways it displaced many of the loyalties and commitments that had preceded it, some of which had, in any case, been 'shattered by the death' of Monsignor Fay the previous year. As Joan M. Allen has noted in her valuable study of the influence of Fitzgerald's Catholicism upon his art, 'the beloved priest, his second father, was dead, and Zelda Sayre took his place in Fitzgerald's life' (59). Following Fay's death, Fitzgerald moved quickly in an attempt to fill the spiritual vacuum. As he acknowledged in a February 1920 letter to his friend, the improbably named Isabelle Amorous, 'You're still a catholic but Zelda's the only God I have left now' (*Correspondence* 53). In marrying the woman he did, Fitzgerald ran counter to the unanimous advice of all his friends, who had advised him 'not to marry a wild, pleasure loving girl like Zelda' (*Correspondence* 53). Even Zelda's own mother told him: 'It will take more than the Pope to make Zelda good; you will have to call on God Almighty direct' (Allen 62). With Zelda Sayre at his side, however, Fitzgerald began that 'rush into Bohemia' that Leslie, in January 1919, had explicitly cautioned him against (*Correspondence* 37).

According to one of the Fitzgeralds' biographers, James R. Mellow, it is possible to conclude that by November 1919, and having received Scribner's letter accepting *Paradise* for publication the previous month, Fitzgerald had already begun 'to create for himself the irreversible image of the playboy and the hard drinker' (80).

A further reason for Fitzgerald's turning away from a closer spiritual affiliation with Catholicism at that time may have been his increasing absorption within Edmund Wilson's sphere of influence. Edmund 'Bunny' Wilson was a respected friend and critic of his work, and, just as Leslie and Fay were urging Fitzgerald to emphasise what Leslie termed 'the mystical note' (*Correspondence* 66) in his writing, and to acknowledge Rome as 'the only permanent country the only patria to which we can all belong' (*Correspondence* 37), so Wilson was equally adamant that Fitzgerald should turn firmly away from what he called, in an August 1919 letter to Fitzgerald, 'the phosphorescences of the decaying Church of Rome' (Wilson, *Letters on Literature* 44). Wilson's influence upon Fitzgerald was certainly derived at least partly from his already established reputation and influence as a magisterial New York literary editor (from 1920 to 1921 he was, for instance, a co-editor of *Vanity Fair*), and Fitzgerald referred to him as his 'intellectual conscience' ('Crack-Up' 49). Indeed, according to Wilson himself, 'from college days, when I had been a year ahead of him ... he had come to regard himself as somehow accountable to me for his literary career' (*Shores* 375). At a time when *Paradise* had still not been accepted by Scribner's and its young author was still very much in need of channels of publication, it may not be surprising that in August 1919 he replied to Wilson's letter in terms intended to mollify his attack upon Fitzgerald's faith: 'I am ashamed to say that my Catholicism is scarcely more than a memory – no, that's wrong, it's more than that; at any rate I do not go to the church nor mumble stray nothings over crystalline beads' (Turnbull *Letters* 345).

Shane Leslie realized the truth of *This Side of Paradise* when he wrote to Fitzgerald after its publication: 'I think it is a Catholic-minded book at heart and that you like Fay and myself can never be anything but Catholics however much we write and pose to make the bourgeois stare!' (*Correspondence* 66), but its bedrock Catholicism was never adequately acknowledged until the appearance of Joan M. Allen's study in 1978, an appraisal more recently consolidated by Benita A. Moore's book *Escape into a Labyrinth: F. Scott Fitzgerald, Catholic Sensibility, and the American Way* (1988) and Walter Raubicheck's 2002 essay, 'The Catholic Romanticism of *This Side of Paradise*'. Raubicheck rightly concludes that the novel's 'investigation of the mores of [Fitzgerald's] time was based on a moral foundation that underlies his moral idealism, a foundation that is essentially Catholic' (65). These views of Fitzgerald's spiritual orientation were also noted as early as 1924 by his contemporary Ernest Boyd, an Irish-born critic who became an important figure in New York literary circles of the 1920s – he published a biography of H.L. Mencken in 1925. Boyd wrote that 'where so many others are conscious only of sex, Fitzgerald is conscious of his soul. His Catholic heaven is not so far away that he can be misled into mistaking the shoddy dream of a radical millennium as a substitute for Paradise' (120–1). Writing in 1945, William Troy also had noted that 'least explored of all by his critics were the permanent effects of his early exposure to Catholicism, which are no less potent because rarely on the surface of his work' (192). As a young man faced with the swiftly mutating life and attractions of New York, the norms of Fitzgerald's upbringing were under pressure as he wrote his first novel, yet its hero is furnished with a reliable moral compass, since 'Amory acknowledges his sense of morality and connects it to established religion. Although he sometimes doubts and blasphemes, he sharply rebukes an unconventional girl friend who is completely atheistic, invariably centers his self-examination on religious principles, and makes his intellectual confessions to Monsignor Darcy' (Gindin 111). Amory Blaine is a hero who is faced with a number of moral tests along the way, yet he remains conscious of the morality of his thoughts and actions. He recognises the extent to which a Christian imperative is 'the only assimilative, traditionary bulwark against the decay of morals' (259) he finds present in American life, and connects religion to the maintenance of civilised order in the face of potential barbarism: 'until the great mobs could be educated into a moral sense someone must cry: "Thou shalt not!"' (259). Amory's Catholic conscience is personified by Monsignor Darcy, whose Christian faith is wrapped up within romantic rhetoric. He writes to Amory, 'You make a great mistake if you think you can be romantic without religion' (204). He identifies the presence of what he calls 'the mystical element' in Amory, something Darcy says 'flows into us that enlarges our personalities, and when it ebbs out our personalities shrink' (204). With this credo, he cautions Amory against the risks of a terminally 'shrivelled' and shrunken self: 'Beware of losing yourself in the personality of another being' (204).

Amory's commitment to an ethical absolutism is closely connected to the novel's concern with the presence of evil. This is manifest as a non-negotiable inevitability in the narrative, the assumption being that diabolical energies are immanent and arrive unannounced in our midst. In the chapter that follows immediately upon Darcy's warning, the last of Amory's loves, the bohemian and promiscuous Eleanor Savage, exploits the tones of Swinburnean decadence in poetry that expresses her gothic atheism

> What if the light is but sun and the little streams sing not!
> We are together it seems ... I have loved you so ...
> What did the last night hold ...
> What leered out of the dark in the ghostly clover ...?
> God! ... till you stirred in your sleep ... and were wild afraid ...
> ... we are chronicle now to the eerie. (222–3)

On first sight of Eleanor, Amory sees beauty and witchery combined, as the lightning of a stormy night shows up her face and her 'burning eyes' appear as those of 'a witch, of perhaps nineteen' (210). She calls herself 'a romantic little materialist' (212), and even sounds like a flower-child of later twentieth-century liberation, as she tells Amory that 'just one person in fifty has any glimmer of what sex is. I'm hipped on Freud and all that' (220); he thinks of her as 'a feast and a folly' (213), and in his erotic transport, 'his paganism soared' (213). The persona of Rupert Brooke, who wrote the poem 'Tiare Tahiti' (in which, as discussed above, Fitzgerald found the novel's title), is now detached from the novel's epigraph (' ... Well, This side of paradise / There's little comfort in the wise') to become incarnate within Amory as a voluptuous haunting, for 'Amory tried to play Rupert Brooke as long as he knew Eleanor', while she tells him, 'you look a good deal like the pictures of Rupert Brooke'. Together they occupy what she calls 'a sort of pagan heaven', much akin to the pagan paradise (214) in Brooke's poems such as 'Waikiki' (1913), which she reads to Amory as he lives through 'reflexes of the dead Englishman's literary moods' (214). Their elations are indeed vicarious and second-hand; they 'turned to Brooke, and Swinburne, and Shelley' (214), whose lyrics are required to do considerable labour in place of Amory and Eleanor's love that is never more than a notion: 'they must bend tiny golden tentacles from his imagination to hers, that would take the place of the great, deep love that was never so near, yet never so much of a dream' (214). Their narrative indeed links very closely to that present in Brooke's 'Waikiki' – which tells 'An empty tale, of idleness and pain, / Of two that loved – or did not love – and one / Whose perplexed heart did evil, foolishly, / A long while since, and by some other sea' – so that it may be read as a concise subtext for this entire episode of *Paradise*. The 'Young Irony' chapter is but one further interrogation of evil, as Eleanor's thoughts turn towards what she calls 'her black old inside self, the real one, with the fundamental honesty that keeps me from being absolutely wicked by making me realize my own sins' (219). Before their final parting, as 'they stood there, hating each other with a bitter sadness' (222), what Amory calls Eleanor's 'blasphemy' provokes his defence of Catholicism and his retreat from materialism: 'like most intellectuals who don't find faith convenient ... you'll yell loudly for a priest on your death bed' (221).

Fitzgerald's concern with moral balance is already intimated in his first novel's title: on this side of paradise, Fitzgerald's story can perhaps be understood as an allegory in which, as critic Sy Kahn has argued, 'American Youth is caught between the forces of Good and Evil' (35). Yet this view only takes us so far in the effort to understand Amory's journey, which in important terms is more than allegorical, for Amory is also aware of the immanence of evil in the world, as his friend Dick Humbird's death and its revenant aftermath indicates. Towards the end of his story and following upon his relations with Eleanor, Amory fears that his 'virtue-tank' is empty; as he puts it in a frank Q&A: 'I've no more virtue to lose ... all through youth and adolescence we give off calories of virtue ... that's why a "good man going wrong" attracts people ... Q. – All your calories gone? A. – All of them. I'm beginning to warm myself at other people's virtue. Q. – Are you corrupt? A. – I think so. I'm not sure. I'm not sure about good and evil at all any more' (238–9). In this morally parlous state, Amory is open to terrifying visitations and visions from the underworld, as 'this dialogue merged grotesquely into his mind's most familiar state – a grotesque blending of desires, worries, exterior impressions and physical reactions' (239).

The novel's reviewers were confounded by its 'disconcertingly realistic' willingness to entertain a supernatural order/disorder at the heart of life (R.V.A.S. in Kazin 49), Heywood Broun (in the *New York Herald Tribune*, 1920), for instance, finding that Amory's 'frenzy of terror and ... hallucinations' were not only inexplicable in context – 'the explanation was hidden from us' – but also incompatible with the novel's other contexts – 'not altogether characteristic of Princeton' (51); and it is only relatively recently that critics such as Stephen Tanner (in his essay 'The Devil and F. Scott Fitzgerald') have been willing to assess these aspects of Fitzgerald's theology appropriately. This may be at least partly explained by the intervening passage of time, almost a century of inhumanity, the horrors of which have made the concept of evil and the devil incarnate now almost commonplace. In the death-camps of the Second World War, the protracted horrors of Soviet gulags and the Bosnian genocide, many could believe that evil had made its perfect home. George Steiner's magisterial essays upon twentieth-century evil have insisted on an ultimate rationale:

> Much has been said of man's bewilderment and solitude after the disappearance of Heaven from active belief. We know of the neutral emptiness of the skies and the terrors it has brought. But it may be that the loss of Hell is the more severe dislocation. It may be that the mutation of Hell into a metaphor left a formidable gap in the coordinates of location, of psychological recognition in the Western mind. The absence of the familiar damned opened a vortex which the modern totalitarian state filled. To have neither Heaven nor Hell is to be intolerably deprived and alone in a world gone flat. Of the two, Hell proved the easier to recreate.... Needing Hell, we have learned how to build and run it on earth.... No skill holds greater menace. (*In Bluebeard's Castle* 55–6)

And Stephen Tanner's essay, though it does not mention Steiner, does discuss Andrew Delbanco's book of 1995, *The Death of Satan: How Americans Have Lost the Sense of Evil*, which argues that 'Satan died in American culture partly because of a preoccupation with personal ambition and wealth, matters which of course were principal concerns for Fitzgerald' (Tanner 75). Certainly, in *Paradise*, Fitzgerald's discourse is nothing if not direct in its willingness to provide both a gothic *mise-en-scène* – as Amory and Eleanor 'rode to the highest hill and watched an evil moon ride high, for they knew then that they could see the devil in each other' (206) – as well as a more robust literalism of approach to the matter that finds its way into James L.W. West's 'Chronology and Characters' Appendix to the Cambridge edition of the novel, where the reader finds that in May 1916 'Amory sees the Devil in New York City' (399). The novel uses its satanic references as a lucid shorthand for extinct virtue; as Walter Raubicheck reminds us, 'the devil is associated with … characters who lose their souls to gain the world' (61), with Dick Humbird representing, for Amory, 'tempting but false values' (Tanner 67). Emancipated from a merely figurative idiom, evil is expressed as a power that keeps breaking through the porous walls of Amory's advancing secularism. For Stephen Tanner, however, Fitzgerald's moral roots 'were in an older, prewar America, a world with supernatural sanctions, a world of conscience and guilt' (71); he was raised in a world much more willing to countenance the devil as an active force in the midst of life. In this regard, Tanner draws an important comparison between Fitzgerald and Flannery O'Connor, an American writer whose short stories dramatise an explicitly Catholic theology. More recently, Norman Mailer's final novel, *The Castle in the Forest* (2007), shows a similar determination to personify devils as actors in a deeply embattled moral universe structured along Manichaean lines, whereby humanity is perennially plagued by the struggle between good and evil, a theme that resonates also in Anthony Burgess's novel, *Earthly Powers* (1980). Certainly *Paradise* confirms Joan M. Allen's argument that it 'is actually the product of a deeply religious sensibility.... the most overtly Catholic novel in his canon' (83), while Paul Giles, in his book *American Catholic Arts and Fictions*, provides a very helpful discussion of 'the implicit discourse of Catholicism' (187) in Fitzgerald's work, particularly with regard to *The Great Gatsby*. The novel is willing to countenance not only the devilish visitations already discussed, but also Amory's awareness of the better angels around him. The presence of evil, manifest as a proximate 'aura ... tainted as stale, weak wine, yet a horror, diffusively brooding', is only one of 'two breathless, listening forces' that he is able to sense; the other, borne on the breeze that wafts through the windows, he recognises to be the spirit of Monsignor Darcy, who has recently died: 'he knew then what it was that he had perceived among the curtains of the room' (234).

Edmund Wilson criticised Fitzgerald's first novel for 'having no dominating intention to endow it with unity and force', complaining that 'one of the chief weaknesses of *This Side of Paradise* is that it is really not *about* anything' (*Shores* 28). This is overstated. The novel does have an underlying spine of organising sense that moves Amory forward from his rather unstructured experience as 'the egotist' and ends with his becoming 'a personage', having acquired a platform of self-knowledge. Although the novel ends anticlimactically and provisionally, Amory's emotional and intellectual strivings and his eventual reconciliation with life's misfortunes are more appealing, at least in comparison to the unwholesome collapse of personal integrity that defines Anthony Patch at the close of his next novel, *The Beautiful and Damned*.

3

A Triumph of Lethargy: *The Beautiful and Damned* (1922)

'Thank God I'm thru with it' (Turnbull, *Letters* 171). As he completed the finishing touches to the final draft of his second novel in late 1921, Fitzgerald's accompanying sigh of relief is almost audible in these words to his editor Max Perkins. An early title for the novel had been *The Flight of the Rocket*, but when *The Beautiful and Damned* was eventually published on 4 March 1922, its reception by reviewers in many ways reflected Fitzgerald's own private judgment of its flight as one burdened by some internal malfunctions, as he confided to Perkins that he was 'almost, but not quite, satisfied with the book' (Turnbull, *Letters* 170). *This Side of Paradise* had indeed rocketed Fitzgerald into early fame, with its 'witty, flippant and lighthearted' style (Meyers 85–6), but two years later, many readers and a significant majority of critics would in contrast see its successor as engaged with a very different register, in the words of Jeffrey Meyers, 'ponderous and tragic, twice as long ... more static' (85). Fitzgerald chose as the novel's epigraph 'the victor belongs to the spoils' and though this is attributed to its main character, the dissipated Anthony Patch, Fitzgerald's own lifelong tendency to live beyond his financial means ('his identity was inextricably tied to money, yet he never learned how to handle it' (Barks, 'Collecting Fitzgerald' 184) had forced him to sell the novel's serial rights to *Metropolitan Magazine* in which it had its first instalment in September 1921. He had therefore no control over the significant cuts the magazine's editors made to the text he had given them, and *Metropolitan* published a version of it that while emphasising the plot and its progress managed to remove most of its philosophical underpinnings as well: overall the six instalments saw a quarter of Fitzgerald's original text omitted by the magazine's editors.

His efforts to repair the damage when preparing the magazine text for publication by Scribner's were, however, less than vigorous.

As he began the task, his letter to Perkins of August 1921 told of his enervation and despair:

> I am sick alike of life, liquor and literature. If it wasn't for Zelda I think I'd disapear [*sic*] out of sight for three years. Ship as a sailor or something + get hard–I'm sick of the flabby semi-intellectual softness in which I flounder with my generation. (*Life in Letters* 48)

In this mood, 'reluctantly, he went to work to revise a manuscript in which he no longer believed' (Le Vot 97). For all of his life Fitzgerald maintained that view. As Cathy Barks has observed, 'evidence of Fitzgerald's honest appraisal of his own work can also be found in his inscriptions. In an inscription dated 1939 in a copy of *The Beautiful and Damned*, Fitzgerald writes: "This book oddly enough is responsible from its title for the phrase 'beautiful and dumb.' I doubt if it has any other distinction"' (Barks, 'Collecting Fitzgerald' 183), while in another, undated, inscription he wrote with typical candour: '"Beautiful but Dumb" was this book's contribution to its time. It has awful spots but some good ones. I was trying to learn' (*Correspondence* 620). Although he recognised the novel's faults, as he worked on the manuscript he was unable to accomplish the wholesale changes he knew were necessary. He even indulged in some wish-fulfilment, as in November 1921 he wrote to Edmund Wilson that he had 'almost completely rewritten' the book (*Life in Letters* 49) though the record shows that while he did make extensive changes to Book 1 of the novel, changes to Book 2 were minimal and there was no revision at all to Book 3. If Fitzgerald himself was 'sick alike of life, liquor and literature' he was hardly cheered by the novel's cover design which, he complained to Perkins, pictured a man who was 'a debauched edition of me' (Turnbull, *Letters* 171). Zelda drew her own alternative version, which seemed to embrace rather than counter the theme of dissipation. Perhaps recalling Anthony Patch's bitter self-appraisal in which he saw himself as 'a pretentious fool, making careers out of cocktails … he was empty, it seemed, empty as an old bottle' (51), Zelda's illustration depicted a nude girl bathing in a champagne glass, or as Nancy Milford in her biography of Zelda puts it, 'a childlike mermaid sloshing happily in a cocktail' (97).

Despite Fitzgerald's misgivings, the novel sold around 50,000 copies, with Scribner's having to go to three printings in 1922. Reviews were less than appreciative, although H.L. Mencken saw the novel as one which if 'not a complete success ... is nevertheless near enough to success to be worthy of respect. There is fine observation in it, and much penetrating detail, and the writing is solid and sound'. He saw it as building upon *Paradise*, since with its writing 'Fitzgerald ceases to be a *Wunderkind* and begins to come into his maturity' (Meyers 89). One review presented the novel's central characters, Anthony and Gloria Patch, as inhabiting a milieu very close to that of *Paradise*, existing not in 'the ordinary moral universe' but rather 'that detached, largely invented region where glittering youth plays at wit and love' (Meyers 89), and although Edmund Wilson (to whom Fitzgerald had sent the manuscript of *The Beautiful and Damned* for editing comments) in a private letter found the novel to have 'a genuine emotional power which he has scarcely displayed before', his eventually published (but, perhaps significantly, anonymous) appraisal of Fitzgerald's work in *The Bookman* of 1922 was, while typically sharp in its understanding of Fitzgerald's strengths as a writer, also cruel in its discriminations. The opening paragraphs of his essay contrive to present him as both 'exhilaratingly clever' as well as intellectually deprived, so that 'to meet F. Scott Fitzgerald is to think of a stupid old woman with whom someone has left a diamond':

> Scott Fitzgerald is, in fact, no old woman, but a very good-looking young man ... yet ... it is true that Fitzgerald has been left with a jewel which he doesn't know quite what to do with. For he has been given imagination without intellectual control of it; he has been given the desire for beauty without an aesthetic ideal; and he has been given a gift for expression without very many ideas to express. (Wilson, *Shores* 27)

Though in a footnote on the same page of his collection of essays *The Shores of Light* (1952) Wilson attributed the 'stupid old woman' anecdote to the novelist Edna St Vincent Millay ('who met Scott Fitzgerald in Paris in the Spring of 1921'), his inclusion of it in the essay, and at its very start, is at best gratuitous, at worst malicious. With its distasteful gendered/gerontic slur, it was surely intended to set the tone for the whole essay, which on the whole damns Fitzgerald by faint praise, presenting him as a gifted naïf.

The essay's importance lies in Wilson's reputation as one of America's most influential literary critics. Fitzgerald, as with any young writer, needed his work to be appraised in robust and honest terms, and his respect for Wilson's acumen was understandable, if more than a little obsequious (in his essay of 1936 'The Crack-Up' he dubbed Wilson 'my intellectual conscience' [49]). His response to Wilson's essay does, however, say a great deal about his insecurities at that time, when, having published his second novel as still a young man of only 26, the receipt of 'more unqualified support from the friends he respected would have gone some way towards bolstering Fitzgerald's always fragile artistic self-confidence' (Hook, *Literary Life* 45). Probably expecting Fitzgerald's censure, Wilson had prior to its publication sent a draft of the essay to him for comment. Fitzgerald's responding letters of January and February 1922 are a candid insight into his self-appraisal in those early years. He begged (rather than demanded, which some authors would certainly have done) that Wilson remove from the draft what would assuredly have been damaging references to 'the legend about my liquoring' which were, he feared, already 'terribly widespread'. What is extraordinary is that his friend 'Bunny' Wilson's draft should have included such references at all and that Fitzgerald should have had to point out the obvious to him: 'this thing would hurt me more than you could imagine – both in my contact with the people with whom I'm thrown – relatives + respectable friends ... and, what is much more important, financially' (*Life in Letters* 50). In a postscript to the same letter Fitzgerald even bends over backwards in an effort not to offend Wilson's own critical sensitivities: 'I am consoled for asking you to cut the ... alcoholic paragraphs by the fact that if you hadn't known me you couldn't or wouldn't have put them in', but he also adds what a critic of Wilson's stature should already have recognised, that such writings are 'really personal gossip' (352).

Certainly, Wilson's essay 'did nothing in the short-term or the long-term to help Fitzgerald's reputation' (Hook, *Literary Life* 45) and only the *nonpareil* genius of *The Great Gatsby* and the tragic radiance of *Tender is the Night* could have salvaged that reputation from some aspects of Wilson's brutal critique. Perhaps the most baffling part of the whole correspondence and, as Andrew Hook notes, 'what is really astonishing [,] is Fitzgerald's enthusiastic response to Wilson's article' (45). That response displays an acceptance of Wilson's censures that is so blatant as to make one wish it was ironically intended, a species of mock-masochism. Such thinking is probably indeed wishful, however, as referring to Wilson's essay he tells him,

> I am guilty of its every stricture ... I don't see how I could possibly be offended at anything in it ... I like it, I think it's an unprejudiced

> diagnosis and I am considerably in your debt for the interest which impelled you to write it ... I enjoyed it enormously. (*Life in Letters* 50)

Again Hook is absolutely right to see that 'only a severe case of artistic and intellectual self-doubt could have produced such a reaction' (45). Perhaps too it might also be seen as the understandable reaction of a young and still needy writer to Edmund Wilson's status and his overbearing, arrogant disposition in the matter. Despite Fitzgerald's complimentary overtures it is clear that Wilson took some umbrage at Fitzgerald's requests, since in his next letter of February 1922 the young novelist is again having to defend his reputation, telling Wilson that 'a pre-publication review which contained private information [i.e. Wilson's references in his essay to Fitzgerald's drinking, for instance] destined (in my opinion) to hurt the sale of my book was something of which I had a legitimate right to complain' (*Life in Letters* 55). When the essay was finally published, however, Wilson contrived to get his way (anonymously) by way of a rhetoric of insinuation and association, telling his readers, for instance, that 'Fitzgerald, when he wrote the book [a reference to *Paradise*], was drunk with Compton Mackenzie' (*Shores* 28). He sustains the critique by impugning Fitzgerald's Irishness, which he defines by quoting Bernard Shaw's description of the Irish imagination, which is 'such a torture that you can't bear it without whisky' (31). Turn the page and one finds that he is at it again, characterising Fitzgerald as a happily inebriated sprite who goes dancing 'amuck on a case of bootleg liquor' (32). Wilson gives a compliment with one hand only to take it back with the other; if *The Beautiful and Damned* is a novel with some serious ethics to it, then for Wilson, this moral dimension is one 'that the author did not perhaps intend to point' (34). For the most part, Wilson's essay is unconscionable in its *ad hominem* assault upon its subject. Its most serious indictment comes in the final paragraph, where Fitzgerald's supposed faults are presented as representative of his generation and he is sketched as at best a guileless and typical victim of what Wilson dubs 'the Age of Confusion' – the Jazz Age – morally unhinged and given over to hedonistic indulgence:

> it may be that we cannot demand too high a degree of moral balance from young men, however able or brilliant, who write books in the year 1921: we must remember ... that they have had to derive their chief stimulus from the wars, the society and the commerce of the Age of Confusion itself. (35)

With such a review from friend Bunny soon to be followed by one titled 'Friend Husband's Latest' from wife Zelda, who charged the novel with leaning heavily upon her own *bon mot*, Fitzgerald in 1922 may have felt with some justification that his new novel could do no worse than take its chance in the general run of reviews outside his home circle. What André Le Vot refers to as 'the insolence of Zelda's book review' (117) came about after she had been asked by another of the couple's friends, Burton Rascoe, to appraise the novel for the *New York Tribune*. He wanted some publicity for the newspaper's new book department which he was managing and encouraged her to 'view it, or pretend to view it, objectively and get in a rub here and there' so that 'it would cause a great deal of comment' (Milford 99). The result must only have added to Fitzgerald's discomfiture as his wife very publicly drew attention to the literary debts she believed he owed her:

> On one page I recognized a portion of an old diary of mine which mysteriously disappeared shortly after my marriage, and also scraps of letters, which, though considerably edited, sound to me vaguely familiar. In fact, Mr. Fitzgerald – I believe that is how he spells his name – seems to believe that plagiarism begins at home. (Bruccoli and Bryer 333)

Although before publication in January 1922 Fitzgerald had acknowledged Zelda's influence upon the novel, he did so in a rather barbed reference to what he called 'the complete, fine and full hearted selfishness and chill-mindedness of Zelda' (*Life in Letters* 51), a comment which seems a little short of uxorious.

The Beautiful and Damned does have an autobiographical basis, though perhaps Wilson's comment – 'it is all about him and Zelda' (Wilson, *Letters* 56) – overstates the relationship between its fictive environment and the Fitzgeralds' own lives. In two comments made a decade apart, the author himself seemed to be divided about the matter, telling his wife in 1930, 'I wish The Beautiful and Damned had been a maturely written book because it was all true. We ruined ourselves' (*Life in Letters* 189), while towards the end of his life in 1940, with Zelda in a sanatorium, and when he was living with Sheilah Graham in Hollywood, he wrote to his daughter Scottie:

> Gloria [Patch] was a much more trivial and vulgar person than your mother. I can't really say there was any resemblance except in the beauty and certain terms of expression she used, and also

> I naturally used many circumstantial events of our early married life. However the emphases were entirely different. We had a much better time than Anthony and Gloria had. (*Life in Letters* 453)

Fitzgerald's critics, however, have been much less willing to follow him in this context, with Richard Lehan, for instance, arguing that 'the woman Anthony marries seems much like Zelda ... a kind of vamp whose demands upon Anthony are excessive and debilitating' (80), while Henry Dan Piper also contends that Gloria Patch 'derived from Zelda' and that Fitzgerald 'was writing much too close to actual experience' (92). Jeffrey Meyers even argues that the symbiotic relationship between life and art was one over which Fitzgerald could not or would not exert control, so that eventually he became 'confused at times between his imaginative and his real existence' and 'behaved like his own fictional characters' in a fatally predictive interplay. Unable to extricate himself from this cycle he 'would eventually be overcome by the very doom he had foreshadowed in *The Beautiful and Damned*' (88). The truth in the end lies probably somewhere in between, and it would be surprising if this novel, which Fitzgerald began sketching out 'a bare three and a half months into his own honeymoon' (Mellow 129) did not eventually show intense signs of the turbulent and passionate primary relationship he had just embarked upon.

Of the novel's more recent critics, Andrew Hook is especially supportive of what he regards as its virtues, condemning the critical consensus that has prevailed in the years since publication – 'the critical tradition that insists that Fitzgerald's early novels are immature, apprentice works' (*F. Scott Fitzgerald* 30). Although Hook's defence of the novel rests upon his view that 'it is a remarkable book' (*F. Scott Fitzgerald* 32) which is 'eminently readable' (*F. Scott Fitzgerald* 43), he yet finds it difficult to defend the novel against salient faults, such as when its forward progress is sacrificed to indulgent philosophical *longueurs*. Hook acknowledges these to be troublesome lapses in narrative progress: 'when Anthony and Gloria and their friends discuss life and its meaning – or lack of meaning – then the pace and tension ... are inclined to flag' (*F. Scott Fitzgerald* 38). His headline praise for the novel may also seem at odds with his other, albeit reluctant, criticisms of its narrative integrity, as he acknowledges 'it is true that Fitzgerald offers no single explanation of the decline that begins as soon as the marriage ceremony [of Anthony and Gloria] is over. A variety of factors, some of them contradictory, seem to be involved' (*F. Scott Fitzgerald* 37).

Inconsistencies and contradictory lapses in its narrative design and point-of-view are perhaps the most common complaint of critics on this novel, a fault even acknowledged by the author himself, who told a friend: 'I devoted so much more care myself to the detail of the book than I did to thinking out the general scheme' (to Bishop, Piper 92). Still, for James L.W. West III, although *Paradise* may be 'the better book', *Beautiful* is in comparison less dislocated, since 'the narrative is coherent; the characters are consistent ... and the themes are carefully articulated throughout' ('The Question of Vocation' in *Cambridge Companion* 48).

Fitzgerald's second novel certainly marked a real advance by incorporating within its drama clear signs of what has been regarded as the core theme of his art, 'the need for illusion, and the tragedy that springs from its inevitable failure' (Cross 37). This is exemplified in different contexts and expressions throughout the narrative and realised on some heightened occasions with a special intensity of focus. Anthony Patch, at these moments, is given to see through the shallow surface of his life as the veil of superficial consciousness parts, and with sudden, sharp insight he approaches a valid existential revelation, as in the following example, entitled 'Breath of the Cave', where we find him engaged in solitary survey, outside of what one might call ordinary time. The narrator begins by describing the sounds of the warm New York night reaching Anthony 'through his wide-open windows', a symphony that is at first organic and innocent in meaning, 'like a child playing with a ball', while also 'a thousand lovers were making this sound', giving the illusion 'that, in a little while, life would be beautiful as a story, promising happiness' (*The Beautiful and Damned*. Harmondsworth: Penguin, 1972. 125. All further references are to this edition). But the illusory nature of this beauty is soon revealed by a more discordant note, intimating another life, more urgent, insistent and much less welcome in its meanings:

> A new note separated itself jarringly from the soft crying of the night. It was a noise from an area-way within a hundred feet from his rear window, the noise of a woman's laughter. It began low, incessant and whining – some servant-maid with her fellow, he thought – and then it grew in volume and became hysterical ... It would break off for a moment and he would just catch the low rumble of a man's voice, then begin again – interminably; at first annoying, then strangely terrible. (125–6)

For Anthony here, the symphony climaxes with an urgent epiphany, his recognition of 'some animal quality in that unrestrained laughter' (126) that cumulatively conveys not happiness but horror. The laughter eventually reaches 'the quality of a scream' which in the end is capable of silencing all around: 'a silence empty and menacing as the greater silence overhead' (126). The narrated encounter here accrues particular meaning since it occurs on the eve of Anthony's wedding to Gloria Gilbert, an event to which it is associated by contexts both temporal and material: it is given the force of a warning which he experiences viscerally, as though the very oxygen is about to be sucked out of his existence. Escaping such a deathly threat means achieving complete sequestration through transcendence, a transport to a dream-world of non-gendered freedom where the air is figured as plentiful and his worries cannot reach him:

> The room had grown smothery. He wanted to be out in some cool and bitter breeze, miles above the cities, and to live serene and detached back in the corners of his mind. Life was that sound out there, that ghastly reiterated female sound.
> 'Oh, my *God!*' he cried, drawing in his breath sharply.
> Burying his face in the pillows he tried in vain to concentrate upon the details of the next day. (126)

Here is an early instance of Fitzgerald's willingness to read the material world for the external signs of man's spiritual condition in terms of both congruence and discord. For Jay Gatsby in the moments before his death, the fallen world of appearances was apprehended as 'a new world, material without being real' (136), and for Dick Diver, faced at the close of *Tender is the Night* with the sight of his wife Nicole and her lover Tommy Barban together on the Riviera sands, betrayal is realized as an image of bleak transcendence: 'black and white and metallic against the sky' (Everyman ed. 319). In the passage from *The Beautiful and Damned* above, fears of untrammelled female carnality are disclosed by repeated motifs of asphyxiation. As that 'ghastly reiterated female sound' reaches 'a high point, tensed and stifled', it causes Anthony to draw in his own breath 'sharply' as, 'burying his face in the pillows', he is unable 'to strangle his reaction' to it and suffocates in a room 'that had grown smothery' (126) as 'the breathless impendency' of his marriage bears down upon him (127). The passage is loaded with tropes that become the raw material of a gathering terror. In *The Beautiful and Damned*, 'life would be beautiful as a story' (125) for Anthony if only the creaturely conditions for that life could be sustained. Those conditions are, however, all connected not to the actualities and logic of commitments made in the real world of an impending nuptial contract but rather to their pleasantly vague possibility. In the passage above the narrator makes it clear that the sounds Anthony hears and associates with 'life' are promissory tokens rather than pressing realities. Such sounds are therefore 'evanescent and summery, alive with remote anticipation' (125): their life is the currency only of his lazy conjecture. Marriage, on the other hand, he now realises as he stares at 'the morning pallor of his complexion' (126) in his bathroom mirror, will certainly have its actual costs – in real currency, and in real time, beginning with the platinum and emerald wedding ring that Gloria 'had insisted on' (127), there on his dressing-table in front of him, an object which he handles with nervous fingers. The tally of his new responsibilities had after all just begun: 'it seemed absurd that from now on he would pay for all her meals. It was going to cost' (127). The wedding ring is hardly a romantic icon here, more the first bill he owes to the marriage.

'The Breath of the Cave' is a capsule rendering of Fitzgerald's core theme, tightly dramatised and focused upon 'the need for illusion' (Cross 37), and containing clear intimations of the tragic irony of failure in that regard. As the morning breaks in yellow light for Anthony on his wedding day, its dance along the carpet of his room confirms an ironic, almost cosmic joke, 'as though the sun were smiling at some ancient and reiterated gag of his own' (127). The old joke, one is encouraged to think on this wedding day morn, is assuredly at Anthony's expense (something along the lines of 'new dawns may be false dawns'), though his response suggests it is a joke he does not share: 'Anthony laughed in a nervous one-syllable snort. "By God!" he muttered to himself, "I'm as good as married!"' (127). The beautiful is, one senses, about to enter the first circle of the damned.

The novel's interest in the theme of damnation itself was likely encouraged by Fitzgerald's admiration for Harold Frederic's novel of 1896, a masterpiece of American realism, *The Damnation of Theron Ware*. That he knew of Frederic's work is clear from an intertextual reference in *This Side of Paradise*, where, along with other examples of American realism by Frank Norris and Theodore Dreiser, it is cited as one of 'several excellent American novels' that Amory Blaine had been 'rather surprised by' after having been introduced to them by 'a critic named Mencken' (195). According to Piper, Fitzgerald had been attracted to it 'not only because it was an outstanding novel but one that had dealt sympathetically with the American conflict between Catholic and Protestant that he himself had experienced' (88). *The Beautiful and*

Damned can also be read as thematically engaged with related issues, and a vignette such as 'The Breath of the Cave' can contribute to a theological reading of Fitzgerald's writing as it developed from the early Princeton stories and *This Side of Paradise*. For instance Stephen Frye, in his essay 'Fitzgerald's Catholicism Revisited', has drawn attention to what he calls 'a spiritual conflict in Fitzgerald' (65), a conflict deriving from his necessary exposure to 'the intellectual influences of a secular age' as they 'confronted the theological notions that governed Fitzgerald's early life' (65). This conflict is manifest textually in 'the desire to encounter God [which] remains deeply rooted in the hearts of Fitzgerald's characters' (73). 'The Breath of the Cave' is one further textual instance of what Frye calls 'a complex interplay between dream and reality, physicality and illusion, which becomes apparent in both character and description' in the novel, so that '*The Beautiful and Damned* manifests an essentially doctrinal view of the relationship between the transcendent and the immanent' (65). In such terms, 'The Breath of the Cave' again exemplifies what H.W. Häusermann (as noted by Frye) in his study of 'Fitzgerald's Religious Sense' describes as the author's 'constant wavering between reality and illusion' (Häusermann 82). Overall, Frye is right to see in Fitzgerald's novel the clear signs of 'his residual Catholic sensibility, his lingering belief in paradise itself' (74) and to conclude that such background beliefs are a very important influence in Fitzgerald's art, one that may drive the kinds of conflicts evident there. More than half a century ago, writing in *Accent* magazine five years after Fitzgerald's death, William Troy was even then able to note that 'least explored of all by his critics were the permanent effects of his early exposure to Catholicism, which are no less potent because rarely on the surface of his work' (192). The neglect of this important enquiry has now to some extent been rectified and the critical discourse as used by Häusermann, Frye (and Raubicheck in terms of his treatment of *Paradise*) combines with that of other critics working from an understanding of the romantic impulse informing Fitzgerald's art. In *Paradise* Thayer Darcy writes in a letter to Amory Blaine, 'you make a great mistake if you think you can be a romantic without religion' (199).

The damnation of beauty theme is first broached in the quasi-Faustian satiric dialogue that takes place at the close of the novel's first chapter. There, in a section entitled 'A Flashback in Paradise', 'The Voice' is the supernatural arbiter of the spirit of 'Beauty' and her reincarnated fate, telling her that in a 15-year embodiment she will become a 'susciety girl ... a sort of bogus aristocrat'. 'Beauty' is indeed to experience damnation by exposure to the bogus, the banality and materialism of America in the 1920s: 'You will find much that is bogus. Also, you will do much that is bogus' (30). 'Beauty' is presumably reincarnated as Gloria, who at a central stage in the novel is terrified by the sinister presence of Joe Hull. As Milton R. Stern rightly comments, since

> there is no vantage point of moral perfection on the part of anyone involved in the action of *The Beautiful and Damned* ... in order to provide a measure for his characters' damnation, Fitzgerald had to revert to his trick of the devil-figure, from which he copied even such details as the devil's conspicuously odd feet. (151)

The personification is not as convincingly handled as in the case of Dick Humbird in *This Side of Paradise*, however, and is trite; as Maury Noble, with whom Joe Hull has arrived at one of Anthony and Gloria's parties, tells Anthony: '"Why, I've known him all my life"', to which Anthony responds: '"The devil you have!"' (196), the reader does begin to sense that the scene will not be one treated with much subtlety. Gloria – alone, inebriated and lying naked in her bed between sleeping and waking while a suitably gothic storm rages outside, is visited by the swaying shadow of a man at her bedroom door, a 'menacing terror, a personality filthy under its varnish, like smallpox spots under a layer of powder ... it was Hull, she saw, Hull' (201). Through different lenses, all of these discourses encounter the same vision in Fitzgerald's novels, one that was aware of 'the need for illusion, and the tragedy that springs from its inevitable failure' (Cross 37). In terms of Fitzgerald's developing aesthetic, one of Anthony Patch's most important conclusions is the following, which deals with the robust structuring of illusion/stagecraft, its shapes and purposes, in a world where youthful hope unravels:

> He found himself remembering how on one summer's morning they two had started from New York in search of happiness. They had never expected to find it perhaps, yet in itself that quest had been happier than anything he expected forevermore. Life, it seemed, must be a setting up of props around one – otherwise it was disaster. There was no rest, no quiet. He had been futile in longing to drift and dream; no one drifted except to maelstroms,

no one dreamed, without his dreams becoming fantastic nightmares of indecision and regret. (231)

The pessimism here is certainly profound; still, so long as the 'props' are in place they act as a stay against life's horrors. If, in the first poem of his *Four Quartets* (1936), Fitzgerald's contemporary T.S. Eliot would also acknowledge 'human kind/Cannot bear very much reality' ('Burnt Norton'), Fitzgerald's narrator goes further to suggest that for Anthony Patch dreams are themselves unbearable. It is not so much life but the dreams of life that become tainted.

All of this is a mighty blueprint for what is figured in and through Jay Gatsby, whose 'props' are an elaborate stay against the death of his dreams. In the end Anthony and Gloria Patch 'appear as merely pitiful figures, quite incapable of ever forming that cultured aristocracy to which they aspire' (Cross 39) and Anthony's props increasingly become the quick fixes of alcohol. Yet Fitzgerald's subsequent novels, especially *Tender is the Night*, provide their characters with a greater potential for success in that regard. Indeed, following upon *The Beautiful and Damned*, thc heroes of Fitzgerald's fiction increasingly embrace the *modus vivendi* that is only glimpsed in some desperation by Anthony Patch in the passage cited above. Those heroes realize the need to set up props so as to sustain life as artifice – in more developed terms, we see this in Jay Gatsby's elaboration of wealth with one end in his sights, while in *Tender is the Night*, Dick and Nicole Diver personify Fitzgerald's friend Gerald Murphy's notion of life as invention; as Abe North says of the Divers' Riviera beach colony, they 'have to like [the beach]. They invented it' (17). Gatsby believed that the logic of the heart would in the end triumph over what he took to be Daisy's marriage of convenience. For him that marriage was only a provisional settlement that Daisy Fay had had to make by becoming Daisy Buchanan, so that he can finally exclaim to Tom Buchanan with complete conviction: '"She only married you because I was poor and she was tired of waiting for me. It was a terrible mistake, but in her heart she never loved anyone except me!"' (102). This statement may inspire in some readers an understandable measure of incredulity, as Gatsby's version of life as a setting-up of props is shown to have overwhelmed its original design so as to become what is for him a totalising reality. Tom Buchanan's reaction to Gatsby's statement – '"You're crazy!"' – is nothing if not understandable. As a species of emotional logic, Gatsby's exclamation may exhibit the reductive madness of reason but it is nevertheless compelling, so compelling that we would not be at all surprised were Daisy to acknowledge its complete truth and walk out of Tom's life forever. As Richard Chase put it, 'Gatsby has a tragic recklessness about him ... something of that almost divine insanity one finds in Hamlet or Julien Sorel or Don Quixote' (131). It would, certainly, have been much better for both Gatsby and Daisy if, following Oscar Wilde, she had said to Gatsby years previously, 'Who, being loved, is poor?', for we are sure that, speaking in the simple language of the heart, that is what Gatsby, with all his wealth, believed to the end.

Within *The Beautiful and Damned*, however, 'It is the manner of life seldom to strike but always to wear away' (168). Accordingly, the decline of Anthony and Gloria Patch is presented as attritional, abject and inevitable, so that, as William Troy remarked, it is 'not so much a study in failure as in the *atmosphere* of failure' (188), and this becomes the subject matter of the novel's latter stages. That atmosphere is the stuff of Anthony's very environment, and the novel, from the earliest chapters, begins to apply to him the appropriate metaphors which seem naturally those of unstructured and ill-defined organisms so that, for instance, 'his day [was] usually a jelly-like creature, a shapeless, spineless thing' (48). The friends he holds in esteem include the likes of fellow Harvard alumnus Maury Noble (who is based upon Fitzgerald's friend George Jean Nathan, to whom, along with Max Perkins and Shane Leslie, Fitzgerald dedicated *The Beautiful and Damned*, 'in appreciation of much literary help and encouragement'), who provides Fitzgerald's narrator with opportunities for satirising Anthony's shapeless, spineless social setting. With this novel Fitzgerald was beginning to use a narrative voice (as he would more famously in the case of Nick Carraway in *The Great Gatsby*) whose intervention in the story's telling was an effective means of complicating the unfolding presence of the central characters. For instance, in an early scene involving Maury, narrative voice is used to render Anthony's worst traits of decadent indolence, so that 'one Saturday night when Anthony, prowling the chilly streets in a fit of utter boredom, dropped in at the Molton Arms he was overjoyed to find that Mr Noble was at home' (41). This feline browsing finds its partner in Maury, whose pomposity is mocked in similar terms, as retreating from the wintry November chill the two enjoy their boon-companionship warmed by 'a drink or two of Bushmill's, or a thimbleful of Maury's Grand Marnier', with Maury 'radiating a divine inertia as he rested, large and catlike, in his favourite chair' (41). If Anthony and Gloria

Patch and their circle are, as many critics have accepted, a thinly-veiled self-portrait of Scott, Zelda and their friends, then in a passage like this it is a portrait of contempt, as Anthony basks in the glow of Maury's smug, Buddha-like insouciance:

> There he was! The room closed about Anthony, warmed him. The glow of that strong persuasive mind, that temperament almost Oriental in its outward impassivity, warmed Anthony's restless soul and brought him a peace that could be likened only to the peace a stupid woman gives. One must understand all – else one must take all for granted. Maury filled the room, tigerlike, god-like. The winds outside were stilled; the brass candlesticks on the mantel glowed like tapers before an altar. (41)

Henry Dan Piper may be correct to judge that 'too much of the humor of *The Beautiful and Damned* consisted of private jokes' (87), but this passage allows for a spruce satire that engages a number of targets very efficiently. Maury Noble (as noted above, a character intended partly as a satirical portrait of contemporary drama critic and wit George Jean Nathan, whose self-indulgent code of life he once described as consisting of 'eating and drinking what you feel like when you feel like doing so, never growing indignant over anything, trusting instead to tobacco for calm and serenity, and bathing twice a day') embodies an insider joke recognisable to Fitzgerald's contemporaries, but the more important joke is at Anthony's expense, as he basks in an alcoholic torpor with Maury and his threadbare nostrums – 'one must understand all – else one must take all for granted' – for company. It may also be significant that Maury's peaceful 'glow' is 'likened only to the peace a stupid woman gives' – perhaps Fitzgerald's narrator here supplies a barbed riposte to Edna Millay's slur upon Fitzgerald's *naiveté*, a slur exploited by Edmund Wilson in his essay cited above, which commences with Wilson's use of Millay's comment that 'to meet F. Scott Fitzgerald is to think of a stupid old woman with whom someone has left a diamond'. If Fitzgerald did intend here an insider joke, with Maury/Millay spouting the empty emanations of 'a stupid woman', their 'tigerlike, godlike' aura assuredly finds easy lordship over Anthony's 'jelly-like' self.

In his increasingly rare moments of complete sobriety, however, Anthony is able to see truthfully into the life he was wasting – 'it worried him to think that he was, after all, a facile mediocrity', as 'he found in himself a growing horror and loneliness', while even 'the idea of eating alone frightened him' (49). And not only in *The Beautiful and Damned* but overall, Fitzgerald's fiction does show a complex relationship with the pathology of fear. In his first novel, too, it is fear that is the tacit condition, the 'fear of poverty and the worship of success' (260) that become Amory's twin rationale. In several forms, fear became an increasingly potent sign of catastrophe in Fitzgerald's writing, a reflection perhaps of his own acknowledged instabilities, expressed in the saturnine recognitions of his autobiographical essay 'The Crack-Up' (1936) that in his 'self-immolation was something sodden-dark' (52). In this regard as in much else, 'The Crack-Up' is a key to Fitzgerald's deteriorating state of mind in his final decade and the terms he uses there to describe his condition are uncannily reminiscent of many such terms he ascribed also to the heroes of even his earliest fiction. Chief amongst his anxieties was his acknowledged fear, which he stressed in italics in 'The Crack-Up' that he *'had become identified with the objects of my horror or compassion'* (52), again reminding us of that 'growing horror and loneliness' we find not only in Anthony Patch but also in the hero of his first novel, Amory Blaine, who, the narrator of *This Side of Paradise* tells us, has 'a dread of being alone' so that 'he attached a few friends ... he was unbearably lonely, desperately unhappy' (33). In his *Notebooks* Fitzgerald would write that 'the enemy of men is Fear' (326), and his novels are replete with salient examples from Amory and Anthony through Tom Buchanan in *The Great Gatsby* (whose neuroses include fears deriving from catchpenny racism – 'if we don't look out the white race will be – will be utterly submerged'[19]) to the many characters of *Tender is the Night* who contribute to the instability of its shifting milieux.

Such fears may derive from or at least be one by-product of the need to adapt to the emerging culture of rapid modernist flux in which Fitzgerald not only participated but also helped to express and define – the Jazz Age, with its restless energies. As the American Century entered its adolescence in the 1920s, its youthful exuberance was played out upon what Kirk Curnutt describes 'as a tempestuous stage of ethical accommodation and adjustment' (*Cambridge Companion* 46). Modernism was the product of not only new energies but stemmed from and was accelerated by the collapse of an older order of nineteenth-century modes of feeling and belief. It is associated therefore with both creation and collapse, and the arts that are most typically Modernist are those 'that respond to the scenario of our chaos' (Bradbury and McFarlane 27). Modernism was the child of both discredited parentage and unstable offspring:

> Of the destruction of civilization and reason in the First World War, of the world changed and reinterpreted by Marx, Freud and Darwin, of capitalism and constant industrial acceleration, of existential exposure to meaninglessness or absurdity ... It is the art consequent on the dis-establishing of communal reality and conventional notions of causality, on the destruction of traditional notions of the wholeness of individual character ... when all realities have become subjective fictions. (Bradbury and McFarlane 27)

Such an art is likely to give rise to representations of character under pressure of definition – precisely what we have in a good deal of Fitzgerald's fiction – and in *The Beautiful and Damned* too we have in Anthony and Gloria Patch a portrait of character without purpose, of character adrift and struggling to cohere. The cultural boundaries that separate the old order from the new are nowhere more ironically described than in the memorable scene where Adam Patch, the aging tycoon and prohibitionist who holds the purse-strings to his grandson Anthony's inheritance, arrives unannounced at the latter's apartment to find he and his friends in a drunken state. Ted Paramore, an acquaintance of Anthony's from his Harvard days and one of the very few there who isn't inebriated on arrival, is happy at first to observe the rest, perhaps as the narrator suggests, 'in order at some future time to make a sociological report on the decadence of American life' (222). Paramore's sobriety soon gives way, however, to his own participation in a drunken 'swan dance' choreographed by Gloria Patch, but in the end completed ignominiously by Paramore as he staggers 'almost into the arms of old Adam Patch, whose approach has been rendered inaudible by the pandemonium in the room' (225). Since the worthy 'uplifter' had 'that morning made a contribution of fifty thousand dollars to the cause of national prohibition' (225), it is little wonder that his immediate departure is associated 'with hellish portentousness' for his grandson, who on Adam Patch's death soon after, is immediately disinherited from his $40-million-dollar estate. It is significant that Fitzgerald's narrator directly invokes fear as both the cause and consequence of Anthony and Gloria's liquor-filled decline, as they both seemed 'weaker in fibre' (228) and Gloria faces up to 'the slow decline of her physical courage' (228). The morning after Adam Patch's unwelcome visitation, 'they awoke, nauseated and tired, dispirited with life, capable only of one pervasive emotion – fear' (228). In 1925, Paul Rosenfeld wrote of Fitzgerald's theme in *The Beautiful and Damned*, 'not another has fixed as mercilessly the quality of brutishness, of dull indirection and degraded sensibility running through American life of the hour' (72), and certainly, through such scenes as the above the novel unflinchingly charts the dystopian undercurrents of the Jazz Age.

In his 1922 review of the novel, Gilbert Seldes argued that Fitzgerald's creation of Gloria Patch redeems it somewhat from the relative failure to sustain Anthony's character as anything more than a stereotype of decadent decline. Seldes notes that 'as Anthony recedes Gloria becomes more and more vivid' and that 'in the second half of the book Gloria slowly acquires being' (331). This is right, and she gradually begins to challenge the decadence and waste exemplified by Anthony and their earlier married life together. Her complaint against Anthony is not that he is an idler but rather that his idling is not systematically underpinned by an appropriate philosophical rationale – 'she would never blame him for being the ineffectual idler so long as he did it sincerely, from the attitude that nothing much was worth doing' (175). Though Warner Berthoff overstates in his comment that the novel is 'a mock-up of *Tender*' (424), in the light of the Fitzgeralds' friendship with the Murphys, which was to begin in France two years after the publication of *The Beautiful and Damned*, its critique of Anthony's self-waste, played off against Gloria's recognition of an alternative lifestyle of idealised loafing, was a preamble to a theme that would eventually be much more fully explored in the portrait of Dick and Nicole Diver (largely based upon the Murphys) in *Tender is the Night*. Both Anthony and Gloria pay only lip-service, however, to a style of life which would allow them to have self-respect as 'efficient people of leisure' (174), while Anthony blames Gloria for his own entrapment within a destructive laziness – 'you make leisure so subtly attractive' (175). In *Tender is the Night*, the skills of using leisure to create an ideal existence rather than abusing it to destroy potentially fruitful human energies would soon become an essential element of the Spanish proverb, 'living well is the best revenge', a life where 'the majesty of leisure' (176) would find its most exemplary embodiment. Indeed, Anthony had once told Gloria that he 'didn't see why an American couldn't loaf gracefully' (175), an exact description of the leisured lifestyles embodied by the Murphys and the Divers. They are models who exemplify a use of leisure which is Aristotelean rather than Epicurean in kind – leisure presented as at best an expression of spiritual freedom, a positive interpretation of leisure activity as an end in itself. In the case of *The Beautiful and Damned*, however, the leisure enjoyed at first by Anthony and Gloria has no integrity at all, since its status is increasingly negative, its mood increasingly that of a kind of *mauvais foi*, based purely upon their hopes of inheriting Adam Patch's millions. Until that moment arrives, many gratifications are deferred, since 'these times were to begin "when we get our money" (228); it was on such dreams rather than on any satisfaction with their increasingly irregular, increasingly dissipated life that their hope rested'. In one of the final insights we have into Gloria's state of mind, we find that Fitzgerald has characterised her as an embodiment of creaturely endurance in the face of life's inherent tragedy:

> She wondered if they were tears of self-pity, and tried resolutely not to cry, but this existence without hope, without happiness, oppressed her, and she kept shaking her head from side to side, her mouth drawn down tremulously in the corners, as though she were denying an assertion made by someone, somewhere. She did not know that this gesture of hers was years older than history, that, for a hundred generations of men, intolerable and persistent grief has offered that gesture, of denial, of protest, of bewilderment, to something more profound, more powerful than the God made in the image of man ... it is a truth set at the heart of tragedy that this force never explains, never answers – this force intangible as air, more definite than death. (335–6)

This may seem overblown and unconvincing when applied to Gloria, who is after all largely responsible for her own dissipated state, but the passage shows that Fitzgerald was at least aware of a need to deepen the novel's engagement with such larger themes, using Gloria's abject condition above as a hook to hang them on. For Arthur Mizener, as for most other critics, however, *The Beautiful and Damned* is unable to provide 'an adequate cause for [Anthony and Gloria's] suffering ... in the end you do not believe they were ever people who wanted the opportunities for fineness that the freedom of wealth provides. They are pitiful ... but they are not tragic' (in Kazin ed. 32).

As a study of human deterioration, decline and fall, the novel is nothing if not detailed and thorough – and its autobiographical debts are certainly strong. As noted above, however, Fitzgerald himself acknowledged that the novel's detailed treatment of its subject all but overwhelms any larger themes that might have provided a more shaping context, telling his friend and fellow writer John Peale Bishop that 'I devoted so much more care myself to the *detail* of the book than I did to thinking out the general scheme' (Piper 92). The autobiographical basis of the novel may also explain this failure, since in 'writing much too close to actual experience' (Piper 92) the novel loses perspective. Fitzgerald had the honesty to own up to such faults, recognising that 'it has awful spots', but there are also signal achievements, among them its evocation of place, of New York in all of its urban press. As Richard Lehan observed in his study *F. Scott Fitzgerald and the Craft of Fiction* (1966), '*The Beautiful and Damned* is bedrocked in physical detail' (81), while more recent studies of this context, such as those of Nathalie Cochoy and Pascale Antolin, find that the novel 'interlaces the melancholic expression of amorous desire and the evocation of the modern city' (Cochoy 69). In such terms, Cochoy argues, the lost 'illusions of [Anthony's] youth' culminate as he 'becomes the spectator to the regenerative magic of New York' (77). In this reading, New York becomes much more than a background *mise-en-scène*, more a place imbued with 'the mysterious alchemy of the cityscape ... a carnivalesque city that incessantly draws its regenerative force from its ruthless power of destruction' (78–9). For Pascale Antolin too, 'New York plays an active role in shaping character and plot' in *The Beautiful and Damned*, and she contends that 'the city provides a mirror image, a reflecting surface to the heroes' emotions, and cityscapes turn out to be mindscapes as well' (110). In such terms both of these critics further extend and helpfully complicate initial approaches to the subject such as were taken by Blanche H. Gelfant's pioneering study of 1954, *The American City Novel*.

Finally, *The Beautiful and Damned* is a staging post on the road towards the supreme achievement of the novel that was to follow it three years later. While the detailed evocations of the characters of the earlier novel are sometimes authentic – as in the case of Joseph Bloeckman, the movie-man who becomes Anthony's rival for Gloria's affections – its story fails to transcend the limitations of such detailed representation of character and environment, and shows clearly the leanings upon such masters of American realism and naturalism as Theodore Dreiser. Above all, the narrative appears to be almost trapped within its detail. In his best writing, Fitzgerald allowed his great gift for poetic evocation to do the work that many pages of detailed treatment of character and place in *The Beautiful and Damned* can only try for. As Henry Dan Piper wrote, Fitzgerald 'was temperamentally unsuited to the conventions of naturalism. He was too much of a poet' (Bradbury and Palmer 66–7). The reader of his second novel is almost suffocated by the pervasive ennui and pointlessness of Anthony and Gloria's self-consuming *milieu;* even those reviews which praised the novel conceded that the reader 'wearies of the egotistic Gloria and becomes disgusted with the swineries of Anthony' (Beston 337). In the end, as Arthur Mizener puts it, Anthony and Gloria 'are pitiful and silly, rather than beautiful and damned' (*Scott Fitzgerald and His World* 61).

4

Inside the Hyena Cage: *The Great Gatsby* (1925)

Remembering his visit to Long Island and the Hamptons in 1999, the British peer Baron Hattersley recalled how attractions of the nearby sea strand – 'orioles swooping on the still pool to catch invisible insects, pure white pebbles in the golden sand and a seaplane which looked as though it has flown in from the world between the wars' – were for him yet overwhelmed by the magical memory of Jay Gatsby, who might also have walked those shores. Along with Gatsby's friend and remembrancer Nick Carraway, 'I thought of Gatsby's wonder when he first picked out the green light at the end of Daisy's dock.' Though it may not surprise us that a politician would admire what he calls Gatsby's 'wholly absurd indomitability' – his refusal to acknowledge that he can never beat the odds, or even that there are any odds against him – Hattersley's further point is more compelling: 'The importance of the story is not that he failed to win [Daisy Buchanan] but the way in which he wooed and lost … Gatsby is the great tragic hero of 20th century fiction' (14). This is right – and most certainly a large part of his enduring appeal. But more than this is the poetry of Jay Gatsby, the lucidity of his self-sacrificial dream which partakes of what Fitzgerald called 'the magical glory'. As he put it: 'Thats [*sic*] the whole burden of this novel … the loss of those illusions that give such color to the world so that you don't care whether things are true or false as long as they partake of the magical glory' (*Life in Letters* 78). Gatsby personifies a manifold paradox that many of us can readily identify with: the person for whom worldly success brings no emotional reward; the steadfast lover whose lifelong dedication is dashed. In these and other ways, Gatsby, we sense, stands for an idealism that personifies the best of us. And while many critics have acknowledged that Fitzgerald's hero is more than faintly absurd and have noted the ways in which he contributes to the novel's comedic elements, yet Gatsby is one of those who strive after a well-nigh impossible dream; to all those who have tried and will try to set sail upon the sea of dreams in their own 'little boats', Dante in *The Divine Comedy* gives a warning from the almighty Empyrean: 'go back to your own shores; don't commit yourself to the open sea' (R.W.B. Lewis, *Dante* 160). But to such sage advice Fitzgerald's hero is heedless; he is one whose romantic compass is born within him and points in one direction only. His heroic striving eventually takes him far beyond the shores of safety; disdaining any anchor, he strives 'against the current, borne back ceaselessly into the past' (*The Great Gatsby*, ed. Matthew Bruccoli, 1991; all further references are to this edition).

Many readers of Fitzgerald's greatest novel have noticed how fugitive and ephemeral Gatsby appears to be; indeed, measured in terms of the narrative's overall length, his presence is slight. In the arithmetic of one critic, he 'does not speak his first line until the story is one-fourth of the way along, and he is dead by the time it is three-quarters finished' (Piper 120); Gatsby's significance, however, not only far outweighs such literalism but is enhanced by it. When he was drafting the novel, Fitzgerald at one stage decided to cut around 18,000 words to do with Gatsby's background context in order to enhance his mystique of character. Like a ghost, his absence provokes murmurs of anticipation within the circle of those like Lucille, one of his party guests, who seeks more palpable reassurances of the man's identity: 'Lucille shivered. We all turned and looked around for Gatsby. It was testimony to the romantic speculation he inspired that there were whispers about him from those who had found little that it was necessary to whisper about in this world' (37). Fitzgerald creates a hero who is attenuated, who is in many ways never really at home in the world, an isolate whose loneliness is profound and definitive, alone in life – and in death, as Gatsby's father waits in vain for other mourners to arrive. His vigil ends with a short and sad closure: 'But it wasn't any use. Nobody came' (135).

Widely acknowledged as a masterpiece of American social fiction, the power of *The Great Gatsby* also derives at least partly from the emphasis Fitzgerald lays upon his essentially lonely hero. Indeed, the theme of loneliness increasingly became a defining feature in Fitzgerald's work and he began to regard it as a complex condition of some paradox, to be explored, and in a sense inhabited and relished, as with this entry in his *Notebooks*, so reminiscent in its cadence and phrasing of Nick Carraway's evocation of Gatsby, loneliness is presented as an existential haunting of the self: 'She was alone at last. There was not even a ghost left now to drift with through the years. She might stretch out her arms as far as they could reach into the night without fear that they would brush friendly cloth' (65). Fitzgerald's writing often identifies loneliness as a key zone in which his characters are often tested and defined. Loneliness was not always a negative state in the Fitzgerald aesthetic, but rather the headline facet of a generic condition that can also be expressed in variant ways as 'aloneness' and 'isolation'. Aloneness, the state of being alone, of *choosing* to be alone, was a part of his aesthetic development, a necessary prerequisite of his coming-of-age as a writer. Loneliness for the artist would allow absolute self-absorption, and looking back on his life in 1935 he wrote to his daughter, 'I didn't know till [I was] 15 that there was anyone in the world except me, + it cost me *plenty*.' Here he identifies aloneness as absolutely formative, the central feature of his boyhood. But he also saw himself as constitutionally suited to the classic model of the sequestered artist, telling Laura Guthrie, 'I am really a lone wolf, and though I wanted to be one of the gang, I wasn't permitted to be until I proved myself ... Everyone is lonely – the artist especially, it goes with creation. I create a world for others' (Turnbull, *Scott Fitzgerald* 265). This perception of himself as a lonely artist who *willingly* surrenders his own participation in society so as to create a social fiction for his readers, and who acknowledges isolation as the essential *donnée*, might come as a surprise to the many who regard Fitzgerald as not only the chronicler but also the manifest exponent of America's nervous energy in the 1920s – 'the heat and the sweat and the life', as Father Schwartz describes amusement-park New York in Fitzgerald's 1924 story, 'Absolution' (411). For if, as his friends Gerald and Sara Murphy believed, according to the Spanish motto 'living well is the best revenge', then Fitzgerald's life also codified the Jazz Age calculus – those who get *too* close to the heat burn twice as brightly, but also live half as long.

Still, again to Laura Guthrie, he wrote in 1935, 'if you want to be a top-notcher, you have to break with everyone. You have to show up your own father ... You've got to go a long, lone path' (Turnbull, *Scott Fitzgerald* 264–5). His contemporary Ernest Hemingway once wrote that 'hunger was good discipline' (*A Moveable Feast* 62), and for Fitzgerald, too, social self-denial became a doorway leading to creative flood. In France and at his best in the summer of 1924, he wrote to Edmund Wilson from the Côte d'Azur, 'my book is wonderful [and] so is the air + the sea. I have got my health back ... write me of all data, gossip, event, accident, scandal, sensation, deterioration, new reputation.' The book was, of course, *The Great Gatsby*, which he completed while living at St Raphaël on the Riviera that same year, and his letter very clearly draws the contrast between the far-away world of American social energy, of metropolitan excess, and the local one of air and sea and creative dedication. One is tempted to say that only within the cradle of the latter could he have written about the former, and that his expatriation was also an effort, however futile, to escape his destiny as an American artist; indeed, only a year later he was able to write in a letter to Marya Mannes, 'America is so decadent that its brilliant children are damned almost before they are born – Can you name a single American artist except James + Whistler (who lived in England) who didn't die of drink?' (*Life in Letters* 130). For Fitzgerald, in that *annus mirabilis* of 1924, loneliness was yet the key to great things – and he knew it as visceral truth. In May he wrote to Thomas Boyd from Hyères:

> I'm going to read nothing but Homer ... and history 540–1200 A.D. until I finish my novel + I hope to God I don't see a soul for six months. My novel grows more + more extraordinary; I feel absolutely self-sufficient + I have a perfect hollow craving for lonliness [*sic*], that has increased for three years in some arithmetical progression + I'm going to satisfy it at last ... I shall write a novel better than any novel ever written in America. (*Life in Letters* 68–9)

But only a year later he could pen a bitter-sweet testimony to this paradise now lost to the crowd, the good loneliness gone, and quite clearly recognised to be so as with a list of names that recalls those who attended Jay Gatsby's parties, he tells John Peale Bishop in a famous letter,

> there was no one at Antibes this summer except me, Zelda, the Valentinos, the Murphy's, Mistinguet, Rex Ingram, Dos Passos, Alice Terry, the Mclieshes, Charlie Bracket, Maude Kahn, Esther Murphy, Marguerite Namara, E. Phillips Openhiem, Mannes the violinist, Floyd Dell, Max and Chrystal Eastman, ex-Premier Orlando, Ettienne de Beaumont – just a real place to rough it, an escape from the world. (*Life in Letters* 126)

Loneliness, the good loneliness, would be not only the seedbed for a novel that was, in its author's view, to be better than any ever written in America, but would also become one of its key motifs. Fitzgerald's 'craving for loneliness' was to be 'satisfied at last' in the novel that gave us a New York that could be emptied of everything but the sense of possibility and promise. For his characters it became indeed a city where solitude elicited both promise and fear. Working in New York, Nick tells us that 'at the enchanted metropolitan twilight I felt a haunting loneliness sometimes, and felt it in others' (47), while for his lover, Jordan Baker, the lonely metropolis is also a potent lure: 'I love New York on summer afternoons when everyone's away', she says, 'there's something very sensuous about it – overripe, as if all sorts of funny fruits were going to fall into your hands' (97). When everyone's away – well then, in that solitude – anything could happen, even Gatsby, who becomes in Nick Carraway's vision the epitome of the lonely hero, his aloneness an integral part of his world, most obvious when he is surrounded by others, a spotlight impresario whose deepest dominion is yet that of an inhibited spirit. Perhaps this is more than a metaphor, since in Nick's perception Gatsby's isolation is bestowed as an essential aspect of his world, his environment; it is strongly associated with the spaces in which he lives and moves, and from his mansion house it is mobilised as an elemental and almost ectoplasmic rush,[2] as Nick tells us that 'a sudden emptiness seemed to flow now from the windows and the great doors, endowing with complete isolation the figure of the host who stood on the porch, his hand up in a formal gesture of farewell' (46). That 'sudden emptiness' is also prefigured in Nick's first envisioning of his neighbour, who 'gave a sudden intimation that he was content to be alone' (20). Aloneness is given to us as a crucial element of the man's poise, so that whenever Nick's 'eyes fell on Gatsby' we're prepared to believe that there he will forever be, 'standing alone on the marble steps and looking from one group to another with approving eyes' (41).

Perhaps, then, it doesn't surprise us that as Nick faces his thirtieth birthday it promises little for him but what he calls 'a decade of loneliness' (106), and that he should be drawn to this in Gatsby, drawn to find himself after Gatsby's murder 'on Gatsby's side, and alone' (127). One of the novel's most enigmatic passages which make loneliness a key factor occurs at the end of the sixth chapter, where we have Gatsby's vision of what can only be called primal transcendence. This passage is one of the most crucial in the whole novel because it refers us to the binary division that defines the dialogue between then and now ('and so we beat on, boats against the current, borne back ceaselessly into the past'), between the man that Gatsby could have been before he fell in love with Daisy, and the man he became. This binary cut brings about disorder and division in Gatsby's life; it intimates that what was gained in loving Daisy was much less than what was lost. The line of division separates the higher from the lower, the greater from the lesser, the ideal from the real, and it marks out a spiritual fissure from which Gatsby would never recover: he 'saw that the blocks of the sidewalk really formed a ladder and mounted to a secret place above the trees – he could climb to it, if he climbed alone, and once there he could suck on the pap of life, gulp down the incomparable milk of wonder' (86). Here, the ascent to wonder, truth, essence – to what Nick calls 'the mind of God' (86), can only be enjoyed alone; indeed, being able to climb 'alone' to the summit is the very *precondition* of this access.

Such climbing alone towards what he called 'something really my own' (*Life in Letters* 84) was absolutely germane to Fitzgerald's achievement in writing *Gatsby*. A part of that journey towards a truly creative summit was certainly due to his decision to move to France and the Riviera. He 'would take the Long Island atmosphere that I had familiarly breathed and materialize it beneath unfamiliar skies' 'My Lost City' (27), a classic case of expatriation yielding creative results.

Of course he travelled to and resided in St Raphaël with Zelda, and if we are to rely upon what he wrote in his *Ledger* on 24 August 1924 they were perfectly happy during that period. Her novel of 1932, *Save Me the Waltz*, excels in beguiling evocations of its summer Riviera setting and atmospheres and Fitzgerald's biographers have rarely resisted the temptation to see its main characters as but thinly veiled portraits of the Fitzgeralds themselves. With its epigraph from Sophocles' *Oedipus, King of Thebes*, the novel's evocation of the Mediterranean sublime quickly sets the tone of Keatsian languor:

> We saw of old blue skies and summer seas
> When Thebes in the storm and rain
> Reeled, like to die.
> O, if thou can'st again,
> Blue sky—blue sky!

and the Keatsian echoes become even more explicit as the novel's main characters Alabama and David Knight move 'into Provence, where people do not need to see unless they are looking for the nightingale'.[3] There, 'it was fun being alive' (78) and at 'Les

Rossignols', the Knights' home in St Raphaël, the languor of the South is present as 'the villa with its painted windows stretched and yawned in the golden shower of late sun' (78). The Knights' agreement that 'It's a marvellous, marvellous place, this France ... we are now in Paradise – as nearly as we'll ever get' (79) closely follows Fitzgerald's own relish of the reciprocity between life in what Keats's 'Ode to a Nightingale' called 'the warm South' and the fertility of his art. As he wrote to Max Perkins in February 1926, 'we're coming home in the fall, but I don't want to. I'd like to live and die on the French Rivierra [*sic*]' (*Life in Letters* 137).

In his 'Preface' to a later edition of *Save Me the Waltz*, Harry T. Moore describes the novel as 'rather literally autobiographical' (viii), giving us a 'story of exterior sunlight and interior shadow' (x), while Ruth Prigozy more recently affirmed it as 'clearly autobiographical, an attempt to deal with [Zelda's] childhood, the severe tensions in her marriage – plus an extra-marital relationship – and, above all, her breakdown' (*F. Scott Fitzgerald* 104). That relationship, with a a young navy lieutenant from the French air-force base at nearby Fréjus, Edouard Jozan, who Zelda flirted and danced with in the casino at nearby Juan-les-Pins, is fictionalised as a central element of the novel. Throughout his life Jozan always denied any full-blown affair with Zelda, and according to Andrew Turnbull's biography the affair ended when 'Fitzgerald forced a showdown and delivered an ultimatum which banished Josanne from their lives' (*Scott Fitzgerald* 153). It is probably an index of Fitzgerald's absorption in writing *The Great Gatsby* that for some time he was apparently unaware of the changing nature of his wife's flirtation with Jozan. And for some observers, it may also be an index of Zelda's jealous awareness of her husband's commitment to his work that she was prepared to go as far as she did by indulging the affair. Even Nancy Milford, in her defensive biography of Zelda, condemns her definitively for her actions 'as indeed she had ... broken the trust between them in their marriage' (124), while Zelda herself, in a letter to Scott of 1930, acknowledged 'there was Josen [*sic*] and you were justifiably angry' (*Life in Letters* 191). According to Gerald and Sara Murphy, the affair and its aftermath caused Zelda to take an overdose of sleeping pills, in what Matthew Bruccoli calls 'her suicide gesture' (*Epic Grandeur* 206).

The Jozan affair would figure not only in *Save Me the Waltz* but also years later in *Tender is the Night*, where Nicole Diver's lover, Tommy Barban, seems closely based upon Edouard Jozan. For Jeffrey Meyers in his biography of Fitzgerald, Zelda's actions with

Jozan told Scott that 'he could no longer trust his wife to be faithful. The purity of their marriage had been tainted, their innocence lost' (117), and certainly in his *Notebooks*, Fitzgerald wrote 'that September 1924, I knew something had happened that could never be repaired' (113). Within the art of *The Great Gatsby*, however, some critics have found Jozan's presence as an informing element; for James R. Mellow, for instance, Zelda's 'romance with Edouard Jozan provided the motivation for Daisy's two betrayals of Gatsby: first when he is a young infantry officer in France, then in the confrontation scene in the Plaza' (218); while for Andrew Turnbull, Fitzgerald's 'work may even have profited' from the Jozan affair. 'Who can say but that Fitzgerald's jealousy sharpened the edge of Gatsby's and gave weight to Tom Buchanan's bullish determination to regain his wife?' (153).

Fitzgerald's *Ledger* entry of August 1924, which reads 'Good work on the novel. Zelda and I close together', suggests that in the immediate aftermath of the affair there was what Mellow's biography describes as 'a return to normality' (210) and implies an intimate relationship between the novel's forward progress and their own unity, a relationship that for perhaps the last time in his short life would work with and not against the grain of his art.

All of the conditions had coincided to produce an atmosphere within which Fitzgerald's creativity could grow and prosper. By leaving America behind he was able to free himself from what he referred to in a letter to Perkins as 'dozens of bad habits', and he confessed that much of the three years that had passed since the publication of *The Beautiful and Damned* had been spent 'uselessly ... in drinking and raising hell generally' (*Life in Letters* 67). Life in the Villa Marie, among cypress and parasol pine trees and wafted by the breezes from the blue Mediterranean (he called St Raphaël 'the loveliest piece of earth I've ever seen without excepting Oxford or Venice or Princeton or anywhere' [*Life in Letters* 68] and the colours of the Côte d'Azur make their way into *The Great Gatsby* itself in the narrator's reference to 'the late afternoon sky' of New York city which, seen by Nick Carraway from Myrtle Wilson's love-nest apartment, 'bloomed in the window for a moment like the blue honey of the Mediterranean' [29]), furnished him with a *genius loci* for study and contemplation that was significantly a world away from the parties and dissipation of New York. His beautiful talent, instead of being wasted, was now free to express itself. As he put it, 'I feel I have an enormous power in me now' (*Life in Letters* 67), and most significantly, he was able to recognise that the power gave access to what seemed to him a new kind of creativity:

> I don't know any one who has used up so much personal experience as I have at 27 … in my new novel I'm thrown directly on purely creative work – not trashy imaginings as in my stories but the sustained imagination of a sincere and yet radiant world. (*Life in Letters* 67)

The terms he uses here to describe the creative context, his being 'thrown directly on purely creative work', suggest much about the deepest sources of *The Great Gatsby*'s power. The notion of an imposed confrontation with an art that was essentially creative rather than at least partly derivative is an accurate description of *Gatsby*'s animus, as Fitzgerald cut loose from a fictional discourse that had fed too often upon his own life experiences, leaving that source all but exhausted and 'used up'. According to Sheilah Graham, Fitzgerald's lover of his last years, 'he considered [*Gatsby*] the least autobiographical of his works' (*The Real F. Scott Fitzgerald* 46). The new novel would reach out far beyond his own experiences, so much so that many commentators both then and since have had difficulty in explaining the radical shift that allowed Fitzgerald to move out from the biographical cul-de-sac of *This Side of Paradise* and *The Beautiful and Damned*, towards the magisterial reach displayed in *The Great Gatsby*. Andrew Turnbull, for instance, noted that since the earlier novels, Fitzgerald's 'sensibility had undergone a mysterious change, which can only be explained as a phenomenon of growth. He had put away the harsh smartness which he considered to be the greatest flaw of his earlier work. Here in its place was a taut realism but also a gossamer romance … a lyric compassion. Fitzgerald had found his voice. (157)

My own reading of this 'mysterious change' is rather to believe Fitzgerald himself when he wrote that *The Great Gatsby* derived from 'the sustained imagination' he was able to bring to his writing of it. This was only possible given the right conditions, and in St Raphaël in the summer of 1924, those were ones of benign expatriation supported by conditions of relative domestic harmony and social sequestration. For the first and last time all this gave rise to a focus so intense as to allow no scatter, and *The Great Gatsby* came to complete life. This is not to underestimate the hard labour that went into Fitzgerald's imagining of *Gatsby*; as he wrote to Perkins from Italy in December 1924,

'I know Gatsby better than I know my own child ... Gatsby sticks in my heart. I had him for a while, then lost him + now I know I have him again' (*Life in Letters* 91), the latter phrasing suggesting a labour of focal hide-and-seek on the author's part, leading eventually to a complete possession of subject by author that could only have come about as a result of the conscription of both imagination and will. When he finally sent the completed manuscript of *Gatsby* to Perkins in October 1924, it was accompanied by a letter which said, 'I think that at last I've done something really my own' (*Life in Letters* 84), emphasising again his absolute grasp upon his art.

Fitzgerald's description of *Gatsby* as having been derived from the 'sustained imagination of a sincere and yet radiant world' (Turnbull 154) bears further examination in context. What could be connoted by an imagined world 'sincere and *yet* radiant'? Had Fitzgerald written of his novel's world as 'sincere and radiant', its meanings would have been more straightforward. For him the virtues of 'sincerity' may have seemed conventionally at odds with those of 'radiance', and it seems likely that the world he is referring to is at least partly the world personified by Jay Gatsby at his best. If so, then his description may supply a very important indication of what he regarded as the essence of Gatsby's 'greatness'. This indication is especially important since, in a fascinating sentence referring to his novel's title, he wrote to Perkins, 'The Great Gatsby is weak because there is no emphasis even ironically on his greatness or lack of it' (*Life in Letters* 95). If Fitzgerald's remark does stress his own understanding of Gatsby's dream as one distinguished by its 'sincere and yet radiant' qualities, then it engages very powerfully with one of the novel's most important ideological confrontations: the clash between public norms and life as redeemed by imaginative possibility. Tom Buchanan, Gatsby's main adversary, and in many ways a more perfectly realised character than Gatsby himself, impugns Gatsby's sincerity, charging him with being a fraud. While of course this is a hypocritical charge (since Tom, married to Daisy, is conducting an adulterous affair with Myrtle Wilson), it is mud that sticks. In terms of the public norms that Tom subscribes to, Gatsby is indeed a fraud with a bogus biography and the whiff of mendacity about much that he says and does. His dazzling past is a confection, spun out as '"God's truth"' in one of the novel's most memorable passages, where Fitzgerald gives us Gatsby as a ludicrous mountebank, whose clichéd autobiography may provoke a piteous laughter:

> 'I am the son of some wealthy people in the middle-west – all dead now. I was brought up in America but educated at Oxford

> because all my ancestors have been educated there for many years. It is a family tradition ... After that I lived like a young rajah in all the capitals of Europe – Paris, Venice, Rome – collecting jewels, chiefly rubies, hunting big game, painting a little, things for myself only, and trying to forget something very sad that had happened to me long ago.' (52)

The effect risks the risible, and indeed, listening to it, Nick almost laughs in Gatsby's face, 'the very phrases were worn so threadbare that they evoked no image except that of a turbaned "character" leaking sawdust at every pore as he pursued a tiger through the Bois de Boulogne' (52). Far from being in any way 'sincere', most of Gatsby's recollections are completely false, just as his very name is a lie. Jay Gatsby was born James Gatz, a poor farmhand who knew more of ploughshares than jewels, more of North Dakota loam than rubies from Rome. The above passage, however, does shed ironic light upon two important issues: that the loneliness that exudes from Jay Gatsby can partly be explained as deriving from a past without substance, while its shallow rhetoric is itself an eloquent condemnation of all that Tom Buchanan represents and values. Buchanan himself is in any case hardly an arbiter of good taste and breeding; we are told that his 'acquaintances resented the fact that he turned up in popular restaurants with [Myrtle] and, leaving her at a table, sauntered about chatting with whomsoever he knew' (21), the implication being either that these 'acquaintances resented' this arrogant display on Myrtle's behalf or, perhaps just as likely, envied Tom's willingness to challenge those public decencies in such flagrant terms, resenting the public relaxation of an accomplished adulterer.

In Nick's preamble, he tells us that Gatsby 'represented everything for which I have an unaffected scorn' (6), but immediately continues to summarise the virtues of the man which give rise to his paradoxical 'greatness'. In this treatment, what Gatsby 'represented' is distinct from that which he essentially is. While Nick's discrimination here might well have been more clearly expressed, my reading of it is that the 'representations' of Gatsby's life are seen by Nick as empty pretence, that which passes for social history and which is utterly different from that which he essentially is. He is redeemed in Nick's view by inward imaginative capacities which are the most authentic engines of his life, a covert climate of the mind and heart. With these attributes, Gatsby is given to us as a kind of superman endowed with supersensitive potentialities, 'as if he were related to one of those intricate machines that register earthquakes ten thousand miles away … an extraordinary gift for hope, a romantic readiness such as I have never found in any other person' (6). Within this inward sphere the rhetoric of public norms is needless and unvoiced; instead we find a lonely shadow-sided discourse that is Gatsby's truest idiom. Here, within the healing silence of the self, 'what preyed on Gatsby, what foul dust floated in the wake of his dreams' (6), cannot reach him. The almost haunted impersonality that attaches to Gatsby-in-public derives from what one might call a discipline of self-distancing, of self-estrangement, a spirit in abnegation.

Away from that public sphere, however, things are very different, as Nick's first sighting of the man shows. He catches sight of Gatsby in darkness, emerging from the shadows of his mansion: 'But I didn't call to him for he gave a sudden intimation that he was content to be alone – he stretched out his arms toward the dark water in a curious way, and far as I was from him I could have sworn he was trembling' (20). The 'sincerity' of Gatsby's ardour is here not in doubt; we are likely to read it as a completely honest expression of immense feeling, rendered even more intense since it is as far removed from the highly-mannered poise Gatsby exhibits at his parties as it is possible to be. It is sincerely felt emotion that causes him to tremble, and how full of wonder Fitzgerald's touch is here – the 'minute' object of Gatsby's trembling gesture so effectively dramatised as being for him a potent lure, despite being seaward and faraway. The 'single green light', no matter how distant, is 'yet radiant' for Gatsby, burning brightly as the only true hope of redemption in his world. 'Sincere and yet radiant' are the qualities of Gatsby in Nick's first fleeting vision of him. In such a scene, we can readily believe that the private gesture is the truest gesture. It is this, the innocence and the purity, which Nick finds in Gatsby at his best, and his proximity to him means that he comes close to breathing the same air. Trying to express such transport is, however, at times beyond Nick's powers:

> Through all he said, even through his appalling sentimentality, I was reminded of something – an elusive rhythm, a fragment of lost words, that I had heard somewhere a long time ago. For a moment a phrase tried to take shape in my youth and my lips parted like a dumb man's, as though there was more struggling upon them than a wisp of startled air. But they made no sound and what I had almost remembered was uncommunicable forever. (87)

As an example of *ars memoriae*, Fitzgerald's novel achieves much, and although his narrator's memory is defeated here, it is yet a crux since it links again to Gatsby's essence. The elusive lyric that Nick struggles to recall may have much to do with what one might call a preconscious memory of pure self. It concludes the novel's sixth chapter and is preceded and provoked by one of the novel's most important passages which itself is concerned with the remembrance and reconstruction of things past, a remembrance that reaches downward to the very roots of the subconscious. The passage gives us Gatsby's identity as essentially incomplete, and positions his life story as that of a searcher for his lost self who 'wanted to recover something, some idea of himself perhaps, that had gone into loving Daisy. His life had been confused and disordered since then, but if he could once return to a certain starting place and go over it all slowly, he could find out what that thing was....' (86). The lost element here is that this 'something' had been an ingredient of his love for Daisy – but pre-dated that love. Considered more closely still, the passage intimates that what 'had gone into loving Daisy' was indeed 'gone': an essential constituent of his being had been lost, sacrificed to that love, and leading in the years since to existential confusion and disorder. In such terms it is necessary to read his subsequent determination to win Daisy back as an effort at the repair, recovery and reconstitution of his divided self. The autobiographical aspects of this crucial scene are suggested in one of Fitzgerald's last letters to his daughter, Scottie, an extraordinarily frank admission that not only was his marriage to Zelda Sayre a piece of poor judgement ('The mistake I made was in marrying her'), but that it dealt a serious blow to the integrity of his life as an artist. As a youth, he tells of how he lived 'with a great dream' (*Life in Letters* 363). The dream was bound up with his youthful realisation that the work of writing and creating through words was his talent: 'the dream grew and I learned how to speak of it and make people listen'. This was, however, put at decisive risk by the decision to marry Zelda: 'the dream divided one day when I decided to marry your mother after all, even though I knew she was spoiled and meant no good to me'. Marriage to Zelda dealt a serious blow to the holistic, deeper structure within which the work of art could be created: 'But I was a man divided – she wanted me to work too much for her and not enough for my dream. She realized too late that work was dignity and the only dignity' (*Life in Letters* 363). As already noted above, such tropes of division and afflicted creativity are further utilised in a passage told by Nick but clearly meant to be a close recapitulation of Gatsby's own telling; about to kiss Daisy for the first time, his thoughts are very far from her:

> They stopped here and turned toward each other ... Out of the corner of his eye Gatsby saw that the blocks of the sidewalk really formed a ladder and mounted to a secret place above the trees – he could climb to it, if he climbed alone, and once there he could suck on the pap of life, gulp down the incomparable milk of wonder.
>
> His heart beat faster and faster as Daisy's white face came up to his own. He knew that when he kissed this girl, and forever wed his unutterable visions to her perishable breath, his mind would never romp again like the mind of God. (86)

For a man about to kiss the love of his life for the first time, this passage is odd indeed, disclosing much less about any pulsating passion for Daisy than it does about Gatsby's awareness of the risks to a separate spiritual integrity. The kiss seems more a sign of spiritual loss than one of Eros unchained. Gatsby's love for Daisy never seems sexual; according to Richard Chase, Gatsby fails to see Daisy 'as she is; he does not seem to have a sexual passion for her. He sees her merely as beauty and innocence – a flower indeed, growing natively "on the fresh green breast of the new world"' (Chase 129). Gary Lindberg also agrees that Daisy and Gatsby's 'sexual activity itself seems oddly insignificant' (136). The 'ladder' is an image of escape from the fever and fret – and perhaps even the sexual passion – of life encumbered; it leads upwards to a heavenly womb where, far above the trees, there is 'a secret place' for him. Alone there, like an infant at the mother's breast, he can always rely upon the simple flow of wondrous and 'incomparable milk'. This 'unutterable vision' is a version of bliss without responsibility – and is also mobilised through tropes of freedom, the childlike freedom to 'romp again like the mind of God', a dictionary search showing that 'to romp' is to run around or play in a boisterous way like a child romping in the playground. Against this is the kiss, which is associated with mortality, accompanied by Daisy's breath, which itself is all too 'perishable'. With Gatsby's kiss, Daisy's love is imagined as a flower that blossoms – and, as the tragic story of *The Great Gatsby* shows, dies. Even while acknowledging the 'appalling sentimentality' of all this, Nick Carraway is still tempted by its references ('an elusive rhythm, a fragment of lost words') towards shafts of deeper understanding which, for him, remain forever ineffable.

This reading allows us to see that Gatsby's grail is not only to recover Daisy Fay, but, more importantly, to recover 'some idea of himself ... that had gone into loving Daisy'. The fragrance of that first flowering kiss had long ago been replaced by 'the foul dust that floated in the wake of' his dream of a perfect love. And for Edmund Wilson in his letter to Fitzgerald of 11 April 1925, the day after receiving the novel, this focus upon dystopian energies was the novel's single flaw – 'the only bad feature of it is that the characters are mostly so unpleasant in themselves that the story becomes rather a bitter dose before one has finished with it ... Not that I don't admire Gatsby and see the point of the whole thing, but you will admit that it keeps us inside the hyena cage' (Wilson *Letters*, 121). Leaving aside Wilson's apparent failure to recognise that *The Great Gatsby* was intended to be a tragic romance and as such unlikely to provide the 'more sympathetic theme' (Wilson *Letters*, 121) he wished for, his striking metaphor that invites an image of Gatsby as a further creature imprisoned inside American society's 'hyena cage' (though the image leaves open the question of whether Gatsby is himself both victim – occupant and/or contributory architect of that 'cage') was also something that Max Perkins had early noted on reading the novel's first draft, subsequently referring to Gatsby as 'an innocent tool in the hands of somebody else' (Berg 65), a description that could well apply to Myrtle and George Wilson, probably this novel's most obvious 'victims' trapped within the cage of financial dependency.

That Fitzgerald's imagination was exercised by the theme of adult innocence is evidenced in his short story, 'The Curious Case of Benjamin Button', published three years before the appearance of *Gatsby*. About a man who ages backwards, this story can be seen as to an extent a shadow-text for *Gatsby*, giving us a fantasy picture of aged innocence. Richard Chase at least argues that Gatsby 'does not pass from innocence to experience – if anything it is the other way around, the youth who climbed aboard the millionaire's yacht being more worldly than the man who gazes longingly at the green light across the bay' (129). Jay Gatsby is indeed in many ways an innocent abroad whose story in such a light reiterates a legendary cast of heroes of classic American literature such as James Fenimore Cooper's Nathaniel 'Natty' Bumppo, Mark Twain's Huckleberry Finn and Herman Melville's Ishmael of *Moby Dick*, all personifications of the innocent hero. However, a reading of Gatsby as innocent victim of 'the hyena cage' throws into question his identity as an exploiter of others – a gangster trading in bootlegged liquor in Prohibition

America, one whose contacts are as dubious as Meyer Wolfshiem, who fixed baseball's World's Series of 1919. Richard Chase finds, however, that neither Gatsby nor Carraway nor Fitzgerald himself 'shows any interest in these activities', reading them instead as a sketchy and minor sideshow to the larger drama of Gatsby's 'transcendent ideal' (Chase 129). Marshall Walker also concludes that 'the underworld associations have ceased to matter' (115), since in Nick's eyes Gatsby is already redeemed as 'an idealist who is compelled to a meretricious way of life in order to realise his dream in a society obsessed with money' (114).

The notion of Gatsby as victim is introduced at the very start of Nick's narrative, which itself begins by acknowledging that his own habit of reserving 'all judgements' has been both an advantage and a disadvantage by opening up 'many curious natures to me' as well as by making him 'the victim of not a few veteran bores' (5). For all the charges against him, however, Gatsby was never accused of being boring: to most he is an enigma, while to Nick the very attractiveness of Gatsby's persona makes him a victim of others' needs and interests, 'preyed on' by the 'foul dust [that] floated in the wake of his dreams' (6). This famous phrase asks for further consideration since it links, most intriguingly, to a similar aquatic metaphor which is found in the novel's even more famous final sentence: 'so we beat on, boats against the current, borne back ceaselessly into the past' (141). Humanity, figured here as so many fragile craft in life's open seas with their own wake in tow, are seen as struggling 'against the current', that is, against the natural force which is driving them backwards, against the direction they yearn to achieve, which is the exceptional future – the future of their 'dreams' as yet unrealised. This metaphor allows that those, like Gatsby, who *strive* for the future ('the orgastic future that year by year recedes before us' [141]) and its promise of the as-yet-unrealised dream of human fulfilment, are 'all right at the end' (6), just so long as they maintain that resolve so that 'tomorrow' they will 'run faster, stretch out our arms further' (the quasi-Olympian coinage suggests the elevated effort and endeavour that is required), then 'one fine morning' (141) the consummation will be reached on the shores of redemption, where human dreams are realised. Once they weaken, however, once that striving lessens, then they too will slip backwards, caught by the current, and forced by it 'into the past' (141), so joining and becoming a part of the 'foul dust' that floats parasitically 'in the wake' of the exceptional few. The logic is brutal: sink or swim, strive or be caught. The trope suggests a common vulnerability, a common fate of polluted hope and a harrowing fall from transcendence that can be redeemed from complete inevitability only by the few. The imagery is also reminiscent of Saul Bellow's novel *The Victim* (1947), which, written in the immediate aftermath of the Holocaust and war which began as Fitzgerald's life ended, is itself a study of souls yearning for ballast in a sea of despair. Bellow's novel charts the strange tyranny visited upon Asa Leventhal by his nemesis Kirby Allbee, both men seen as victims and victimisers. With its epigraph from Thomas De Quincey's *The Pains of Opium*, the narrative charts what De Quincey called 'the tyranny of the human face' in all of its yearning pressure:

> Be that as it may, now it was that upon the rocking waters of the ocean the human face began to reveal itself; the sea appeared paved with innumerable faces, upturned to the heavens; faces, imploring, wrathful, despairing faces that surged upward by thousands, by myriads, by generations.

The Great Gatsby's most explicit scene of human suffering is that of the Valley of Ashes, an environment unforgettable in its ghastliness. Life there takes the form of a living death, and one senses that Hades is close by. There too we find the signal presence of a mephitic marker, for the foul dust that characterises 'the solemn dumping ground' is itself 'bounded by a small foul river' (21), the whole scene overlooked by the brooding eyes of Dr. T.J. Eckleburg – supposedly a billboard advertisement, though perhaps significantly the text does not use this term or any alternative word, so emphasising the symbolical, mystical properties of the image. Here is the novel's vision of an earthly perdition. There is no escape from it, as Myrtle and George Wilson's life and death both show, though at first Myrtle is presented as being the sole occupant of the valley who exists beyond its defining atmosphere: 'a white ashen dust ... veiled everything in the vicinity except [Wilson's] wife, who moved close to Tom' (23). The implication seems to be that while Myrtle's vitality burns, it protects her from the living death that the dust symbolises. Even in the only sight we have of her actually at work in the Wilson garage, Nick, on his way to New York with Gatsby, glimpses her 'straining at the garage pump with panting vitality as we went by' (54). Our final image of Myrtle, however, is the striking one of her mortal capitulation and dissolution as she 'knelt in the road and mingled her thick, dark blood with the dust' (107). The novel uses such environments and their imagery to express its metaphysic. Fitzgerald's theology permits hope of redemption, but it is small. It offers what George Steiner has called

> the indistinct intimation of a lost freedom or of a freedom to be regained – Arcadia behind us, Utopia before [which] hammers at the far threshold of the human psyche. This shadowy pulsebeat lies at the heart of our mythologies ... We are creatures at once vexed and consoled by summons of a freedom just out of reach. (*Real Presences* 153)

Nick Carraway's final sight of the contemptible Tom Buchanan suggests that deliverance from the nets of materialism is not possible; on New York's Fifth Avenue he leaves him as Buchanan 'went into the jewelry store to buy a pearl necklace – or perhaps only a pair of cuff buttons' (140). At the other end of the material scale is his mistress, Myrtle Wilson, given to us as a truly pathetic creature whose entrapment within the coils of a reductive money system is both ironic and sad. As she remembers her first meeting with Buchanan on a crowded commuter train, she conflates her rationale for her imminent acts of adultery from sexual gratification ('I was so excited that when I got into a taxi with him I didn't hardly know I wasn't getting into a subway train') to a fearful, plaintive recognition of her own mortality: '"All I kept thinking about over and over was "You can't live forever, you can't live forever"' (31). If this life is all there is, then the winner is she who takes all, or at least as much as she can get of what Buchanan money can buy:

> 'I'm going to make a list of all the things I've got to get. A massage and a wave and a collar for the dog and one of those cute little ash trays where you touch a spring, and a wreath with a black silk bow for mother's grave that'll last all summer. I got to write down a list so I won't forget all the things I got to do.' (31)

'Got to do ... got to get' – Jay Gatsby's greatness is not in the end to be measured in such material terms – in Carraway's final words, the passing material measures of Gatsby's flagrant wealth give way to an ineradicable spiritual profundity. The obscene word 'scrawled by some boy' on the white steps of Gatsby's mansion is easily 'erased' (140) by Nick, and the mansion too becomes 'inessential', melting away in front of his eyes to reveal the essence beneath, still flowering in the purity of virgin soil, 'the old island here ... the old unknown world' (140–1) of American possibility and, by extension, human possibility. Gatsby 'did not know that [his dream] was already behind him ... but that's no matter' (141): it's not the location of dreams that counts, it's the *striving* for them that matters, it's Gatsby's determination 'to fix everything just the way it was before' that counts – what he's 'going' to do (86). He 'wanted to recover something, some idea of himself perhaps' – again it's a goal, in the future: our redemption is measured by the courage with which we meet the 'summons of a freedom just out of reach' (*Steiner, Real Presences* 153). Whereas Myrtle must always pay to Buchanan the carnal price of her shopping with his money ('sitting on Tom's lap Mrs Wilson called up several people on the telephone ... When I came back [Tom and Myrtle] had disappeared' [26], presumably, into the bedroom), at Gatsby's house people 'came for the party with a simplicity of heart that was its own ticket of admission' (34). His lavish parties are a democratised experience, 'second to nothing because it had no consciousness of being so' (81), and conditioned only by 'the rules of behaviour associated with amusement parks' (34). 'He doesn't want any trouble with *any*body' (36), which is not a threat but rather a warranty of material satisfaction guaranteed, so that even when Lucille happens to tear her party dress accidentally on one of Gatsby's chairs, 'inside of a week I got a package from Croirier's with a new evening gown in it ... it was gas blue with lavender beads. Two hundred and sixty-five dollars' (36). In his West Egg mansion, where even the flowers in his garden seem a botanical phenomenon, their fragrance endowed with Gatsby gold ('the pale gold odor of kiss-me-at-the-gate' [71]), in what Donald Monk calls 'a world infatuated with the superficial' (94), Gatsby is king, his moneyed favours bestowed with accomplished style.

The Great Gatsby is social fiction and a novel of manners. As such the reader will expect to find satire, and Fitzgerald does not disappoint. For Brian Way it is precisely 'the element of social comedy, which gives the novel its predominant tone and colouring' (100). Most of the novel's characters, large and small, are presented with at least some elements of comedy either in what they say and/or in their outward representations. Fitzgerald's earliest collegiate writings – for *The Tiger* and *The Nassau Literary Magazine*, two Princeton University publications – show what seems to be a natural talent for the spoof and the send-up, aimed particularly at the foibles of the wealthy and privileged. In these apprentice publications 'Fitzgerald developed a style' (Bruccoli and Bryer xiii), and the style was often one that relished the pleasures of parody, as in one of his earliest examples of such whimsy, 'The Usual Thing, by Robert W. Shameless' (1916), which skits the work of author Robert W. Chambers and is not too far away from the society evoked in certain scenes and characters to be found in *Gatsby*, including Daisy Buchanan and her world of fashionable *ennui*:

> Tea was being served at the Van Tynes. On the long lawn, the pear trees cast their shadows over the parties of three and four scattered about. Babette and Lefleur had secured a table in a secluded nook, and as the sun glimmered and danced on the burnished silver tea set, she told him the whole story … while he reached into the little mother of pearl satchel that hung at his side for cigarettes …
>
> 'Hush,' she breathed, 'the servants, one is never alone. Oh! I'm tired of it all, the life I lead …
>
> It's horrible,' she went on, 'Nothing to eat but food, nothing to wear but clothes, nowhere to live but here and in the city.' She flung her hand in a graceful gesture towards the city.
>
> There was a silence. An orange rolled from the table down to the grass, then up again on to a chair where it lay orange and yellow in the sun. They watched it without speaking. (Deffaa 61–2)

A parody assuredly, yet reading this alongside the famous scene in *Gatsby* where Daisy Buchanan's precious pose is set against a similarly languorous background, is to acknowledge its hoax resemblances to the apprentice fiction above. From the overly punctilious butler, to Daisy's mannered inertia, this is a society that seems always to be teetering on the edge of the ludicrous:

> 'Madame expects you in the salon!' he cried, needlessly indicating the direction. In this heat every extra gesture was an affront to the common store of life.
>
> The room, shadowed well with awnings, was dark and cool. Daisy and Jordan lay upon an enormous couch, like silver idols, weighing down their white dresses against the singing breeze of the fans.
>
> 'We can't move,' they said together …
>
> Gatsby stood in the center of the crimson carpet … Daisy watched him and laughed her sweet exciting laugh; a tiny gust of powder rose from her bosom into the air …

> Our eyes lifted over the rosebeds and the hot lawn and the weedy refuse of the dog days along the shore ...
>
> 'What'll we do with ourselves this afternoon,' cried Daisy, 'and the day after that, and the next thirty years?'
>
> 'Don't be morbid,' Jordan said. (90–2)

Gatsby – with his pink suit and ludicrous automobile ('a rich cream color, bright with nickel, swollen here and there in its monstrous length with triumphant hatboxes and supper-boxes and tool-boxes, and terraced with a labyrinth of wind-shields that mirrored a dozen suns' [51]) – is in many ways so far removed from the recognisably human as to be a comic subversion of humanity. From start to finish, whether Nick sees him 'balancing himself on the dashboard of his car' (51) as though a vaudevillian acrobat, or whether in his badly scripted responses to reasonable queries – as when Daisy comments on his gigantic mansion, 'I love it, but I don't see how you live there all alone', to which Gatsby replies, 'I keep it always full of interesting people, night and day. People who do interesting things. Celebrated people' (71) – it is 'the unreality of reality' (77) that is the fundament and spine of Gatsby's world. The half-truth – that his house is indeed often full of people – exposes the ludicrous notion that they are all somehow vetted and retained there according to the extent to which they are 'interesting', while all others are somehow swiftly shown the back-door exit. The famous list of names of 'all these people [who] came to Gatsby's house in the summer' (51) is similarly indiscriminate rather than refined, so making Lucille the perfect guest: 'I never care what I do, so I always have a good time' (36). In Gatsby's case, the humour is most often intended to reveal what Nick calls 'his overwhelming self-absorption' (77), while at the same time throwing into high relief his storm-proof dream of recovering for himself what remains of the love in Daisy's heart.

Tom Buchanan and Myrtle Wilson are also not spared the lacerations of Fitzgerald's satiric barbs. Whenever they are together in public, or best of all, in the same room as Gatsby, comedy is certain to be one side effect of the meeting. The most famous of these is the showdown summit between Tom and Gatsby at the Plaza Hotel, but the earlier meeting between the Buchanans and Gatsby, who has invited them to one of his Saturday evening parties, is perhaps more comic because at this juncture it is more exploratory and less predictable in social terms. In this scene Gatsby, with Daisy and Nick as bystanders, appears to bait Tom, who – wearing his best stuffed shirt – is at his most uncomfortable outside his snobbish

East Egg circle and amid 'the sparkling hundreds' (81) attending the party. Gatsby has been waiting a lifetime for this moment, this opportunity to impress Daisy with the opulent conviviality of his party, and while playing the role of fastidious host to comic effect, also exposes and – perhaps unwittingly at first, but sensing Tom's conspicuous lack of *savoir-faire* – exploits Tom's social discomfiture to similarly amusing result:

> 'Look around,' suggested Gatsby ...
>
> 'You must see the faces of many people you've heard about.'
>
> Tom's arrogant eyes roamed the crowd.
>
> 'We don't go around very much,' he said. 'In fact I was just thinking I don't know a soul here.'
>
> 'Perhaps you know that lady.' Gatsby indicated a gorgeous, scarcely human orchid of a woman who sat in state under a white plum tree. Tom and Daisy stared, with that peculiarly unreal feeling that accompanies the recognition of a hitherto ghostly celebrity of the movies ...
>
> He took them ceremoniously from group to group:
>
> 'Mrs. Buchanan ... and Mr. Buchanan ——' After an instant's hesitation he added: 'the polo player.'
>
> 'Oh no,' objected Tom quickly. 'Not me.'
>
> But evidently the sound of it pleased Gatsby for Tom remained 'the polo player' for the rest of the evening ...
>
> 'I'd rather a little not be the polo player,' said Tom pleasantly. 'I'd rather look at all these famous people in —— in oblivion.' (82)

In a scene such as this all of Fitzgerald's habitual observance of social protocol, the extent to which carefully observed social rituals are a matter of equilibrium and nuance, are put to witty work. His friends Gerald and Sara Murphy, models of sophisticated taste, were often fed up with Fitzgerald's use of them as what Sara termed 'objects for observation'; in a letter to him as he began his work on

Tender is the Night in the summer of 1926, she scolded him: 'you can't expect anyone to like or stand a *Continual* feeling of analysis + sub-analysis + criticism – on the whole unfriendly – Such as we have felt for quite awhile' (*Correspondence* 196). He was certainly capable of smashing, sometimes literally, expectations of mannered social poise and trying the tolerance of his hosts, most egregiously at the Murphys' home on the Riviera, where their daughter Honoria remembered the infamous dinner party during which Fitzgerald, in drunken abandon, threw her parents' 'prized Venetian champagne glasses over the wall of our terrace. My father simply told Scott he was not welcome at the Villa America for a while' (Donnelly 148), while Matthew Bruccoli's biography adds the further choice details that at the same party Fitzgerald 'threw a fig at the Princesse de Caraman-Chimay, punched Murphy [as well as lobbing] the Venetian stemware' (*Epic Grandeur* 253).

If such behaviour seems to show Fitzgerald practicing being an exemplary social misfit, violating the rules and boundaries of bourgeois respectability, his fiction often personifies characters who also transgress the norms of permissible conduct, whether wittingly or otherwise. In the case of Myrtle Wilson, the novel's treatment of her is at its most satirically accomplished in the scene at the Plaza, where her fatuous efforts at social climbing reveal not only her desperation to escape her life in the Valley of Ashes, but its futility. The ordeal of her last hours of life, as she is literally imprisoned by her husband in the dingy room above the Wilson garage – 'her eyes, wide with jealous terror' as she fixes them on Jordan Baker, 'whom she took to be [Buchanan's] wife' (97) – is itself an eloquent commentary upon Buchanan's villainy. In this novel where automobile ownership is for all players an index of social freedom, success and failure, George Wilson is also imprisoned, kept in his place as an abject beggar by Buchanan's cruel refusal to sell him his old car as promised. Wilson is long ago a broken man, 'all run down' (96), just like his own car – a 'dust-covered wreck of a Ford which crouched in a dim corner' (22) of his garage. But the discovery that his wife 'had some sort of life apart from him in another world … had made him physically sick' (96), though once decided on taking the wrong road in pursuit of murdering Gatsby, he finds a final burst of criminal energy. In what is one of his most definitive lines, Buchanan taunts Wilson despicably right to the end:

> 'I didn't mean to interrupt your lunch,' he said. 'But I need money pretty bad and I was wondering what you were going to do with your old car.'

> 'How do you like this one?' inquired Tom. 'I bought it last week.'
>
> 'It's a nice yellow one,' said Wilson …
>
> 'Like to buy it?'
>
> 'Big chance,' Wilson smiled faintly. 'No, but I could make some money on the other.'
>
> 'What do you want money for all of a sudden?' (96)

With the delivery of these last words one can almost see the eyes of Dr T. J. Eckleburg widen in response to the horror of it all.

'Did you ever write a book half as good as *The Great Gatsby*? I tell you, that's a book you can't touch' (Hall 261). When Scott Fitzgerald asked this of Malcolm Cowley in 1932, its rhetoric may have been assisted by the liberal amounts of grain alcohol he was drinking as he spoke. In the years that remained to him however, his fundamental belief in his talent never wavered, though as he wandered from place to place in the years after Zelda's illness set in, and surveyed the various rooms in which he wrote, it may sometimes have seemed to him, as to Nick Carraway rummaging in Gatsby's house at the end, that 'there was an inexplicable amount of [foul] dust everywhere' around him (115). Again with Gatsby, however, he might yet have felt able to dismiss all such material measures as 'just personal' (119), since for both character and author, the personal was to be distinguished from the transcendent. In a key moment in *The Great Gatsby*, Daisy, drowning in the heat, sees Gatsby as a cool saviour:

> Gatsby's eyes floated toward her. 'Ah,' she cried, 'you look so cool.'
>
> Their eyes met, and they stared together at each other, alone in space. With an effort she glanced down at the table.
>
> 'You always look so cool,' she repeated.
>
> She had told him that she loved him, and Tom Buchanan saw. He was astounded. His mouth opened a little and he looked at Gatsby and then back at Daisy as if he had just recognized her as someone he knew a long time ago. (92–3)

Daisy's words, uttered in her 'low, thrilling voice' (11) are here received as dreadful portent by her husband, for even he, whose arrogance and egotism is only matched by his simple-minded stupidity (97), can read their meaning in the immediately prevailing discourse. For on a day that was not just hot but 'broiling, almost the last, certainly the warmest day of summer', when the noon heat arrives with 'a simmering hush' and passengers on board the train bound for East Egg 'lapsed despairingly into deep heat with a desolate cry' (89), the binary opposites of hot and cold become deeply significant. In the language of myth and archetype Daisy may have intuited the right word to apply here – for Gatsby's love, and underpinning that, 'his incorruptible dream' (120) of recovering spiritual completion, are loaded within him, protected from decay as though within a cold-storage container of the heart, where their steady pulse is cool and slow. As the last tragic act begins, 'hot whips of panic' (97) begin to assail Tom Buchanan, but for Gatsby 'the old warm world' (126) had been lost long ago, and before he left Daisy to go to war already 'he knew that he had lost that part of it, the freshest and the best, forever' (119). Indeed, he spends his last moments drifting alone and in the cool element of his swimming pool, which he expressly instructs his gardener not to drain, despite the autumn crispness in the air. There, the arc of his life reaches completion as finally, 'the track curved and now it was going away from the sun' (119).

5

The Tragic Power: Selected Short Stories and *Tender is the Night* (1934)

'His information, to be sure, on the general history of this American phase is remarkable. His most trivial stories have a substantial substratum of information. It should yield more and more revealing, penetrating pictures of American life as he settles gravely down in the twilight of the thirties' (Mosher 80). Writing for *The New Yorker* in 1926, John Chapin Mosher's prediction as to the likely paths to be taken by Scott Fitzgerald's career were to prove remarkably accurate. The twilight years of the twenties were darkened progressively by Zelda Fitzgerald's decline into insanity. Her admission to the Malmaison clinic outside Paris in April 1930, only the first of a series of clinics that would give her some temporary respite in the years ahead, marked almost ten years exactly since the date of her marriage to Scott. Among his 'ten most beautiful words in the English language' he told a reporter in 1932, were 'snap, wine, dark and ineluctable' ("Cellar Door?" in *Conversations* 106). In various manifestations the first three of those words would themselves become markers informing the unravelling of their life together, encoded in a downward spiral which by 1932 must have seemed ineluctable indeed. In their preamble introducing the Fitzgeralds' letters to each other 1930–38, Jackson Bryer and Cathy Barks offer a definitive *summa*. Mosher's reference to Fitzgerald's settling 'gravely down' in the decade's twilight is inflected here in the picture of a couple burdened by 'grave difficulties' as the 1930s began:

> After a decade of marriage, the Fitzgeralds were under every strain imaginable ... [their] relationship, tested at every turn for over ten years, had certainly weakened. And neither Scott, who was only thirty-four but whose alcoholism had caught up with him early, nor Zelda, only thirty, would ever be truly healthy

> again. Under the considerable weight of these grave difficulties, the Fitzgeralds began the third and most challenging phase of their lives together – the thirties. (Bryer and Barks, 77)

If the word 'dark' seemed beautiful to Fitzgerald, many of the short stories he produced in the years between *The Great Gatsby* and *Tender is the Night* would embody the theme of darkness and some would rank among his best. Often referred to by Fitzgerald scholars as *Tender is the Night* cluster stories, they are what Bryant Mangum has called 'essentially dress rehearsals for characters in *Tender is the Night* ... perhaps the most significant group of stories that Fitzgerald ever wrote when they are considered together and in the context of his uniting in them the concerns of the professional writer and literary artist' (*Cambridge Companion* 71). They were indeed stories concerned with inner darkness and personal fears, while also reflecting a larger sense of national calamity. Looking back to 1929, he told an interviewer in 1934: 'the end came and you saw a sickening look of fear and puzzlement grow in girls' eyes' (McBride 113). His willingness to read here the signs of a sudden, more widespread shock, as following the Wall Street Crash of 1929 America itself seemed to awaken suddenly from innocence to face the trials of rank experience, can also be seen in many of the stories he produced between 1927 and 1932. 'The days of carnival', he wrote, would soon echo 'to the plaints of the wounded' ('My Lost City' 30). Twilight was inexorably turning towards darkness in both personal matters as well as in the life of the nation; as he put it in 'Echoes of the Jazz Age': 'Somebody had blundered and the most expensive orgy in history was over' (18).

'All the stories that came into my head had a touch of disaster in them' ('Early Success', 59), Fitzgerald wrote in 1937, and in the three he produced between 1927 and 1928, 'Jacob's Ladder', (1927), 'A Short Trip Home' (1927) and 'Magnetism' (1928), we find the clear signs of sudden fall, the snap of hope and security. In 'Jacob's Ladder', Jake Booth is privy to his share of that 'fear and puzzlement' becoming 'conscious of a faint twinge of fear' which soon grows 'to become an ache' (160, 161) as his film starlet protégé Jenny Prince refuses to reciprocate his new-found passion for her; in 'Magnetism', George Hannaford, who finds success as a Hollywood star 'of the new "natural" type then just coming into vogue' (449), finds that his 'simple and dignified' tastes and 'instinctively gentle' outlook are brought into sudden conflict with 'a world of the volatile and the bizarre' (444) when he is blackmailed as payback by Margaret Donovan, a work colleague with whom he has flirted but who tells him, 'I've loved you for years' (459); while in 'A Short Trip Home' (which Fitzgerald, in a cable to his literary agent Harold Ober, described as 'the first real ghost story I ever wrote' [*As Ever, Scott Fitz-*, 102]), Eddie Stinson's middle-American 'faith in the essential all-rightness of things and people' (438) has to contend with a brass-knuckle wielding ghoul, Joe Varland, the kind of man who hails from 'the dim borderland' (426) where reality and nightmare intersect. He represents the dark side of the American Dream of righteous reward, the type personified in Stinson's nightmares, 'watching me and despising me. Once, in a dream, he had taken a few steps towards me … and I had broken for the door in terror' (426–7). Now Varland is an evil presence returned from the grave, 'dead as hell' (439) (he tells Stinson he's from St. Paul, Minnesota, Fitzgerald's home town), to exert a baleful influence upon Stinson's love, Ellen Baker. Under Varland's Svengali-like influence, she becomes his puppet, invested with sneering mouth and a look of 'tense cunning' (436), her face 'contorted with mirthless, unnatural laughter' (435).

Advancing towards the great work of Fitzgerald's maturity, *Tender is the Night*, these three stories are all conditioned by a pervasive sense of menace and pessimism, so much so that this may be reckoned as their very subject. It is true that George Hannaford and his wife Kay are eventually reconciled; that Jacob Booth is eventually involved at the end of the story with a new kind of 'ladder' that connects him cinematically with Jenny Prince, however vicariously and ironically; and true that Eddie Stinson's 'short trip home' ends with his discovering a revised relationship with Ellen Baker – 'even if I lose her she belongs to me' (442), but all these stories are nevertheless studies in the pathology of menace and hazard, created by Fitzgerald's imagination of disaster. Hannaford indeed finds that 'for a moment his glance had wavered … and he stumbled blindly into disaster' (457). Here are characters brought to a sudden harrowing of experience: they transit between the certainty of orderly lives and lives damaged by shocking circumstance. Life continues for them but these stories' endings show their characters as patched-up people. Invariably, Fitzgerald's narrator treats the aftermath frankly – Ellen who at the start has the beautiful 'bewitchment' (424), of youth, eventually survives Varland's evil bewitchment, but her traumatic stupor in which she 'hunched into a corner staring straight ahead with a sort of film over her eyes, as if she were in a state of suspended animation of body and mind' (438) concludes with only a conditional release from such trauma as she often 'gets silent about nothing' (442). George Hannaford, the film star whose good looks and 'magnetism' are such that he 'drew people right up close to [him] and held them there, not able to move' (459), in the end recoils from the sight of his own face in the mirror, and 'closed his eyes with a sudden exclamation of distaste' (462); while Jacob Booth, bereft of Jenny Prince's living presence, 'cut off from him forever in a high room at the Plaza Hotel' (169), takes his love for her and sublimates it as a zombie-like spectator in a Broadway movie palace, where 'in the fast-throbbing darkness' he is riveted to her abstraction on the silver screen – 'She was there! All of her, the best of her – the effort, the power, the triumph, the beauty' (170). He is, in Bonnie Shannon McMullen's words, 'consigned to the death-in-life of a member of the audience, experiencing the suspended animation of one watching an image on a screen' (19). These stories all seem concerned to take us to the heart of certain instabilities in the fabric of ordinary lives. They question the stability of conventional affection and love; each of their central characters is, as it were, ambushed by circumstances which they cannot control.

Two stories Fitzgerald wrote in 1929, 'The Rough Crossing' and 'The Swimmers' are also both concerned with the fracturing of relationships, with insincere affection and with couples making the best of the void at the heart of their lives together. 'The Swimmers' particularly, though a flawed story, has touches of greatness in it and as the 1920s ended shows Fitzgerald's willingness to again find parallels between local and particular narratives and their larger national significance. The story's title motif itself provides a matrix of symbolical significance and draws again on the aqua-symbolism that Fitzgerald used to such memorable effect in *The Great Gatsby*. Swimming, with its meanings of immersion in an environment both fundamental and private, of buoyancy that is muscular and earned, is also used in the story as a symbol of escape and striving. The activity of swimming and the environment of the ocean are variously explicated in the story, but overall they function as a potent means whereby cultural critiques both simple and profound can resonate.

For Henry Marston, Fitzgerald's embattled protagonist in 'The Swimmers', the cynosure of swimming is personified in 'the girl', an unnamed American 'thoroughbred' (175) who exemplifies all that Marston grows to admire. Choupette, his adulterous French wife, whose cuckolding of her husband provides the story with its darkly cynical propulsion, can only look out to the ocean from the shore of St Jean de Luz and watch without admiration those expert American practitioners of *'le sport'*, regarding them from a distance with Gallic hauteur and seeing them as little more than expatriates of an imbecilic type – 'they push water ... then they go elsewhere and push other water. They pass months in France and they couldn't tell you the name of the President. They are parasites such as Europe has not known in a hundred years' (176). In contrast for Marston swimming is potentially an elemental statement, life-saving and death-denying. So much is shown in the scene immediately following Choupette's statement above, Fitzgerald arranging the story's narrative here so as to reveal her judgement as facile and the action of the American swimmers as admirable and heroic. They, along with Marston (who at this point does not know how to swim but reacts instantly, heedless of his own safety), rush to save the life of the drowning girl fifty yards offshore. Too much 'chocolate ice cream' (177) causes her bodily distress in the water, but her eyes are also 'full of cool secrets' (178), and in gratitude she will eventually teach Marston how to swim, and in doing so how 'to get clean' – for her an unexamined benefit of the sport, but for him a fundamental knowledge as swimming eventually becomes 'a new gate to life' (178), philosophically lucid and liberating. The gate will indeed open to show him 'what was clean and unclean, what was worth knowing and what was only words' (178). In such terms swimming gives him the chance to strengthen in body and mind and so take back what he had lost – healthy vigour and the integrity of manhood recovered from emasculation experienced through marriage to the adulterous Choupette: 'he possessed again the masculine self he had handed over to the keeping of a wise little Provençal girl eight years ago' (179).

Fitzgerald's command of environmental details, used so magisterially in *The Great Gatsby*, is again assured in 'The Swimmers', endowing the *mise-en-scène* with an ambience much more than local. With the story's first sentences the reader is immediately installed alongside Henry Marston, breathing the polluted Parisian air of the Place Benôit, an objective correlative for the pollution that is invading his marriage in the form of Choupette's infidelity. The 'foul asthma' of that 'suspended mass of gasoline exhaust' (171), is inhaled by Marston – a certain miniature reprise of 'the foul dust' that weighs down Gatsby's dreams – 'and it became the odor of the thing he must presently do ... a black horror (171), which is to return home to confront his wife and her lover. Sensibility is invaded, overcome by the morally polluted environment of that *ménage*, as the next paragraph offers a further Gatsby-esque reprise when Marston's 'eyes fell upon a sign – 1000 Chemises. The shirts in question filled the shop window, piled, cravated and stuffed ... 1000 Chemises – Count them!' (171), an intertextual affinity with Gatsby's own array of shirts 'piled like bricks in stacks a dozen high' (72). For both men, such excess offsets their own emptiness *d'amour*, the superabundance of objects revealing the paucity of Marston's exhausted spirit as 'he became too exhausted to care' (171).

Fitzgerald and his critics have recognized the story's flaws in plotting and its contrivances of narrative circumstance – he regarded it as 'the hardest story I ever wrote, too big for its space' (*Bits of Paradise*, 15) – but its hero indeed contains something of Gatsby's spirit, as well as being in some respects Dick Diver's forerunner. For Richard Lehan, 'this remarkable story is surely a transition piece between the Fitzgerald of *The Great Gatsby* and the Fitzgerald of *Tender is the Night* (Bryer ed., *The Short Stories of F. Scott Fitzgerald*, 18), while nearly fifty years ago Robert Sklar was absolutely right to judge the story as a sure antecedent of *Tender*, noting that 'for the significance of its themes and the nature of its imagery "The Swimmers," among all the stories Fitzgerald wrote from 1927 to 1932, is the most important precursor to *Tender is the Night*' (239). The story's fourth and final section in particular strikes out beyond the bounds of any local context to engage with a more profound register, which Melvin J. Friedman describes as 'a kind of hymn to America' (258). In the passage, language and punctuation is used to build maximal rhapsodic intensity, and as Marston once again departs American shores for Europe, having tricked Choupette and her lover into signing off primary custody of his children to him, his insight into the highest human potential of his homeland is loaded with exalted feeling:

> Watching the fading city, the fading shore, from the deck of the Majestic, he had a sense of overwhelming gratitude and of gladness that America was there, that under the ugly debris of industry the rich land still pushed up, incorrigibly lavish and fertile, and that in the heart of the leaderless people, the old generosities and devotions fought on, breaking out sometimes in fanaticism and excess, but indomitable and undefeated ... the best of America was the best of the world. (190 – 91)

In the passage one senses Fitzgerald's confident recovery of the visionary idiom at the close of *The Great Gatsby*, and while as many critics have recognized, 'the tonal quality of the coda and the improbability of the plot are at odds with each other' (Brodwin 186), 'The Swimmers' yet emerges as a crucial fiction in its author's transition during his years of crisis. Ruth Prigozy offers a definitive assessment of the story's significance, stating that it 'raises virtually every question Fitzgerald had ever asked about the relationship between Europe and America, money and power, waste and self-indulgence, character and responsibility, class and caste, incompatibility and adultery; but they are finally all subsumed under one passionate declaration of faith in America' (Prigozy, 'Fitzgerald's Short Stories and the Depression' 120). The declaration of faith that comprises the story's final paragraph is almost a stand-alone passage, a coda that seems to derive more from its author's desire to express its powerful message than upon any intimate relationship with the story itself. It reaches towards a deeper and more compelling focus that conveys a great deal about the tragic grandeur at the heart of American commitment to national values:

> France was a land, England was a people, but America, having about it still that quality of the idea, was harder to utter – it was the graves at Shiloh and the tired, drawn, nervous faces of its great men, and the country boys dying in the Argonne for a phrase that was empty before their bodies withered. It was a willingness of the heart. (191)

Following 'The Swimmers' in 1929 and before the publication of *Tender is the Night* in 1934, Fitzgerald would write such fine short stories as 'Babylon Revisited' (1931), and 'Crazy Sunday' (1932), the former of which is particularly related to *Tender.* As Bryant Mangum states, 'Babylon Revisited' shares 'the novel's mood of loss and regret' ('The Short Stories of F. Scott Fitzgerald' 71) and gives us in Charlie Wales another character who returns to France, to Paris/Babylon, to find there 'the meaning of the word "dissipate" – to dissipate into thin air; to make nothing out of something' (115). But Wales' attempt to make himself something – a father to his daughter Honoria – out of the inebriated nothing he had been – brings with it only displacement and further isolation. He is the prodigal father returning to Babylon lean and chastened – one whisky a day not withstanding – demanding that his air of sobriety be recognized by Marion, his deceased wife Helen's sister, who now has legal custody of Honoria – that his reformation be rewarded with resumed responsibility for Honoria's care. Echoing one of Fitzgerald's most revered beliefs, Wales expresses his wish to elude corrupt contemporary values by attaching himself to an earlier, more durable philosophy: 'He believed in character; he wanted to jump back a whole generation and trust in character again as the eternally valuable element' (114). 'Babylon Revisited' shows, however, that by attempting to detach himself from the norms of his own age, Wales inevitably invites estrangement, distrust, and eventual alienation. His fruitless moves to evade those 'ghosts out of the past' (118), his old boon-companions Lorraine and Duncan, also seem to implicate him in a narrative of guilty downfall in which he is at best unwittingly complicit: 'He would come back some day; they couldn't make him pay forever' (134). The story's final sentence which tells us that Charlie Wales 'was absolutely sure Helen wouldn't have wanted him to be so alone' (134) may for some be read ironically, so revealing the 'larger concerns of the author – here, the inevitability of human loneliness' (Bryer et al, *F. Scott Fitzgerald: New Perspectives*, xiii). It is this, a major ingredient of 'its evocation of a profoundly tragic view of life' (Kennedy, 'Figuring the Damage', 319) which links 'Babylon Revisited' so closely to *Tender is the Night*, the final version of which Fitzgerald began to work upon in 1932, soon after the story's publication. For many readers the parallels between novel and story are manifest, revealing 'the patent connection between Charlie's fall and that of Dick Diver, Fitzgerald's dashing yet ultimately defeated psychoanalyst-hero' (Kennedy, 'Figuring the Damage', 319).

****

As recently as 1996, Matthew Bruccoli – introducing *Tender is the Night* for the Everyman paperback edition of that year – was able to refer to it as an 'underrated masterpiece' (xiii). The extent to which a novel can be recognized as both a masterpiece and yet be underrated raises questions, and Henry Claridge, introducing the Wordsworth Classics edition of the novel in 2004, was also concerned with the possible reasons for its underrated status, stating that 'There can be no doubt that the long period of gestation had deleterious consequences for the finished work we read as *Tender is the Night*' (ix). Dennis Potter in his 'Introduction' to the Folio Society edition of the novel (1987), makes a similar point, referring to what he calls 'the perpetual re-workings of the novel' which 'have undoubtedly left their scars' upon it so that 'even the most generous critic, to say nothing of the patient reader, would have to concede that there is upon occasion a feeling of incompleteness about particular scenes' (11).

The 'gestation' was indeed extended, since Fitzgerald had begun work on the novel nearly ten years before its eventual publication in 1934. Claridge provides a succinct summary of the novel's earliest version:

> In its original form *Tender is the Night* seems to have been conceived of as a murder story ... Like many of his contemporaries, Fitzgerald was fascinated by two celebrated contemporary murders, the Leopold – Loeb case of 1924 and Dorothy Ellingson's murder of her mother in 1925 after a heated argument over her daughter's wild and impulsive behaviour. The murder in Chicago of a boy of fourteen called Bobby Franks by two wealthy University of Chicago students, Nathan Leopold and Richard Loeb, seems especially to have intrigued him. (vi)

Claridge notes that what may have interested Fitzgerald in these murders was the extent to which, in the case of Leopold and Loeb, they could be seen 'as types of malign "genius" and construed as 'victims of the social advantages secured by wealth' (vi), the latter being a clear prefiguration of central themes in *Tender is the Night*. The essay by James L.W. West III, '*Tender is the Night*, "Jazzmania", and the Ellingson Matricide' provides a thorough treatment of the relationship between the Ellingson matricide case and the genesis of *Tender is the Night*.

The novel would go through three plot versions; the second, with working titles such as *Our Type*, *The Melarky Case* and *The World's Fair* being partly 'about Zelda and me' as Fitzgerald told his editor Max Perkins in 1925 (Sklar, 252.). This second version contains a narrative which uses the French Riviera setting, eventually so central to the final version of *Tender is the Night*, while its characterization also contains the seeds which would grow into Dick Diver and others around him in the novel's final version. As Robert Sklar states, 'Frances Melarky, the central character of *Our Type* ... falls in with an American social set on the Riviera where, unable to work, he dips deeper into habits of waste and dissipation' (252). Henry Claridge uses very similar terms in his summary of *Our Type*, noting that Frances Melarky 'falls in with a group of expatriated Americans, whose influence over him ... provokes an ineluctable process of degeneration' (vii). Another of the novel's working titles was *The Boy Who Killed His Mother*, in which the Dorothy Ellingson matricide source made its final appearance with Fitzgerald's plan to have Melarky murder his own mother. As Claridge remarks, however, 'we should be very thankful Fitzgerald never wrote this novel' (vii).

A further plot version was written in 1929, in which Hollywood movie director Lew Kelly and his wife Nicole encounter a young Hollywood starlet named Rosemary on board a Europe-bound liner. While the female names and Rosemary's occupation as set out in this draft survived into the final version of *Tender*, as Bruccoli notes 'These manuscript chapters were never typed, indicating that Fitzgerald lost interest early on' (Bruccoli, 'Introduction' to *Tender is the Night*, Everyman ed., xxiv).

Zelda Fitzgerald's mental breakdown in April 1930 and her treatment first in the Malmaison psychiatric clinic outside Paris, then the Valmont clinic in Switzerland, followed by a longer stay in Les Rives de Prangins clinic near Geneva beginning June 1930, fed into the final version of the novel, in which we find the appearance of a new hero in the shape of psychoanalyst Dr Richard Diver. With Zelda's discharge from the clinic in September 1931, the family left Europe for the last time. She was hospitalized again the following February, in the Phipps Psychiatric Clinic of the Johns Hopkins Hospital in Baltimore, and Fitzgerald recommenced the final Dick Diver version of the novel in January 1932. After the years of drafts and delays, work at last moved swiftly to completion, for written against the backdrop of Zelda's illness and his own alcoholism (one working title of the Diver version was 'The Drunkard's Holiday') the story of Dick and Nicole Diver carried the manifold impress of Fitzgerald's own experience. *Tender is the Night* began to appear in serial form in *Scribner's Magazine* at the end of 1933.

The novel's autobiographical roots are also evident from the very start of the lengthy 'General Plan' of *Tender*, where Fitzgerald acknowledges that 'the hero born in 1891 is a man like myself' and that 'he looks ... like me' (*Epic Grandeur* 335–7). The Plan begins with this 'Sketch':

> The novel should do this. Show a man who is a natural idealist, a spoiled priest, giving in for various causes to the ideas of the haute Burgeoise [*sic*], and in his rise to the top of the social world losing his idealism, his talent and turning to drink and dissipation. Background one in which the liesure [*sic*] class is at their truly most brilliant + glamorous such as Murphys. (*Epic Grandeur*, 335)

By the sands of Antibes in the home they built and named Villa America, the Fitzgeralds' wealthy friends Sara and Gerald Murphy had created a salon – the centre, as Dirk Bogarde was to describe it, 'of a gorgeous, glittering carousel .... Looking back at them today sprawled in the sun, laughing and dancing, is a little like turning the pages of old bound copies of *Vanity Fair* and *Tatler.* Scintillating, beautiful, remote and far out of reach' (8). For Archibald MacLeish, too, 'there was a shine to life wherever they were ... a kind of inherent loveliness' (Vaill 7), and wherever in *Tender is the Night* Fitzgerald provides a vision of graceful expatriation, there the Murphys are, shining still as the very spirit of expatriate style. They were the creators of those 'many fêtes' that the novel's winsome dedication seems to gift and bless them with, as though in a deed of reciprocal generosity. In a letter to Gerald Murphy, Fitzgerald acknowledged both extensive debts and a profound *entente*: 'the book was inspired by Sara and you, and the way I feel about you both and the way you live, and the last part of it is Zelda and me because you and Sara are the same people as Zelda and me' (Tomkins 5).[4] The way the Murphys lived would indeed become the luminous blueprint for an American arcadia in *Tender,* and though Fitzgerald would often permutate the theme of paradise lost in his life and writing, only here in his final completed novel does he succeed in tracing fully the tragic arc of sublimity declining to ruin.

'Please do not use the phrase "Riviera" ... not only does it sound like the triviality of which I am so often accused, but also ... its very mention invokes a feeling of unreality and unsubstantiality' (*Life in Letters* 247). So wrote Fitzgerald to his editor Max Perkins in 1934, setting out his ideas for the advertising of *Tender is the Night,* and fearing that in the debt-haunted America of the 1930s an emphasis upon Riviera glamour would potentially damage the novel's sales. Yet his recognition that together with its reputation for triviality, the Riviera would generate a further set of images concerning 'unreality' is of more interest in retrospect. In a letter to Fitzgerald written soon after the novel's publication, Gerald Murphy would also invoke unreality, though as a key feature of the book's meaning and truth. If Andrew Turnbull saw that Fitzgerald had discovered 'perfection in the real world' of Europe and the Murphys, Murphy himself realised that *Tender is the Night* folded this perfect reality into the artifice of an even more transcendent design: 'I know now that what you said in "Tender is the Night" is true. Only the invented part of our life – *the unreal part* – has had any scheme any beauty. Life itself has stepped in now and blundered, scarred and destroyed' (*Correspondence* 425, my emphasis).[5] Looking back through the atmosphere of Fitzgerald's novel, Murphy was able to see that expatriation had provided him partly with the climate in which creativity could flower, if not with the prerequisite condition for entry into the beautiful land of unreality/artifice. In another related phrase invoking the potential of the human imagination, Murphy also told Fitzgerald, 'it's not what we do, but what we do with our minds that counts' (Tomkins 123), thus giving modern inflection to that dangerous liaison which for Henry James had so characterised the European scene for American visitors. In James' fiction, the European environment is often experienced as a beguiling playground where they are transformed into lotus-eaters. So Roderick Hudson declares himself to be 'an idle useless creature, and that he should probably be even more so in Europe than at home' (22). Activity for James' expatriates is often sublimated by their attraction to European passivity. As Hudson muses, 'it is evidently only a sort of idealised form of loafing: a passive life in Rome, thanks to the number and quality of one's impressions, takes on a very respectable likeness to activity' (23). Although Fitzgerald's novel too is concerned with expatriation as *flânerie*, it also counters this with a revised model of the expatriate *engagé*, the 'man with repose' (the phrase is Diver's own, coined in the opening paragraph of Book 1, Chapter 12), one who could, like Murphy himself, exemplify a model of calm and creative being, of 'what we do with our minds', self-consciously trying for new means of survival amidst the ruins of an inter-war Europe.

It was Edmund Wilson who first persuaded the young Fitzgerald to continue his cultural education in France, urging him to 'come to Paris for the summer. Settle down and learn French and apply a little French leisure and measure to that restless and jumpy nervous system. It would be a service to American letters: your novels would never be the same afterwards' (Wilson, *Letters on Literature and Politics* 63). Wilson was right about that, for having enrolled in Gerald and Sara Murphy's school of style in the summer of 1924, Fitzgerald found there, along with 'many fêtes', the influence of a refined *ménage* which seemed to him an ideal expression of human life. But in the aftermath of the Great War, such a context could also embody style as heroism. As Fitzgerald himself remarked, Dick Diver 'is after all a sort of superman ... an approximation of the hero'; he recognises that 'taste is no substitute for vitality but in [*Tender is the Night*] it has to do duty for it. It is one of the points on which he must never show weakness as Siegfried could never show physical fear' (Turnbull, *Letters* 587). For Fitzgerald, as for Ernest Hemingway, style, taste, deportment, became an index of existential integrity.

'Grace under pressure' was Hemingway's definition of courageous poise,[6] and grace and style were two sides of the same coin, a currency that becomes the gold standard by which Diver judges himself and others. The novel lays stress upon his exceptionalism in this regard, as his tranquil enclave is progressively attacked by the invasion of 'life itself', stepping in to blunder, scar and destroy. In many ways this novel is about betrayal, Dick Diver's 'betrayal at the hands of a world he thought he could manipulate' (Vaill 229), a betrayal so closely based upon Gerald Murphy's own. Murphy remembered telling Fitzgerald:

> For me only the invented part of life is satisfying, only the unrealistic part. Things happened to you – sickness, birth, Zelda in Lausanne, Patrick in the sanatorium, Father Wiborg's death – these things were realistic, and you couldn't do anything about them. 'Do you mean you don't accept these things?' Scott asked. I replied that of course [I] accepted them, but I didn't feel they were the important things really ... The *invented* part, for me, is what has meaning. (Vaill 226)[7]

Reality in this sense is something that one is the victim of, arriving upon one's head in random blows of unreasonable fate. It is certainly no coincidence that the sign outside Villa America, the Murphys' home in Antibes, (which would become the Divers' 'Villa Diana' in the novel), was designed by Murphy himself to show a dramatically split graphic, with the broken star and stripes in sharp contrast to each other. As described by Amanda Vaill, "The effect is striking visually, but also metaphorically: somehow the villa, like its owners, exists in two worlds at once – France and America, the real and the imagined" (160).

And in *Tender is the Night* it was that 'unreal' world, that imagined great good place which had its fleeting correlative in the beach apartheid close by Gausse's Hôtel Des Étrangers. There, for those within Dick Diver's orbit of invention, the unimportant matter of 'reality' gives way to something else, 'something [that] made them unlike the Americans [Rosemary] had known of late' (*Tender is the Night* [New York: Scribner's, 1934] 6. All further references are to this edition). This 'something' is rooted in Diver's ability to create a new, playful sense of being for his group of fellow expatriates. His first appearance is indeed that of a master of comic invention, 'a fine man in a jockey cap and red-striped tights', entertaining his guests who are enthralled by his vitality. Rosemary understands that 'under small hand-parasols' (5) this group of Americans are being subtly altered by Diver's 'quiet little performance' (6), becoming, in fact, something atypical in the process as he 'moved gravely about with a rake, ostensibly removing gravel and meanwhile developing some esoteric burlesque held in suspension by his grave face' (6). The narrator's identification of the particular type of comedy is important: burlesque is a generic term for parody, caricature and travesty and is particularly effective when customs, manners, institutions – individually or as types – are ripe for debunking. Targeting the ridiculous by incongruous imitation, burlesque presents the trivial with ironic seriousness. Audience pleasure comes largely from recognising the subject of the ridicule, and in this scene Dick Diver provides a textbook burlesque directed at a subject identified in Mrs Abrams' comment to Rosemary a few lines later, 'there seems to be so darn much formality on this beach' (7). The phrase reiterates the narrator's own earlier scene-setting comments upon expatriate beach-life on the summer Riviera, where in tedious occupancy 'British nannies sat knitting the slow pattern of Victorian England ... to the tune of gossip as formalized as incantation' (4). A stultifying formality therefore reigns supreme here, as 'a dozen persons kept house under striped umbrellas, while their dozen children pursued unintimidated fish through the shallows' (4). This is the dominant reality in place at Antibes, 'the atmosphere of a community upon which it would be presumptuous to intrude' (5).

While there is certainly a strong element of *épater le bourgeois* in Diver's stylized performance, this first glimpse reveals even more about the style of his relationship to those in his circle – the effort to control the discourse, the ability to define for them an alternative, more charged correspondence between inner life and outer reality. The language gives it away – his group being "held in suspension by his grave face," an early instance of that magical dialectic so manifest at the Divers' dinner parties at Villa Diana, where leisure and conviviality transcend themselves to approach an ultimate civility of human relationship and therefore to inhabit "the rarer atmosphere of sentiment":

> There were fireflies riding on the dark air and a dog baying on some low and far-away edge of the cliff. The table seemed to have risen a little toward the sky like a mechanical dancing platform, giving the people around it the sense of being alone with each other in the dark universe, nourished by its only food, warmed by its only lights. And, as if a curious hushed laugh from Mrs. McKisco

> were a signal that such a detachment from the world had been attained, the two Divers began suddenly to warm and glow and expand, as if to make up to their guests … for anything they might still miss from that country well left behind. (34)

Here, the imagery of transcendence is considerably more advanced: the table becomes a stage, the guests transported as though to a *chambre separé* where an occult, hierarchical bonding can take place. The cameo scene at the beach had introduced the idea of Diver as gifted entertainer, a man capable of holding his audience in suspension – an image repeated here in the wonderfully exact conceit of the table as a floating 'mechanical dancing platform' – and in the scene above he appears more completely as a magus bestowing an almost mystical union, stemming from his apparent *expansion* of presence. The scene is justifiably renowned. It is perhaps the most elaborate instance of Fitzgerald's notion of Diver as 'after all a sort of superman', endowed with special powers that allow him to 'warm and glow and expand' in a spirit of ultimate conviviality. In terms of this chapter the scene also personifies Murphy's idea of life as invention, of the transformative fruits of 'what we do with our minds' as well as exemplifying a new vision of an enlightened leisure class. That idea finds its way without amendment into Fitzgerald's imagination of the Divers, as Abe North tells Rosemary that Dick and Nicole 'have to like [the beach]. They invented it' (17).

In a letter of 1934 to Max Perkins, Marjorie Kinnan Rawlings wrote of *Tender* as a 'a book disturbing, bitter and beautiful … Fitzgerald visualizes people not in their immediate setting, from the human point of view – but in time and space – almost, you might say, with the divine detachment' (Tarr 140). The novel's vision of serenity is of course intensified by the bitter cargo that lies in wait for Dick Diver and others in his circle, but in a scene such as the above, Rawlings is absolutely right – the angels do hold sway. Fitzgerald admired Matthew Arnold and agreed with his warnings about the gathering threats to civilized values posed by the modern world. In *College of One* Sheilah Graham remembers how he stressed the need to defend against this, recalling his underlined approval of Arnold's ethic 'the question how to live is itself a moral idea' (99). The above scene responds to this question (which is also a question about the virtues of style) in its celebration of life shared with intensity of purpose, a mystical, almost Yeatsian vision of unity. In referring to the novel's 'divine detachment' was Rawlings alluding specifically to just 'such a detachment from the world' as described in the above passage? As W.B. Yeats's charting of spiritual transcendence in his great poem, 'Sailing to Byzantium' (1928) is based upon a necessary renunciation of the physical world, since 'That is no country for old men' (217), so the Divers also dispel any regrets for what the narrator calls 'that country well left behind' (34).

The Divers' dinner party presents a paradigm of carefully cultivated license, of the freedoms deriving in part from what Henry James called 'dispatriation'.[8] Perhaps such a scene comes as close to a vision of benign exile as it is possible to get. R. P. Blackmur, however, pointed to one important paradox at the heart of American expatriates' generic experience, noting that they 'sought to be exiled, to be strangers in a far land, and sweetly to do nothing; that is to say, they wanted to be men of the world divorced from the world' (69). So one version of expatriation is manifest in a rare kind of worldly transcendence, mediated through invention/artifice, but Fitzgerald's expatriates also take their place as 'men of the world', in Blackmur's terms. As Malcolm Bradbury has written, Dick and Nicole Diver

> belong willingly enough to history, which, as Fitzgerald aptly says, manifests itself day-to-day, as style ... Thus they live, like the Fitzgeralds themselves, by history's daily workings, through styles and images, this week's haunting jazz songs and the summer's new resorts. (355)

The Divers certainly show themselves to be alive to the appeal of the avant-garde. They are 'too acute to abandon its contemporaneous rhythm and beat' (76), but even here Dick is untrammelled, inventive (this characteristic Fitzgerald also derived from Gerald Murphy, who is described most wonderfully by André Le Vot as 'the corsair of La Garoupe ... a fount of fashions ... there was something in him of the impresario' [207]) and influential. In a Europe that was becoming increasingly stylocentric, they set the fashions that others followed: 'the sailor trunks and sweaters they had bought in a Nice back street' were 'garments that afterward ran through a vogue in silk among the Paris couturiers' (281). Be it a small patch of sand on a Riviera beach or a dinner party, the Divers' style is appreciated by the *gens de monde*. In a description that recalls Jay Gatsby's lustrous automobile, 'bright with nickel ... and terraced with a labyrinth of wind-shields that mirrored a dozen suns' (*The Great Gatsby* 51), Fitzgerald even has Dick commandeer 'the car of the Shah of Persia' so that his party guests can see Paris on a joyride: 'Its wheels were all silver, so was the radiator. The inside of the body was inlaid with innumerable brilliants' (77).

In a 1927 interview Fitzgerald indicated his appreciation of Gallic civilization in matters of taste and breeding, remarking that 'France has the only two things toward which we drift as we grow older – intelligence and good manners' (Le Vot, 223). Intelligence, good manners, and what Henry Dan Piper would identify as the novel's core theme, 'the tragic power of charm' (228),[9] are all in view when Rosemary first meets Dick Diver. In his voice she finds immediately that promise of romantic, almost effortless invention: 'he would open up whole new worlds for her' (16). She intuits quickly that Diver, Barban and North are different from the men of her previous acquaintance, 'the rough and ready good fellowship of directors ... and the indistinguishable mass of college boys' (19). In contrast these people manifest a new kind of self-possession. Rosemary sees that they share an essential difference, one that at this early stage seems Fitzgerald's answer to the jibe at American expatriate degeneration in Hemingway's *Fiesta* (1927):

> 'You're an expatriate. You've lost touch with the soil. You get precious. Fake European standards have ruined you. You drink yourself to death. You become obsessed by sex. You spend all your time talking, not working. You are an expatriate, see? You hang around cafés.' (133)

Instead of atrophy in the type, however, Rosemary finds integrity, for: 'Even in their absolute immobility, complete as that of the morning, she felt a purpose, a working over something, a direction, an act of creation different from any she had known' (19). These men are not only integrated with their immediate environment, they are also involved creatively with it, intuitive *auteurs*. It is perhaps also significant that the group is here easily embraced by organic, natural imagery – they are 'complete' like the morning itself – they have not, in fact, 'lost touch with the soil'. Compare this depiction to the narrator's treatment of the effeminate Campion in the same section: he is the man *without* repose, rejected by the natural as he 'tried to edge his way into a sand-coloured cloud, but the cloud floated off into the vast hot sky' (11).

Barban, Diver, North: each in his own distinctive way personifies a version of selfhood that challenges orthodoxy; each exemplifies a disjunction between ego and collectivity that enables him to exploit possibilities of feeling and response which others have either abandoned or failed to realize. In this sense *Tender* is a novel that confronts concepts of identity and convention. The condition of being an expatriate can be precisely that – a condition of being. Yet there are those who are able to escape confinement within expatriate stereotypes, to escape the poverty of encountering life through a toneless lens. The novel's twelfth chapter begins with the characters (Diver, the Norths, Rosemary) poking fun at neurotic American mannerisms, played off against Dick Diver's notion of himself as the "man with repose" (51). Scrutinising their fellow diners in a high-class Paris restaurant, Diver's claim that 'no American men had any repose, except himself' (51)[10] is put successfully to the test, as one by one they showed the signs of nervous impulse: 'a man endlessly patted his shaven cheek with his palm, and his companion mechanically raised and lowered the stub of a cold cigar. The luckier ones fingered eyeglasses and facial hair ... or even pulled desperately at the lobes of their ears' (52). This scene is a vignette of all that bourgeois respectability cannot contain, being maladjusted to its environment, a condition exacerbated for these Americans by their displacement in Europe. It is a society of no repose, peopled by a moneyed class that is ill-at-ease with itself, filled with wanderers who are uncomfortable with themselves and their bodies.[11] If this is typical of postwar expatriate café society, it is a portrait without wit or elegance. The patrons' restless tics and twitches are signs of a more general enervation in the culture.

Fitzgerald's chronicle of modern neurosis interacts with the surrounding sociological, cultural, economic setting. Expatriation is a factor in all of those contexts and style is used as an index of the eclipse of the old order. As Nicole Diver realizes when she and Dick visit the beach at Antibes together for the last time, it has become a place 'perverted now to the tastes of the tasteless' (280). Its boundaries have quite literally disappeared, crumbled beneath the sand – 'Let him look at it – his beach ... he could search it for a day and find no stone of the Chinese wall he had once erected around it, no footprint of an old friend' (280). In its stead there is a new style of expatriate presence – an idiom of abject mediocrity, the presence of no style at all. This new reality is entirely without nuance, a democratised mass without discrimination. Fitzgerald's narrator is withering in judgement here, telling us that 'Now the swimming place was a "club", though, like the international society it represented, it would be hard to say who was not admitted' (281). As in the novel's opening scenes on the beach, body and form are used to indicate essential values. There are still the beach umbrellas, but simply too many to matter, so many in fact that Nicole has to watch 'Dick peer about for the children among the confused shapes and shadows of many umbrellas' (280). When the bodies are individuated, they are unlovely, a perception apparently acknowledged even by their owners, since 'few people swam any more in that blue paradise ... most of Gausse's guests stripped the concealing pajamas from their flabbiness only for a short hangover dip at one o' clock' (281). Here is repose without style. If the Divers, and the Murphys on whom their lives were based, were 'masters in the art of living' (Tomkins 7) on the Riviera, they were shown the way by convincing old-world aristocrats who had come there to die – in the grand style. In a passage stripped almost verbatim from another published in *The Saturday Evening Post* of 1924,[12] Fitzgerald's narrator paints a beguiling picture of that *ancien régime*. The very names of Cannes, Nice, Monte Carlo whisper 'of old kings come here to dine or die, of rajahs tossing Buddha's eyes to English ballerinas, of Russian princes turning the weeks into Baltic twilights in the lost caviare days' (15). Though Diver is no blue-blood,[13] the narrator's description of him as representing 'the exact furthermost evolution of a class' (21) suggests that in sensibility if not in breeding he is the natural inheritor of what is left of that civilisation.

Certainly Diver's return is to a place that has by 1929 become effete, and the narrator is careful to make that return carry overtones of *lèse majesté*: 'Probably it was the beach he feared, like a deposed ruler secretly visiting an old court' (280). In valediction, 'his beach' has become in the narrator's words (though the strong implication is that they represent Nicole's thoughts) 'perverted now to the tastes of the tasteless' (280), an intriguing language that suggests the rape of a natural environment by a counterworld of vulgar kitsch. All of the subtlety, the deep amity that went into the Divers' art of living has given way to rampant philistinism. The Riviera summers of a lost, aristocratic order are most certainly gone, buried under a whole apparatus of meretricious form. Both style and the natural (for in Fitzgerald's aesthetic, they are congruent) have been overwhelmed by an odious flourishing of 'new paraphernalia': 'the trapezes over the water, the swinging rings, the portable bath-houses, the floating towers, the searchlights from last night's fêtes, the modernistic buffet, white with a hackneyed motif of endless handlebars' (281). Diver was right to fear the beach, or at least what has been done to it. Again we see that in this novel style is emblematic of cultural change, though in this case the change is an affliction. Even Nicole 'was sorry' (280) for Dick, whose instincts seem lost amid such meaninglessness. Yet of the two, Nicole is better equipped to adjust towards the future: whatever one side of her ancestry suggests, her essential self easily shakes free of old-world values. The capacity to adapt to modern conditions, however unseemly, is an integral part of her deepest structure. She is in this respect profoundly centred in the modern. Whereas for Dick adaptation often involved an imaginative assimilation of new prospects, for Nicole change is rather a matter of reversion to origins, since she 'had been designed for change, for flight, with money as fins or wings. The new state of things would be no more than if a racing chassis, concealed for years under the body of a family limousine, should be stripped to its original self' (280). In this radical sense she is much more at home in the new world than her husband, whose expatriation, as the above return to the beach suggests, has become akin to a state of profound homelessness. Indeed, his exiled condition will increasingly resemble that of a refugee, driven from place to place by social upheaval and personal crisis. In this sense Diver is a representative figure, for as George Steiner has written, the twentieth century inaugurated 'the age of the refugee', an environment of extreme alienation: 'No exile is more radical, no feat of adaptation and new life more demanding. It seems proper that those who create art in a civilization of quasi-barbarism which has made so many homeless, which has torn up tongues and people by the root, should themselves be poets unhoused and wanderers across language' (*Extraterritorial* 11).

Faced by the 'feat of adaptation' now required of him in this subverted culture, Diver's capacities are ineffectual. He is defeated not by European standards, but as Hemingway's Bill Gorton put it, by 'fake European standards' (*Fiesta* 133) which have turned the simplicity of the Divers' beach colony into a mixture of amusement park and 'club'. Modernity is here defined by such pretence and artificiality, and although Jacqueline Tavernier-Courbin is right to draw attention to the sensuality of the novel's Riviera setting, to its appeal deriving from 'a life lived in closer harmony with the body and with nature' (226), she over-emphasises the contrast between Dick and Nicole in this regard, for he is more than capable of sensual engagement. It is indeed Nicole herself who acknowledges this, remembering wistfully their *vie plaisante* – a life emanating from Dick's openness towards natural energy, 'the ritual of the morning time, the quiet restful extraversion towards sea and sun – many inventions of his, buried deeper than the sand under the span of so few years' (321). For Nicole now, Dick has become 'a tarnished object of art' (282) and her new state of resurgent vitality can only emerge fully once she has departed his orbit, 'his beach'. The narrator goes so far as to tell us that 'she hated the beach, resented the places where she had played planet to Dick's sun' (289). The operative term in this figure is, however, that of life as playful invention. Nicole refuses any longer to be defined in these terms, opting instead for the reality of banal betrayal.

In 1935 Gerald Murphy wrote to Fitzgerald of his premonitory fear that his happiness would be lost to 'life itself', telling him that 'in my heart I dreaded the moment when our youth and invention would be attacked in our only vulnerable spot, the children' (Tomkins 125). Diver's 'inventions', now buried under Riviera sand, are exactly analogous to Murphy's youthful fount of 'invention': both have been destroyed by the advance of an amoral realism. For though George Steiner has reminded us that 'the liberating function of art lies in its singular capacity to "dream against the world," to structure worlds that are *otherwise*' (*Extraterritorial* 34), Fitzgerald's novel insists that the imagination of Dick Diver can only resist reality's darkening shadow for so long. Nicole is right – Dick has indeed become 'a tarnished object of art', and as his own 'dreams against the world' are increasingly threatened by the appeal of baser appetites, so Nicole is the beneficiary. Her affair with Barban is conditioned not by the application of style or tasteful discrimination but by the appeal of an opposing motive – the attraction of moral chaos: 'all summer she had been stimulated by watching people do exactly what they were tempted to do and pay no penalty for it' (291). As she crosses herself with Chanel Sixteen and waits for Barban, her 'earnest Satan', (294) she has no vision, no plan; she only knows that the change is coming and that she will not stand in its way. Her primary desire at this stage is not even marital emancipation, instead 'she enjoys the caviare of potential power ... she wanted a change' (291). With 'the plush arrogance of a top dog' (301) she knows that nothing can prevent her taking what she wants and needs: a new freedom, an unfettered license to indulge her passion.

For the present Nicole is a free agent, but Fitzgerald's narrator clearly signals that in the future her moral bills will be called in. Adultery ensures her entry to the postwar mess of collapsing values, to what Adamov called '*le temps de l'ignominie*'[14] (106). Her 'vulgar business' (291) with Barban is, she realizes, an unemotional act of self-indulgence. In the final push to claim her freedom and at the same time give Doctor Diver *his* liberty, she uses all weapons at her disposal, even her 'unscrupulousness against his moralities' (302). Just like the new breed of expatriates who 'pay no penalty' for self-indulgence, so Nicole has the freedom of knowing that she need never commit herself to anything. Her visionary reach is, however, limited, and 'she does not seem ... to anticipate the subsequent years when her insight will often be blurred by panic, by the fear of stopping or the fear of going on' (291). For now, however, an act of easy betrayal is the line of least resistance, and after her return to Diver from Barban '[s]he wandered about the house rather contentedly, resting on her achievement. She was a mischief, and that was a satisfaction' (300). As Fitzgerald's narrator reminds us, one of Nicole's most potent weapons is that she is equipped 'with the opportunistic memory of women'; this allows her to tell Barban accomplished lies about her passion for him, and to hardly remember the times "when she and Dick had possessed each other in secret places around the corners of the world' (300). Yet what Tavernier-Courbin calls 'the complicated and intellectual world of Dick Diver' (229) survives as the truest one nevertheless, and in the end Nicole's rebellion could never damage it radically, nor defeat his deep-rooted moral intelligence, 'sometimes exercised without power but always with substrata of truth under truth which she could not break or even crack' (301). In the end, 'Nicole felt outguessed, realizing that ... Dick had anticipated everything' (311).

J. Gerald Kennedy finds correctly that writing by American expatriates 'tends to reflect both an intensified awareness of place and an instinctive preoccupation with the identity of the alienated self' (26) and indeed the final scenes of *Tender* show that, for Diver, place was in the end perhaps even more important than people.[15] There is both practicality and humour in his farewell to his Riviera housekeepers: 'he kissed the Provençal girl who helped with the children. She had been with them for almost a decade and she fell on her knees and cried until Dick jerked her to her feet and gave her three hundred francs' (311). He dispenses with the formality of polite manners at the close as he tells his fellow expatriate Mary North, 'You're all so dull' (313). When, demanding a final showdown with Diver, Barban interrupts the Divers' joint visit to the barber at the Carleton Hotel, Fitzgerald even provides a considerable element of the ludicrous in Diver's matter-of-fact refusal to allow him any opportunity for macho posturing or the confrontation he wanted. This interruption is only the first of a series of apparently farcical breaks in the proceedings, one of which is the commotion caused by the incongruous arrival of the Tour de France outside. The meeting subsequently takes place nearby, at the ironically named Café des Allées, but not before Tommy gets his row from a still fully towelled and resentful Nicole – '"But my hair – it's half cut"' (307). She 'wanted Dick to take the initiative, but he seemed content to sit with his face half-shaved matching her hair half-washed', his dishevelled appearance being obviously reflected in the exhausted backmarkers and losers of the Tour de France, 'indifferent and weary' (310). Yet Diver is still the master-of-ceremonies, maintaining a code of permissible expression – '"Well, then," said the Doctor, "since it's all settled, suppose we go back to the barber shop"' (310), thus concluding a scene of abject reality which could not be transfigured. 'So it had happened – and with a minimum of drama' (344), and Nicole was right – Dick had anticipated everything.

His final action is, explicitly, to 'take a last look at Gausse's beach' (311) rather than its many occupants, who in those last moments include Nicole and Baby Warren, and finally Nicole and Tommy. It may be hardly surprising that the sight of Nicole and Tommy is precisely what he wishes to avoid at the last, but even the elements are now armed against his moods: '[a] white sun, chivied of outline by a white sky' (311-12) delineates betrayal in sharp relief, etched as myth, 'a man and a woman, black and white and metallic against the sky' (313). Colour and realistic perspective are here subordinated to the bleak monochrome of archetype. For although Dick is looking down on the beach and thus on his wife and her lover "from the high terrace" (314) above, Fitzgerald chooses sky, rather than the more logical sand to provide the boundless backdrop for a mythic theme. Any poetry of place, of subtle invention is impossible in such a harsh light. The Riviera set was still dazzling, but Diver's show was over. Perhaps in the end the beach was the only place that Diver could call home, the only place in which he had been not estranged, but in ownership, as Nicole recognizes: 'This is his place – in a way, he discovered it. Old Gausse always says he owes everything to Dick' (312). Indeed this impression had from the start been facilitated by Fitzgerald's language that domesticated the beach in homely metaphor as a 'bright tan prayer rug' (3). It may be Gausse's beach in fact, but it was more creatively and exclusively '[*o*]*ur* beach that Dick made out of a pebble pile' (20).

For Fitzgerald himself what might be termed 'good expatriation' was very much linked to relative isolation from the crowd, more akin to voluntary exile than expatriation. 'No one comes to the Riviera in summer, so we expect to have a few guests and to work' (161), says Nicole in a dream of hope. Loneliness as a theme increasingly became a defining zone in Fitzgerald's life and work, one in which his characters were tested and challenged. In loneliness he found a kind of emancipation, a freedom from the tyranny of social obligations. He also saw himself as constitutionally suited to the classic model of the sequestered artist.[16] For Fitzgerald on the Riviera in his *annus mirabilis* of 1924, expatriation was about being alone to work, and as already noted, loneliness was the key to great things – and he knew it, writing in a letter of that year as he worked on *The Great Gatsby* 'I hope I don't see a soul for six months ... I feel absolutely self-sufficient + I have a perfect hollow craving for lonliness [*sic*]... I shall write a novel better than any novel ever written in America' (*Life in Letters* 68). Yet only a year later he would pen a bitter-sweet testimony to this paradise lost to the crowd of expatriates who joined him in France, good expatriation turned bad as he told John Peale Bishop in a famous letter, 'there was no one at Antibes this summer except me, Zelda. The Valentinos, the Murphy's, Mistinguet, Rex Ingram, Dos Passos, Alice Terry, the McLieshes [*sic*] ... just a real place to rough it and escape from the world' (*Life in Letters* 126). Similarly Dick Diver's final meeting with Nicole and Tommy is interrupted not only by the arrival of the Tour de France, but by the ominous figure of an American photographer, in search of Riviera gold and in his way an eloquent expression of all that had gone wrong with Diver's world. Roughing it in splendid isolation on the Riviera is no longer an option with company like his. Rarely was publicity more unwelcome, and privacy more endangered:

> They were suddenly interrupted by an insistent American, of sinister aspect, vending copies of The Herald and of The Times fresh from New York ... He brought a gray clipping from his purse – and Dick recognized it as he saw it. It cartooned millions of Americans pouring from liners with bags of gold. 'You think I'm not going to get part of that? Well, I am.' (309)

This invasion is malign and inexorable, the sullying of the private by the public, a note struck again in the novel's penultimate chapter when Diver noticed that 'an American photographer from the A. and P. worked with his equipment in a precarious shade and looked up quickly at every footfall descending the stone steps' that lead to

Gausse's beach (312). The wolves are now at the very door of Diver's domain, drawn by the scent of exclusivity and difference. The result is a phenomenon we have all had to get used to in the years since, the surrender of the private sphere to the public, with a concomitant erosion of the virtues of private discourse including inward imaginative energies.

This chapter began with memories of the Murphys and their special charisma for F. Scott Fitzgerald, who in *Tender* was able to deepen their influence through his vision of their enlightened expatriation. It is fitting, then, to close with Gerald Murphy's own memory of Fitzgerald, provoked by having seen the 1964 film version of *Tender*. Murphy went to the cinema without Sara, who had refused to go, presumably because she feared that moving pictures would do no more justice to the reality of Riviera life in the early 1920s than the kind of photography satirised by Fitzgerald in the novel. If so, she was right. Murphy recalled that as he watched the movie the vast auditorium was completely empty apart from himself and 'an elderly charwoman sweeping the back rows' (Tomkins 128). The film 'disregarded everything except the battle of the sexes and dismissed the lure of the era with a nostalgic ridiculing of the Charleston' (Tomkins 128). Bad it was, yet driving home afterwards in the snow, Murphy remembered that

> I had a really vivid recollection of Scott on that day, years and years ago, when I gave him back the advance copy of his book and told him how good I thought certain parts of it were … and Scott took the book and said, with that funny, faraway look in his eye, 'Yes, it has magic. It has magic.' (Tomkins 128)

6

The Heart of Hollywood: *The Last Tycoon* (1941)

A year after Fitzgerald's death his unfinished novel *The Last Tycoon* was published, edited for Scribner's by Edmund Wilson. From the start Fitzgerald had connected the novel with renewed vitality, telling his daughter Scottie in a letter of October 1939: 'Look! I have begun to write something that is maybe great ... I am alive again' (*Life in Letters* 419), and on reading the novel in 1941, Zelda Fitzgerald also said it made her want to live again (Turnbull, *Scott Fitzgerald* 326). Such uplift needs to be put alongside moments of darker weight however, tragic insights into the futility of his labours, as in fatigue he sickened towards the imminent death he seemed to see coming upon him in a poem fragment in his death year of 1940:

There was a flutter from the wings of God and you lay dead.
Your books were in your desk
I guess & some unfinished
Chaos in your head
Was dumped to nothing by the great janitress
Of destinies. (Turnbull, *Scott Fitzgerald* 325)

Throughout his final years Fitzgerald was not only working at the Hollywood studios but also, during 1937–8, researching the history of America's dream factory in preparation for *The Last Tycoon*, although the first mention of the novel as a work-in-progress does not occur until 1938 in a letter to his publisher. Already by that date, according to Sheilah Graham, Fitzgerald's companion in Hollywood, he had accumulated a large collection of notes for his novel but had not yet started to write it. Perhaps as early as 1936 he may already have been planning a novel about Irving Thalberg (1899–1936), the motion picture magnate upon whom Monroe Stahr, the hero of *The Last Tycoon*, is based: 'I've long chosen him for a hero ... because he is one of the half-dozen men I have known who were built on the grand scale' (*Life in Letters* 411).

As Fitzgerald's letter of 1931 to Kenneth Littauer explained, 'this has been in my mind for three years' (*Life in Letters* 411).

One reason why a more exact chronology of his work on the novel is relatively difficult to track is that he had convinced himself that the two roles – Fitzgerald the Hollywood movie writer and F. Scott Fitzgerald the novelist writing a new novel about Hollywood with Thalberg at its centre –would, if publicized, lead to him being 'black-balled by the major [Hollywood] studios' (Piper 276). According to one of his biographers, he felt 'obliged to pursue his writing secretly' (Piper 276), even going so far as to deny his editor Max Perkins information about the novel's subject matter. Such fears in several forms were manifest as increasingly potent signs of catastrophic themes in Fitzgerald's life, writ large in the bleak recognition of 'The Crack-Up' that in his own 'self-immolation was something sodden-dark' (52). That his fears and anxieties were indeed flourishing in his last years is clear in the letter he wrote to Perkins in May 1939, denying in bizarre certitude that his novel had anything at all to do with Hollywood: 'I am in terror that this mis-information [i.e. that his novel-in-progress was about Hollywood] may have been disseminated to the literary columns. If I ever gave any such an impression it is entirely false ... It is distinctly <u>not</u> about Hollywood (and if it were it is the last impression that I would want to get about)' (*Life in Letters* 392), while Sheilah Graham remembers he swore his new secretary in Hollywood, Frances Kroll, to keep the 'great secret' that he was writing a book about Hollywood (*The Real F. Scott Fitzgerald* 178). In 'The Crack-Up', published a year or so before his arrival in Hollywood, his opinions on film were far from favourable. He criticised film as

> a mechanical and communal art that, whether in the hands of Hollywood merchants or Russian idealists, was capable of reflecting only the tritest thought, the most obvious emotion. It was an art in which words were subordinate to images, where personality was worn down to the inevitable low gear of collaboration. As long past as 1930, I had a hunch that the talkies would make even the best selling novelist as archaic as silent pictures ... there was a rankling indignity, that to me had become almost an obsession, in seeing the power of the written word subordinate to another power, a more glittering, a grosser power ... something I could neither accept nor struggle against, something which tended to make my efforts obsolescent, as the chain stores have crippled the small merchant, an exterior force, unbeatable –. (49)

This negative attitude extended to Hollywood itself as well as to its film products. About 'the question of going to California' he wrote to his agent Harold Ober in 1935: 'I hate the place like poison with a sincere hatred ... I should consider it only as an emergency measure' (*As Ever* 216).

In this regard as in much else, 'The Crack-Up' essays, which he began writing the year before his arrival in Hollywood, are a key to Fitzgerald's state of mind at that time. According to Jackson Bryer and Cathy Barks, his 'motive for writing the essays was, in part, to end the painful sense of isolation he felt' (218) in the mid-1930s. It was as though he wanted to converse with his readers in a very intimate way. In taking his own neuroses as a subject fit for publication in 'The Crack-Up', he was again ahead of his time, anticipating the literary mode which in 1959 the critic M.L. Rosenthal (in a review of Robert Lowell's *Life Studies*) would call 'confessional', applying the term to the autobiographical strain present in the mid-twentieth-century poetry of, for instance, Robert Lowell, Sylvia Plath, John Berryman and Anne Sexton. 'The Crack-Up' itself provides an authoritative definition and expression of a modern dark night of the soul, even as it finishes with an extract from Matthew 5–13 and the Sermon on the Mount: *'Ye are the salt of the earth. But if the salt hath lost its savour, wherewith shall it be salted?'* (45). Fitzgerald acknowledges that he had to leave town to get away from himself, so that:

> one harassed and despairing night I packed a brief-case and went off a thousand miles to think it over. I took a dollar room in a drab little town where I knew no one ... I only wanted absolute quiet to think out why I had developed a sad attitude towards sadness, a melancholy attitude towards melancholy, and a tragic attitude towards tragedy–*why I had become identified with the objects of my horror or compassion* ... Identification such as this spells the death of accomplishment. It is something like this that keeps insane people from working. (51–2, original emphasis)

A fugitive from himself, Fitzgerald came to fear that he had permanently merged with his subjects. Having in *Tender is the Night* given us Dr Dick Diver as psychiatrist-hero, in 'The Crack-Up' Fitzgerald provides his own candid self-appraisal that is more succinctly stated by the despairing voice of the poet in 'Skunk Hour', the final poem of Robert Lowell's equally frank *Life Studies* (1958): 'My mind's not right.' Or in the extraordinary 'Night Sweat', from the same poet's collection, entitled *For the Union Dead* (1964), there is an even more accurate correlative for the writer's mind sinking through primal despair into a clammy living death:

> Work-table, books and standing lamp
> … for ten nights now I've felt the creeping damp
> float over my pajamas' wilted white …
> Sweet salt embalms me and my head is wet,
> …my life's fever is soaking in a night sweat–
> one life, one writing! … in this urn
> the animal night sweats of the spirit burn.

'In a real dark night of the soul it is always three o' clock in the morning, day after day' (46) Fitzgerald wrote, his 'Crack-Up' essay anticipating Lowell's poem in a classic figuration of the artist's purgatorial self-reckoning, while Andrew Turnbull's biography tells us that by 1939, his penultimate year of life, Fitzgerald had entered 'the time of hospitals, nurses, night sweats, sedatives and despair … half-crazed with worry and isolation, he was also blocked in his work, and "a writer not writing," he once remarked, "is practically a maniac within himself"' (*Scott Fitzgerald* 302). In such a context and in such terms, work in Hollywood offered him much more than a solution to financial distress. Watching others of his generation succumb to irreparable psychological breakdown, his own solution eventually clarified, and recognising the hole he was in – 'it is something like this that keeps insane people from working '– he knew that to save himself from a similar fate or worse, he would have to accomplish a radical severance from the burnt-out life he had been leading, which work at the Hollywood studios provided him with:

> I had stood by while one famous contemporary of mine played with the idea of the Big Out for half a year; I had watched when another, equally eminent, spent months in an asylum unable to endure any contact with his fellow men. And of those who had given up and passed on I could list a score. ('Crack-Up' 52)

Fitzgerald finally diagnoses his own ills as exemplary of a more national *agon* consequent upon the ending of the Jazz Age and the Wall Street Crash: 'my recent experience parallels the wave of despair that swept the nation when the Boom was over' ('Crack-Up' 56). The Crash and the Crack-Up – the only way out was to get out and to give up on the ideals of youth since, he concludes, 'a writer need have no such ideals unless he makes them up for himself, and this one has quit' ('Crack-Up' 55). If, as Saul Bellow once wrote (in his novel of 1975, *Humboldt's Gift*), perhaps quoting Sigmund Freud, 'happiness was nothing but the remission of pain' (7), then for Fitzgerald too 'the natural state of the sentient adult is a qualified unhappiness' ('Crack-Up' 55).

As noted in my discussion of *The Beautiful and Damned*, Fitzgerald admired Ernest Hemingway's fiction for its engagement with fear as subject, writing in his *Notebooks* that 'some day when the psychoanalysts are forgotten EH will be read for his great studies into fear' (325). Again and again, however, Hemingway was to accuse Fitzgerald of succumbing to his own fears, in 1951 writing to Charles Scribner that Fitzgerald had 'the in-bred talent of a dishonest and easily frightened angel' (Baker 726), which is close to saying he had no talent at all, while in a letter to Gerald and Sara Murphy just after the publication of 'The Crack-Up', Hemingway compared their troubles to Napoleon's retreat from Moscow, a long march from which Fitzgerald, he said, would have deserted in the first week (Baker 440). Whereas Fitzgerald saw his crisis of the mid-1930s as the final stage of a cumulative breakdown, for Hemingway Fitzgerald's weakness was all but constitutional. With typical cruelty he told Max Perkins that if Fitzgerald had been in the war he would have been shot for cowardice, and later told Malcolm Cowley that 'cowardice' was one of Fitzgerald's abiding problems.

While it is true that in Hollywood towards the end of his life Fitzgerald wrote that 'the enemy of men is Fear' (*Notebooks* 326), nevertheless a confrontation with the enemy, facing it and knowing it, could well be regarded as an act of courage, not of cowardice, and *pace* Hemingway, Fitzgerald's aesthetic had always demanded a close and authentic relationship with those materials he chose to write about. If the modern novel that Fitzgerald's fiction helped to inaugurate was the latest stage in the narrative history of studied introspection, of self-probing discourse, then it was Fitzgerald rather than Hemingway, with his self-censorship, who was their genuine inheritor. Perhaps this is what T.S. Eliot meant in his letter to Fitzgerald *apropos The Great Gatsby* – he called it 'the first step American fiction has taken since Henry James' (Turnbull, *Letters* 218) – that modernist art with its fundamental lyric of self-revelation had found in Fitzgerald a perfect exponent. In his 1933 essay, 'One Hundred False Starts', Fitzgerald acknowledged that he was a writer who had to 'start with an emotion – one that's close to me and that I can understand' (*Afternoon* 132). Even more crucially, the onset of an intimate fear and dread was the very spur to creativity for him; indeed it had almost become a prerequisite for releasing the creative flow. But his last published book, the short-story collection *Taps at Reveille* (1935) had barely sold 3000 copies, and with Zelda's third nervous breakdown and repeated suicide attempts, his letters begin to step up from fearful musings to register a 'rising note of terror' (Dardis 20). While for Jackson Bryer and Cathy Barks, the Fitzgeralds' life story inspires 'admiration and courage', it is also recognised to be a tragic evocation of 'pity and fear' (387). And Tom Dardis, in his study of novelists in Hollywood, *Some Time in the Sun*, found that as he began his work in Hollywood, Fitzgerald 'had good reason to fear that his writing talent had deserted him' (Dardis 19). Faced by the worry and mounting costs of his wife's hospital treatments, along with his inability to sell his stories (his royalties from his books in 1936, a year when they were all in print, amounted to only $81.18 in total), Fitzgerald entered what may have been 'the grimmest hour of his entire professional life as a writer' (Dardis 19).

His final years in Hollywood, however, eventually proved to be a classic of encounter. Though he spent less than three years there and, apart from the 'Pat Hobby' series of short stories, published just one short story with a Hollywood setting while he was living there ('Design in Plaster' [1939]), nevertheless some critics believe that 'in Hollywood Fitzgerald had found his greatest theme' (Piper 280). It was a theme that grew out of the coalition between the place itself, its already powerful mythos – Hollywood the dream factory – and Fitzgerald's own most essential delineations as an artist. The place was both a factory in which he – and other important novelists of the time such as William Faulkner and Aldous Huxley – worked as functionaries of the studio system, and also a dynamic culture which, at its best, escaped reductive commercial constraints, creating moving pictures which gave humanity the chance to dream some of its largest yet most intimate imaginings as they were played out upon the silver screen; as Monroe Stahr tells the English writer George Boxley (based partly upon Aldous Huxley): 'our condition is that we have to take people's own favorite folklore and dress it up and give it back to them' (Bruccoli ed., *The Love of the Last Tycoon*: *A Western* 120. All further references are to this edition).

It is little wonder that Hollywood producers were attracted to his work, for amongst his natural talents he had always been an accomplished scenographer whose fiction, both short and long, was often distinctly organised into formally dramatic scene-settings. In his very first novel, in Chapter 1 of Book 2 of *This Side of Paradise*, we have for instance 'The Débutante', which comprises almost a one-act play complete with scene-settings and stage directions – '*The time is February. The place is a large, dainty bedroom in the Connage house on 68th Street, New York – a girl's room*' (157) along with character briefs to introduce the scripted dialogue – 'After a pause a third seeker enters.... This is CECELIA CONNAGE, sixteen, pretty, shrewd and constitutionally good-humored' (158). Such interruptions to orthodox form in his early fiction are indications of the extent to which Fitzgerald was ready to traverse generic boundaries in search of a more complete scenic imagining. After the failure of his play *The Vegetable* in 1923, however (the 'opening night was a disaster ... people walked out during the second act fantasy which didn't work on the stage', wrote Matthew Bruccoli; or as Zelda Fitzgerald witnessed and wrote to a friend, 'the show flopped as flat as one of Aunt Jemima's pancakes', *Epic Grandeur* 187), he became thereafter something of a dramatist *manqué*. Although he had dallied with screenwriting in 1927 and 1931, at that time 'he never took these short visits to California very seriously' (Dardis 10), mainly because his work as a short-story writer for mass-market periodicals such as the *Saturday Evening Post* was still highly lucrative. At the end of the decade, however, and amidst financial crisis, Hollywood may have seemed a timely opportunity to revive such latent aspirations.

It is an irony that the unfinished state of *The Last Tycoon* permits us to see its episodic artistry even more clearly than perhaps would have been possible had those episodes been integrated within a completed text. In such terms, Fitzgerald's appeal to Hollywood's studio chiefs lay in his potential for taking the promise of movie-as-dream and scripting an episodic correlative for this that might translate into the shared desires and fears of a mass audience. His plans for *Tycoon* indeed indicate that he intended it to be episodic, a novel of moods, what he called à la Flaubert: 'without "ideas" but only people moved singly and in mass through what I hope are authentic moods. The resemblance is rather to "Gatsby" than to anything else I've written" (*Life in Letters* 470–1). In the end though, Fitzgerald's ability to apply his talents to what he called the 'grosser power' of the movies was at best only moderately successful. For though all but three of the thirteen films he had some hand in scripting during his final years in Hollywood were produced, in most of these he worked only as a 'polisher' of the final screenplay, and in only a single instance, that of the screenplay for Erich Maria Remarque's novel *Three Comrades*

(1937–8), was he actually given a screen credit (which he shared with E. E. 'Ted' Paramore) by the MGM studio.

Fitzgerald once told Sheilah Graham, 'if I had lived in another age, I would have been a poet. But there's no money in poetry now' (*The Real F. Scott Fitzgerald* 146). There was certainly money to be made in the movies however, and his work as a Hollywood scriptwriter was to provide him with plenty of it. The $68,000 he earned from his film scripts in 1938 was a very large sum in today's terms, and that at a time when US income tax was almost nonexistent. One only has to compare this figure with the total sales of all of his nine published books for the year 1939, which amounted to only 114 copies, giving royalties of just $33, to see that he could hardly take a disinterested view of Hollywood money. Indeed, Leo C. Rosten's contemporary study of Hollywood's movers and shakers in the late 1930s, *Hollywood: The Movie Colony, the Movie Makers* (1941), tells us that of the nearly 230 writers working there in 1938, Fitzgerald was amongst the top 20 highest paid. It is odd that nothing in Fitzgerald's correspondence of these last years indicates that he was aware that he was one of Hollywood's highest-paid screenwriters, even though this may have been the reason that his first contract, at MGM, was not renewed in January 1939 – he was just too expensive. Although his place within Hollywood's status system may not have been at the very top, nevertheless to renew his contract MGM would have had to increase his weekly pay cheque to $1500 – again a very large sum. According to Edwin Knopf, the MGM story editor whose recommendation to the studio on Fitzgerald's behalf had influenced his appointment there, 'no one worked harder or was more determined to succeed' (Berg 28), while his Hollywood agent, H. N. Swanson, believed that Fitzgerald's producers in Hollywood 'were in awe of him' (Berg 29).

Unlike the more permanent nameplates of other more reliable screenwriters, however, Fitzgerald's office door had only his name on a scrap of pencilled paper and his awareness of such Hollywood status details is writ large in many of his 'Pat Hobby' stories. These comprise a set of 17 stories about a somewhat superannuated writer still trying to make a living in screen city. In 'A Patriotic Short', for instance, Pat Hobby remembers wryly that in the 'fat days of silent pictures' he 'had his great success in Hollywood during what Irving Cobb refers to as "the mosaic swimming-pool age – just before the era when they had to have a shinbone of St Sebastian for a clutch lever"'. Now working only on 'humble short' movies, he enters 'the shorts department ... remembering a certain day over a decade ago in all its details ... his ascent to that long lost office which had a room for the secretary and was really the director's office' (*Collected Short Stories* 312–13). According to Nunnally Johnson, a contemporary of Fitzgerald in the Hollywood of those years, and one of Hollywood's most successful writers (his office door surely had a more permanent name tag – amongst the writing credits of his career were *The Grapes of Wrath* and *How to Marry a Millionaire*), Fitzgerald's 'biggest misfortune, which I doubt that he ever realized, was that they paid him fat money at the very beginning. And even though he blew his chances with inadequate work, he believed that he should continue to draw such salaries or even larger ones' (Dardis 53). His main problem was trying to meet the even larger weight of debts he brought to Hollywood (by his own estimate he owed around $40,000 at the point of his arrival there [*Epic* 423]) along with the ongoing costs of Zelda's treatments and their daughter Scottie's education. As a result, 'he was rarely able to keep more than half the money he was paid' (Dardis 29). Even after his MGM contract came to an end at the start of 1939, however, his work as a Hollywood screenwriter continued and his final pay cheque, for the scripting of the film *The Light of Heart* (based upon Emlyn Williams's drama, Fitzgerald's screenplay was rejected but eventually rewritten by Nunnally Johnson and produced by Twentieth-Century Fox in 1942 as *Life Begins at Eight-Thirty*), earned him $7,000, again a large sum when translated into today's terms.

'I can believe that you may really get at the heart of Hollywood, and of what there is wonderful in it as well as all the rest' (Berg 383). So Max Perkins wrote to Fitzgerald in 1939, urging him in the same letter to 'push on with courage' towards the completion of *Tycoon*, and, according to Sheilah Graham, Fitzgerald's completed novel might well have revealed what was 'wonderful in it as well as all the rest', since he told her 'he wanted his story about the movie world not only to reveal its faults ... but also to extol its virtues and capture its glamor' (*The Real F. Scott Fitzgerald* 174). In fact, as Tom Dardis notes, 'it was only when screenwriting jobs became scarce or nonexistent that [Fitzgerald] finally settled down to writing *The Last Tycoon*' (30), while Frances Kroll, Fitzgerald's secretary in Hollywood, remembers that 'it was late fall in 1940 before Scott was able to give full attention to *Tycoon*. This time he would stay with it to the end' (*Against the Current* 94). She also noticed that 'Scott's invalidism disappeared when he was doing what he liked to do. His energies soared' (*Against the Current* 93). And though Edmund Wilson (with typically unkind judgement in the case of Fitzgerald) could write to Perkins shortly after Fitzgerald's death – apparently without any satirical undertone – 'it is the only one of Scott's books that shows any knowledge of any field of human activity outside of dissipation' (Edmund Wilson, *Letters on Literature and Politics*, 337), he also saw that while in Hollywood Fitzgerald 'had made some sort of new adjustment to life' (Wilson to Christian Gauss, 1941 *Letters on Literature and Politics* 343). These comments recognise the revived sense of purpose Fitzgerald applied to his new novel, which Fitzgerald said was to be 'a constructed novel like Gatsby, with passages of poetic prose when it fits the action but no ruminations or side-shows like Tender. Everything must contribute to the dramatic movement' (*Life in Letters* 467). Many critics have recognised this (indeed the unfinished novel's first edition of 1941 seemed to invite the comparison, published as it was in the same binding along with *The Great Gatsby*), noticing for instance that in Cecelia Brady we have a narrator involved in the plot, so bearing some resemblances to Nick Carraway's narrative role in *Gatsby*.

Yet Cecelia's narrative role is also the unfinished novel's weakest aspect, a drawback allowed even by Matthew Bruccoli, one of Fitzgerald's most partisan admirers and editor of *The Love of the Last Tycoon: A Western*, in the 'Introduction' to which he writes:

> the written material consists of fragments in various states of revision, and Fitzgerald was still solving problems of plot, structure, and point of view. For example, the use of Cecelia Brady as narrator had become too restrictive as the scope and thematic content of the novel enlarged. What Fitzgerald got down on paper constitutes a miraculous work in progress: miraculous because it promises so much of what Fitzgerald intended to achieve in *Tycoon*. (Bruccoli, 'Introduction' xxxii).

Although Bruccoli's 'miraculous' is an odd descriptor here, since it both plays down the work that still remained to be done – particularly the 'problem' of the narrator – yet asks that we consider even the unfinished *Tycoon*'s promise as 'miraculous', there are certainly clear signs that the novel would have had every chance of finally emerging alongside *Gatsby* as one of the author's very best. Fitzgerald likely realized and would have eventually resolved the narrative issue, since among other problems with her narrative positioning, Cecelia's 19-year-old perspective is incapable of carrying the sophisticated insights that were increasingly required as the story grew. In his 1939 letter to Kenneth Littauer, he set out his plans for the novel and its narrative stance:

> By making Cecelia at the moment of her telling the story, an intelligent and observant woman, I shall grant myself the privilege, as Conrad did, of letting her imagine the actions of the characters. Thus, I hope to get the verisimilitude of a first person narrative, combined with a Godlike knowledge of all events that happen to my characters. (*Life in Letters* 410)

As it stands, this narrator, described by Donald Monk as 'the callow Cecelia' (93), provides at best an awkward presence. At times her narrative is described as 'drawn partly from a paper I wrote in college on "A Producer's Day" and partly from my imagination' (30), while too often she has to reintroduce herself when the reader has all but forgotten about her being there at all; so, for instance, at the close of Episode 13 we have the blunt statement that 'this is Cecelia taking up the narrative in person' (86), an intervention that must make many readers wince and wish that she would return to a background impersonality. Her rationale for her apparent narrative omniscience certainly provokes incredulity, and when she lists her sources of information about Stahr's doings, the reader senses the narrative architecture is unsteady and may begin to ask what is the point of a narrator who is personalised if she is dependent upon Prince Agge, Wylie White, the butler and the fly on the wall:

> That was substantially a day of Stahr's. I don't know about the illness, when it started, etc., because he was secretive but I know he fainted a couple of times that month because Father told me. Prince Agge is my authority for the luncheon in the commissary … and Wylie White told me a lot … as for me I was head over heels in love with him then and you can take what I say for what it's worth. (75)

When Stahr dutifully takes Cecelia to the dance floor, he assuredly sees her for what she is – hardly more than a child with an adolescent infatuation, the daughter of a colleague. By this later stage she, too, sees that her love interest is not reciprocated, that her dance partner is 'an absent-minded man' (87) whose thoughts, along with the reader's, are elsewhere: with Kathleen Moore and the developing relationship that has become the story's emotional centre (though, according to Henry Dan Piper, in the unfinished novel 'Stahr's relationship to Kathleen ... was so uncrystallized that Fitzgerald still had considerable revising ahead' [Piper 283]). Cecelia also feels the loneliness of Kathleen's departure, feels that she is 'lonelier than before the girl had gone. For me, as for Stahr, she took the evening with her, took along the stabbing pain I had felt – left the great ball-room empty and without emotion' (87). Her unreciprocated love is itself uninteresting since, by her own admission, he 'was a man any girl would go for, with or without encouragement' (15). If on first introduction Cecelia found that Stahr 'made me feel young and invisible' (15), in the remaining narrative her presence hardly becomes any more defined in his eyes or any more interesting to the reader. Many readers will agree that the narrative 'comes most completely alive at the very moment Fitzgerald drops both her and any pretense of her existence and carries on with the narrative by himself' (Dardis 70). It's not until her narrative is half-way done that she gives us a sketchy, physical self-description: 'I had good features except my face was too round and a skin they seemed to love to touch and good legs and I didn't have to wear a brassiere' (76). She acknowledges that she is no intellectual match for Stahr, whom she presents as a superman and autodidact who had 'a long time ago run ahead through trackless wastes of perception into fields where very few men were able to follow him' (18). In such terms Stahr embodies the Horatio Alger rags-to-riches myth 'in which Fitzgerald still firmly believed' (Piper 269) even until the end of his life. Cecelia even considers that Stahr had created not only himself but also that she was herself movie-made in Stahr's image, for it was 'more than possible that some of the pictures which Stahr himself conceived had shaped me into what I was' (19).

We have little of Cecelia's developed personality but in, for instance, the passages quoted above, we catch once again Fitzgerald's *leitmotif* of the lonely self: in Cecelia's depiction of Stahr as a lonely pioneer who has braved 'trackless wastes' to venture 'where very few men were able to follow him', and in Cecelia's narration of Stahr's relationship with Kathleen Moore ('it was more intimate than anything they had done and they both felt a dangerous sort of loneliness and felt it in each other' [95]), we find inflected echoes of both romance and punishment in contexts that also conditioned the Fitzgeralds' relationship. In one of her most extraordinary, damning and extended indictments of her husband written in 1930 from her Swiss sanatorium, Zelda names the worst of times as deriving from those lonely sorrows caused by Fitzgerald's desertions of her. She sees loneliness as punishment, and in a much more chilling prefiguration of the 3.30 am emptiness of Cecelia's dance-floor loneliness, castigates him for desertion:

> We quarrelled about Dwight Wiman and you left me lots alone.... There was Gerald [Murphy] and Ernest [Hemingway] and you often did not come home ... You were far away by then and I was alone ... You left me more and more alone ... Now that I can't sleep any more I have lots to think about, and since I have gone so far alone I suppose I can go the rest of the way ... You didn't care: so I went on and on – dancing alone, and, no matter what happens I still know in my heart that it is a Godless, dirty game; that love is bitter and all there is, and that the rest is for the emotional beggars of the earth. (*Life in Letters* 192–5)

Yet Zelda could also write of the romance of the lonely self, telling Scott that she 'would like to be walking alone in a Sirocco at Cannes at night passing under the dim lamps and imagining myself mysterious and unafraid like last summer ... What would you like? Not work, I know, and not lone places' (*Correspondence* 256). It seemed that in Hollywood too, loneliness was in the air Fitzgerald breathed in his last years and the man who, for many, would forever be associated with America's party culture in the New York of the 1920s now reserved for his work what dwindling energy he had left. According to Aaron Latham's *Crazy Sundays: F. Scott Fitzgerald in Hollywood*:

> now something had happened to Fitzgerald. Edwin H. Knopf, who was story editor at MGM and therefore one of Fitzgerald's bosses, remembers that the author who had once personified The Prom, The Bonne Fête, The Wild Party, now shied away from large gatherings. 'If it was to be a big party,' Knopf says, 'he didn't want to come.' (13)

Another cameo was provided by the dramatist and screenwriter Frances Goodrich Hackett, who remembers the first time she and her husband saw Fitzgerald at lunch in the huge Hollywood dining-hall known as the commissary:

> The first time I saw Scott ... he was in the commissary sitting alone at a table. He just sat there but he didn't order. What I noticed

> were his eyes. Never in my life will I forget his eyes. He looked as if he were seeing hell opening before him. He was hugging his brief case and he had a Coke. Then suddenly he got up to go out. I said to Albert, 'I just saw the strangest man.' He said, 'That's Scott Fitzgerald.' (Latham 7–8)

One of the oddest and starkest commissary conjunctions was that of Fitzgerald and Groucho Marx, who would occasionally sit at the same lunch table as Fitzgerald and the other Hollywood writers. Ogden Nash remembers that Groucho 'turned things upside down so that you couldn't have a coherent conversation – everything had to be a joke' (Latham 8). Among such company Fitzgerald's lonely presence was hardly appreciative, so that 'while Groucho kidded and talked all the time, Scott would sit as voiceless as Harpo, not even laughing' (Latham 8). Fitzgerald seemed to live inside his own loneliness, not seeming to acknowledge the famous company he was in. Certainly laughter was hardly to be expected from him in these years, as confirmed by his secretary Frances Kroll, who remembered that 'Scott was not a laugher. I don't think I ever recall him laugh out loud. He seemed rather to smile deeply' (Kroll 90). Fitzgerald, like Monroe Stahr, has 'the house he rented', and Stahr dares not mention his tenancy to Kathleen for fear 'it would make him sound lonely' (106). Edwin Knopf remembered well that sometimes Fitzgerald would seek his company and 'would be invited out to the Knopfs' sprawling home on La Mesa Drive in Santa Monica … If he was lonely, he would call me … I finally trained him to do that' (Latham 13).

Rather than Cecelia, it is Kathleen who reminds Monroe Stahr of his dead wife, Minna, but filtered through Cecelia's consciousness, *The Last Tycoon* is in all a story of love doubly unrequited and thus leading to loneliness of the heart, be it Cecelia's love for Stahr, or his for Kathleen. Cecelia Brady, much more than Nick Carraway in *The Great Gatsby*, is an observer who belongs to the inside of the society she describes. She is the daughter of one of Stahr's closest colleagues, the Irish-American producer Pat Brady, who is probably based upon Hollywood mogul Louis B Meyer. Fitzgerald's plans for the novel's conclusion included having Brady hire a gunman to murder Stahr; in a letter of 1939 to Kenneth Littauer of *Collier's* magazine, describing his plans for *Tycoon*, Fitzgerald said that Pat Brady would be 'a scoundrel of the lowest variety', and alluded to the parallels he wanted to draw between Brady and Stahr and what he called 'the deadly dislike of each other between Thalberg and Louis B. Meyer' (*Life in Letters* 408–9). Brady was a Hollywood careerist who 'was in the picture business as another man might be in cotton or steel', while Cecelia herself was 'brought up in pictures' (1), or as Fitzgerald said, 'she is *of* the movies but not *in* them' (*Life in Letters* 409). Like Nick Carraway, Cecelia is both inside and outside the story she tells. As a Hollywood producer's child she might be 'in a position to watch the wheels go round' (1), yet as the sole female narrator of Fitzgerald's novels, she also understands that she is gendered as an outsider when it comes to Hollywood's most intimate discourse. Her vision of Hollywood is therefore one of witnessing an enigma whose workings 'can be understood ... but only dimly and in flashes' (2). As a woman in the Hollywood of the 1930s she also accepts her *de facto* status of earnest supplicant to the reigning Hollywood patriarchy: 'the closest a woman can come to the set-up is to try and understand one of those men' (2).

Understanding the Hollywood of those years without preconception or prejudice was difficult, something that Fitzgerald has Cecelia take up at the start of *Tycoon*, when, remembering her school years, she recalls that 'some of the English teachers who pretended an indifference to Hollywood or its products really *hated* it. Hated it way down deep as a threat to their existence' (1). The language selected here is significant, since it echoes very distinctly Fitzgerald's own prejudices about Hollywood as set out in 'The Crack-Up' and already noted above in this chapter: 'I hate the place like poison with a sincere hatred ... I should consider it only as an emergency measure' (*As Ever* 216). Even as late as April 1940 he was writing in a letter to his wife, 'I suppose a place is what you make it but I have grown to hate California' (Bryer and Barks 334), while in July 1940 from Santa Barbara he wrote to his friend Alice Richardson, 'Isn't Hollywood a dump – in the human sense of the word? A hideous town, pointed up by the insulting gardens of its rich, full of the human spirit at a new low of debasement' (Turnbull, *Letters* 624). Both Fitzgerald and the teachers remembered by *Tycoon*'s narrator saw Hollywood film as a personal threat, since it was regarded as a challenge to the dominance of book culture and the imaginative and cognitive skills seen to be necessary for the appreciation of literature. The fear (immeasurably extended in our own cyber-age) was that what were then regarded as the higher cultural artefacts and forms of serious literature would be overwhelmed and trivialised by the commercially-driven mass products of Hollywood.[17]

But it is not just Cecelia's English teachers who recoil from the Hollywood phenomenon, since 'even before that, when I was in a convent, a sweet little nun asked me to get her a script of a screen play so she could "teach her class about movie writing" as she had taught them about the essay and the short story' (1). The nun's response was to return the script eventually to the young Cecelia 'with an air of offended surprise and not a single comment' (1). The implication is that Hollywood texts posed an heretical challenge not just to the sacred bastions of high culture but also to their preferred ethic. That Fitzgerald intended this passage to carry this kind of weight is further clarified, since in his 'Working Notes' (appended to *The Love of the Last Tycoon*) for this section of the novel, Cecelia gives the script to 'a professor in Freshman' who eventually 'handed it back to me without comment and didn't mention the picture part of the course again' (157). That the 'professor' becomes a nun in the published version of *Tycoon* indicates more accurately the kind of constituency Fitzgerald wanted to cite at this point. In such terms of assessment, the status of a typical Hollywood script would have been regarded as at best dubious in terms of its moral content. It is worth remembering that Hollywood films of these years had become the target of explicit censorship. In the late 1920s and early 1930s Hollywood movies had become more relaxed in their willingness to open up in terms of sexual content, and while the scandals in the private lives of the stars shocked the moral majority in America, simultaneously the mass audience may have been drawn to the movies' flouting of such standards. Fear of government intervention, however, inspired a programme of self-censorship in Hollywood, a watershed that Fitzgerald's narrator connects explicitly with Stahr's greatness as a producer: 'he led pictures way up past the range and power of the theatre, reaching a sort of golden age before the censorship in 1933' (30). As Twentieth-Century Fox studio President Sidney Kent told production boss Winfield Sheehan in 1933, 'I think the quicker we get away from degenerates and fairies in our stories the better off we are going to be and I do not want any of them in Fox pictures' (Leff and Simmons 36). At the same time, the introduction of the so-called Motion Picture Production Code in 1930, administered by Joseph 'Joe' Ignatius Breen,[18] was intended to censor what the Code's 'General Principles' called any movie 'which will lower the moral standards of those who see it … the sympathy of the audience should never be thrown to the side of crime, wrongdoing, evil or sin' (Leff and Simmons 286).

Mainstream Hollywood cinema in the 1920s and 1930s also posed very powerful challenges to the aesthetic norms of the period. Whereas the films of avant-garde European directors such as Sergei Eisenstein are accommodated readily within existing art-historical norms, Peter Wollen argues rightly that Hollywood film was much more resistant to such assimilation: 'There is no difficulty in talking about Eisenstein in the same breath as a poet like Mayakovsky, a painter like Malevich, or a theatre director like Stanislavsky. But John Ford or Raoul Walsh? The initial reaction, as we well know, was to damn Hollywood completely, to see it as a threat to civilized values and sensibilities' (Brookeman 171). In this latter context, *Tycoon*'s narrative preamble offers the reader three choices – the narrator's way, which is to accept Hollywood's existence as a fact of American cultural life ('take Hollywood for granted like I did' as Cecelia puts it [2]); the way of the 'sweet little nun' and the associated constituency of middle-America as cited by Wollen above, which is to 'dismiss it with the contempt we reserve for what we don't understand' (2); or the way offered by the narrative itself as it unfolds, towards a deeper understanding of Hollywood – 'to try and understand one of those men' such as Monroe Stahr who have intellectual access to 'the whole equation of pictures' (2). In these terms, Fitzgerald's portrait of Stahr is in many ways intended as a characterization of a maverick producer who possessed all the keys to the Hollywood kingdom, an insider who was on occasion prepared to fly in the face of the studio system and its prejudices. Indeed, the metaphor of Stahr as an heroic superman who has the power to fly above with encompassing vision is one of the narrator's most memorable idealizations of the man she is infatuated with:

> He had flown up very high to see, on strong wings when he was young. And while he was up there he had looked on all the kingdoms, with the kind of eyes that can stare straight into the sun. Beating his wings tenaciously – finally frantically – and keeping on beating them he had stayed up there longer than most of us, and then, remembering all he had seen from his great height of how things were, he had settled gradually to earth. (21)

More buoyant than Icarus, yet the narrator's panoramic picture of the hero as a youthful visionary is one that cannot in the end avoid its own descent into tragedy when tested by the reality of bodily dysfunction. 'He has survived the talkies, the depression, carried his company over terrific obstacles and done it all with a growing sense of kingliness' (163), Fitzgerald wrote in his 'Working Notes' to *Tycoon*. He saw Hollywood as 'a tragic city of beautiful girls' (Pearce, *Sayings* 43), and his novel in progress was from the start one that fixed Stahr with what he called 'a death sentence' at 35 years old, as 'the mere accident of one organ of his body refusing to pull its weight' incapacitates and kills him ('Working Notes' 163).

'Show me a hero and I will write you a tragedy' (51), wrote Fitzgerald in his *Notebooks*, and his final novel intended to give us both the ingredient and the outcome. In an unsent letter to Norma Shearer, Irving Thalberg's wife, Fitzgerald told her, 'I invented a tragic story … no one has ever written a tragedy about Hollywood' (Piper 266). What Fitzgerald called 'Stahr's idealism and extravagance in the picture business … plans which he has built up like a pyramid of fairy skyscrapers in his imagination' ('Working Notes' 163) were, as with Fitzgerald himself, to be defeated by bodily fatigue and breakdown. Although there are intended similarities between the author and his hero in Fitzgerald's plans for *Tycoon*, with the novel's 'Working Notes' insisting, for instance, that Stahr 'must have had no more aesthetic education after finishing secondary school than I did' (158), in the utilitarian ethos of the Hollywood studio industry Stahr was conceived as tragically unique, a man whose vitality and vision are capable of challenging, and sometimes transcending, material limitations. In such terms he is very much in the grain of Fitzgerald's work as a whole, for if, as William Blazek contends, 'loss and failure are the result of high expectations, then Fitzgerald places great emphasis on aspiration as a value in itself' (*Companion to Twentieth-Century United States Fiction* 280). The narrator also prefers to give us Stahr as a hero who chooses his own precise fate, one who fastens himself to an earnest destiny because he sees the need and the importance of Hollywood films as a *conduit* for the human spirit:

> this was where Stahr had come to earth after that extraordinary illuminating flight where he saw which way we were going, and how we looked doing it, and how much of it mattered. You could say that this was where an accidental wind blew him but I don't think so. I would rather think that in a 'long shot' he saw a new way of measuring our jerky hopes and graceful rogueries and awkward sorrows, and that he came here from choice to be with us to the end. Like the plane coming down into the Glendale airport, into the warm darkness. (21–2)

This lyrical passage gives us Stahr as a hero in the noble line of those whose fate is the greater for being chosen by them, Shakespearean rather than Sophoclean or, more specifically, a hero in the American grain, his origins democratic, progressive rather than reactionary, one who with a quickening sense of Hollywood's epic possibilities, 'came here from choice to be with us to the end' (22).

For Stahr the movies were a timely opportunity to project America to itself, to enhance its mythic possibilities, or as the poet William Carlos Williams wrote in the same period, to give Americans back to themselves through a 'projection of the great flower of which they were the seed' (23). Williams's own book of essays, *In the American Grain*, was also published into and addressed what he regarded as the grave state of the nation in the 1930s, its betrayal of founding values which threatened to destroy a better destiny: 'to-day it is a generation of gross know-nothingism, of blackened churches where hymns groan like chants from stupefied jungles, a generation eager to barter permanent values ... in return for opportunist material advantages, a generation hating those whom it obeys' (68). *The Last Tycoon* can almost be seen as a reply to this bleak culture-reading, giving us in Monroe Stahr a modern tragic hero, a common man out of common stock ('one of a gang of kids in the Bronx ... Stahr's education was founded on nothing more than a night-school course in stenography' [18–19]), one who grew 'out of the jungle over which he presided, yet he did not carry a club', as he told Frances Kroll Ring (*Against the Current* 50).

Stahr works at the heart of the Hollywood money machine but is yet, in Hollywood screenwriter Wylie White's compliment, 'no merchant' (17). The 'down and out' (10) former Hollywood studio chief Mannie Schwartze knows that without Stahr on his side he's reached the end of the road, as at the start of the narrative he selects the place for his suicide at the Hermitage, President Andrew Jackson's home outside Nashville, Tennessee. There, in an odd echo of Nick Carraway's elegiac musings about Jay Gatsby, who 'had come a long way to this blue lawn, and his dream must have seemed so close that he could hardly fail to grasp it' (141), Fitzgerald brings Schwartze also to his sad terminus: 'he had come a long way from some ghetto to present himself at that raw shrine' (13). In the narrator's description, the Hermitage 'looked like a nice big white box, but a little lonely, and vacated still, after a hundred years'. Complete with its death-bird, which 'perched on the chimney pot like a raven' (12), it already resembles the tomb it will soon become for Schwartze. In his final moments, he seeks 'someone who was large and merciful, able to understand ... something to lay himself beside when no one wanted him further, and shoot a bullet into his head' (13). When it seemed to him that Stahr no longer wanted him, he writes his suicide note: 'Dear Monro, you are the best of them all I have always admired your mentality so when you turn against me I know it's no use! I must be no good and am not going to continue the journey' (16).

The opening episodes of *The Last Tycoon* are concerned to further enhance this picture of Stahr as the exceptional man, one who, in the world of Hollywood counterfeit, is the real thing, a hero whose status as such is recognized consensually and legitimised by those around him:

> Men began streaming by him – every second one glancing at him smiling speaking Hello Monroe ... Hello Mr. Stahr ... wet night Mr. Stahr ... Monroe ... Monroe ... Stahr ... Stahr ... Stahr. He spoke and waved back as the people streamed by in the darkness, looking I suppose a little like the Emperor and the Old Guard. There is no world so but it has its heroes and Stahr was the hero ... The old loyalties were trembling now – there were clay feet everywhere – but still he was their man, the last of the princes. And their greeting was a sort of low cheer as they went by. (29)

The last of the princes, Stahr in the eyes of all is their Emperor and hero, the king they can trust – his royal status being derived partly from leadership traits. As noted by Arthur Mizener, 'a gift for organization and command had always been a characteristic of [Fitzgerald's] heroes' (*The Far Side of Paradise* 294), and Stahr is nothing if not a confident commander of others, pragmatic and end-directed. It is likely that significant elements of Stahr's heroism were based upon Fitzgerald's understanding of historic heroes such as Julius Caesar; in J. A. Froude's biography of Caesar which Fitzgerald owned, he found a hero 'who, because of his insight into human nature, was able to direct the most diverse talents, welding them into a loyal, purposeful organization' (Piper 268). As Fitzgerald himself found out to his own chagrin, Hollywood scriptwriters were functionaries of the system created by producers like Stahr, put to work in pairs on creating a story. If there was inadequate progress, as Stahr explains, 'we put two more writers working behind them. I've had as many as three pairs working independently on the same idea' (64). And while Stahr pays lip service to his scriptwriters' sensitivities – telling two of them who are about to be taken off their work on one picture and put to work on another – 'the system was a shame, he admitted – gross, commercial, to be deplored', still it was a system 'he had originated' – 'a fact that he did not mention' (65). Within this piecemeal system only Stahr is able to say with confidence, 'I'm the unity' (64) – a benign dictator at best, but a dictator nonetheless (Cecelia refers to him as 'the oracle' [62]), rigorously committed to the end justifying the means. Yet his influence derives also from rescuing and protective strengths bestowed upon the group. So, 'through the beginnings and the great upset when sound came and the three years of Depression he had seen that no harm came to them' (29). The narrative presents him as an inspirational and paternalistic leader: 'here was Stahr to care, for all of them' (47). Wylie White also recognizes that Stahr's governance of the studio is magisterial, a persuasive combination of factors which are greater than the sum of their parts:

> He felt a great purposefulness. The mixture of common sense, wise sensibility, theatrical ingenuity, and a certain half naive conception of the common weal which Stahr had just stated aloud, inspired him to do his part, to get his block of stone in place, even if the effort were foredoomed. (47)

Unlike Jay Gatsby, Stahr's greatness is in no sense regarded as dubious by those around him, and Fitzgerald gives it further significance in its being the ultimate personification of all that such a hero might be: a benign king, a prince who carries his people with him, a tycoon whose worth is measured not in terms of the dollar and the Dow Jones but rather one whose humanity, like that of President Andrew Jackson in Schwartze's final vision, is maximal: '[he] must have been someone who was large and merciful, able to understand' (13). Even the sadness of the suicide needs succour, 'at both ends of life man needed nourishment – a breast – a shrine' (13).

For Lionel Trilling, 'the root of Fitzgerald's heroism is to be found, as it sometimes is in his tragic heroes, in his power of love' (*Liberal Imagination* 244), and Schwartze's suicide note makes it clear that Stahr is at least respected, perhaps loved by those who work for him ('I have always admired your mentality' [16]), a hero whose motivation and ethic are rooted in a positive creativity. Fitzgerald's original notes for *The Last Tycoon* make the importance of this very clear, as he reminds himself that his novel should give what he called 'an all-fireworks illumination of the intense passion in Stahr's soul, his love of life, his love for the great thing he's built out here ... he's not interested in it because he owns it. He's interested in it as an artist because he has made it' (*Against the Current* 143–4). Again the negative ethic of selfish and material increase is to be challenged by Stahr, who is the personification of Hollywood invention, and as his notes make clear, in this regard Fitzgerald wanted his hero to be contrasted 'sharply with the feeling of those who have merely gypped another person's empire away from them' (Lehan, *Craft of Fiction* 154).

Fitzgerald wrote to Thalberg's wife, Norma Shearer, acknowledging that *Tycoon* was 'an attempt to preserve something of Irving', who 'inspires the best part of the character of Stahr', yet that character also contained, as Fitzgerald said in the same (unsent) letter, 'inevitably, much of myself' (Berg 393). What Trilling calls 'the power of love', and the passionate belief in creativity and making, are writ large in both maker and hero of *Tycoon*, and while in 1939 Fitzgerald seemed to Sheilah Graham to be 'like a gentle invalid, trying to do as much as possible in the race against time' (*The Real F. Scott Fitzgerald* 201), so Stahr is also running against the clock, his body already breaking down. In one of the final episodes Fitzgerald ever wrote, Stahr visits his doctor for his weekly examination and cardiogram – a scene Fitzgerald himself must have known so well. Frances Kroll remembered that 'Scott would obey the doctor's orders to a point. He refused to interrupt the pattern of his work' (104), while in *Beloved Infidel*[19] Sheilah Graham also remembered that the day before he died Fitzgerald twice postponed seeing his doctor, who was due 'to take a cardiogram. Would I telephone him, Scott called, and tell him to come tomorrow? His work was moving too well to be interrupted now' (326). Even after collapsing the night before his death on 21 December 1940, Fitzgerald again refused medical help: 'Scott said no. Dr Wilson was coming tomorrow, anyway. Let's not make any fuss' (327). In Episode 16 of *The Last Tycoon* Stahr's doctor also realizes that, due to his patient's attitude, the cardiograms are useless:

> He was due to die very soon now … you couldn't persuade a man like Stahr to stop and lie down and look at the sky for six months. He would much rather die … Fatigue was a drug as well as a poison and Stahr apparently derived some rare almost physical pleasure from working lightheaded with weariness. It was a perversion of the life force he had seen before. (123)

The extent to which any of this narrative resonated directly with the author's view of his own predicament is difficult to surmise, and the usual cautions regarding finding an overly simplistic relationship between art and life apply; in any case, as Jonathan Schiff reminds us, in Fitzgerald's plan 'the ending of the novel was to involve Stahr's tragic death in a plane crash caused by a bomb in the cargo hold, the result of Brady's contract on his rival's life' (153), rather than a death caused by heart failure.

The dating of the narrative's events is rather vague, indeed Alan Margolies, in his treatment of Fitzgerald's Hollywood fiction, suggests that it is 'not too fruitful to attempt to accurately date the events in the novel' (207). Referentially, however, Margolies's essay 'Fitzgerald and Hollywood' (2002) tracks much of the novel's inventory of popular songs to the mid-1930s, adding, however, that while 'some of the films alluded to in the novel were being made during Fitzgerald's 1931–2 trip to Hollywood; others were being made during his final years there' (207). Several of Fitzgerald's letters suggest that the narrative's events take place no later than 1935, and in a lengthy and important letter of September 1939 to Kenneth Littauer of *Collier's* magazine (Fitzgerald was attempting at the time to negotiate a contract with the magazine for the rights to publish *Tycoon* serially), he tells him clearly that 'the Story occurs during four or five months in the year 1935' (*Life in Letters* 408). The dating is important because the novel-in-progress was also being written against the backdrop of gathering and increasingly murderous European fascism, with the anti-Jewish pogrom of *Kristallnacht*, for instance, occurring throughout Germany and Austria in November 1938, just at the moment Fitzgerald was drafting his novel. His plans for the novel certainly included a substantial political plot which would have engaged with some of the main currents of American life consequent upon the collapse of the American economy and the New York Stock market in September 1929, while the terror and instability of events as they mutated quickly in Europe might also have been addressed with Stahr, perhaps defining a new kind of leadership more pertinent to such times.

It is certainly important to recognise that most of *The Last Tycoon* was written following the declaration in September 1939 of the war in Europe, although, of course, American entry into the war following the Japanese bombing of the American naval base in Pearl Harbor in December 1941 postdated Fitzgerald's death almost exactly a year earlier. A late *Notebook* entry tells of 'hearing Hitler's speech while going down Sunset Blvd. in a car' (252), while Sheilah Graham remembered how 'during 1938 and 1939 we listened on the big old-fashioned radio in [Scott's] living room at Malibu to Hitler's rantings and the terrifying roar of "Heil Hitler"' (*College of One* 55). His letters certainly reveal his distress as he contemplated the war abroad, indicating the extent to which he was not only aware of the war in Europe but also aware of his being deeply affected by it. Writing to Zelda in October 1940, he tells her of how 'living in the flotsam of the international situation, as we all are, work has been difficult' (Bryer and Barks 315), while in a letter of August 1940 he reminds her of the sad reiterations of their joint history, both personal and public, as he saw their daughter Scottie grow up, like themselves, in a conflicted world: 'it is strange too that she is repeating the phase of your life – all her friends about to go off to war and the world again on fire' (*Correspondence* 605). Zelda herself, in a North Carolina hospital, was also in October of the same year aware of the war and its accompanying atmosphere of impending doom, writing to Fitzgerald that no news was most definitely not good news – 'there does not seem to be any news: which some people think of in terms of an advantage, but which, to me, presents itself vaguely in terms of disaster. Well anyway we're better off than the Finns and the Russians' (Bryer and Barks 313) – though of course it was the Russians who, in an unwarranted act of military aggression and imperialist land-grabbing, invaded Finland at the end of November 1939 in the so-called Winter War. 'My feeling is that we are in for a ten year war', Fitzgerald wrote to Zelda in the summer of 1940, while the effect of the war upon Hollywood was one of disorder and dismay; he told her that 'things are naturally shot to hell here with everybody running around in circles yet continuing to turn out two million dollar tripe' (Bryer and Barks 347). He was also well aware that the life of art was also dimmed by war, again telling Zelda in July 1940 that 'the war pushes art into the background. At least people don't buy anything' (Bryer and Barks 354). Fitzgerald was particularly affected by the fall of France in May 1940, and on sending Gertrude Stein's recently published book *Paris France* to Zelda in 1940, expressed his regret at the extent to which its representation of Paris in the city's prewar halcyon days was now darkened – 'it's a melancholy book now that France has fallen' (Bryer and Barks 354) – though Stein's book is itself almost a sustained reflection upon French life in time of war: 'it really takes a war to make you know a country ... living here all winter in a provincial French town I once more realize that a war brings you in contact with so much and so many and at the same time concentrates your isolation' (72). The golden age of Paris in the 1920s had now become historic for the Fitzgeralds and their lost generation – 'it certainly is sad to think that that's all over – at least for our lifetime' (Bryer and Barks 359).

Within this context of instability and war, Monroe Stahr is partly an effort to address Fitzgerald's prediction – in a newspaper interview at the close of the 1920s – that the free world, threatened by fascism, would need a new kind of leader, a leader who 'would come out of the immigrant class, in the guise of an eastside newsboy' (*Conversations* 89). In a letter of 1940 to his daughter, he acknowledges his hardening politics – 'your father is rather far to the left' *(Life in Letters* 436*)* – and at the same time he steered his novel-in-progress towards a conclusion that was intended to engage directly with a very topical political matrix. In Episode 17 of *The Love of the Last Tycoon* (Chapter 6 in the novel's first edition) we find the first real emergence of the political plot that has seemed to some critics, however, the most unsteady and implausible part of the novel. For Brian Way, this plot was at best an eccentric deviation from Stahr's character as already established, at worst a completely wrong turn:

> Stahr was to have found himself at the centre of a struggle between the Writers' Guild (a union in which Communists had some influence) and those studio chiefs like Brady and Fleishacker who saw cinema as a purely commercial enterprise. It was a situation that Stahr could not dominate with his personal style of leadership: as he found himself forced increasingly to descend to the methods of his enemies, his character would deteriorate and his vision be largely lost ... Fitzgerald does nothing to prepare for the abrupt change in Stahr's behaviour – his drunkenness, his stupid aggressiveness, his ugly loss of self-control. This chapter does not augur well for the future progress of the novel, and there is no hint in it of the political sophistication which enabled Norman Mailer to write so well about Hollywood anti-Communism in *The Deer Park.* (162)

For Richard Lehan, the doubts are similar – a blatant inconsistency caused by conflicting representations of Stahr's character:

> He starts as Thalberg – with his energy, vitality, drive, and purpose – and ends as Fitzgerald – sick, frail, vacillating, and tired ... at the end of the unfinished manuscript – as he talks with a Communist labor leader – he is loud and aggressive, boasts, misjudges his man, loses self-control, and makes a fool of himself. The transition from one man to the other is sudden and unjustified. (*Craft of Fiction* 154)

My own view is that while we should recognise the seriousness of the challenges that faced his narrative, they were far from insuperable, and I believe that Fitzgerald had set his sights upon a realistic goal and would eventually have overcome any of the issues alluded to above. If such critics can see the flaws in the unfinished novel, so could a great artist like Fitzgerald, whose writing career had already shown he was nothing if not a meticulous and methodical reviser of his own work-in-progress. At his death in December 1940, Fitzgerald's unfinished novel had already given almost 45,000 words, with under half of his outline covered; perhaps the novel when finished would have run to 125,000 words, more than enough space to resolve whatever was needed for the integrity of the narrative.

He confided to his *Notebooks* that 'as a novelist I reach out to the end of all man's variance, all man's villainy', and in the onward formation of Stahr's character, in his literal fall to earth as he lifts himself off the floor and unconsciousness following Brimmer's assault upon him ('I always wanted to hit ten million dollars but I didn't know it would be like this' [144]), on the penultimate page of *The Last Tycoon*, Fitzgerald is still reaching out to such limits through his characterisation of Stahr. Variance and villainy – concepts that seem almost to anticipate his critics' charge sheet about Stahr's 'sudden and unjustified' bout of drunkenness. To this Fitzgerald's final novel seems to say, 'I'll take you there – and I'll take you back', just as Cecelia shakes Stahr, who is literally under the table, back to consciousness, and finds that 'in a moment he came awake with a terrific convulsion and bounced up on his feet' (145). Although 'over-worked and deathly tired', Stahr, 'afraid of nothing', is still able to rule others 'with a radiance that is almost moribund in its phosphorescence', as Fitzgerald put it in his 1939 letter to Littauer (*Life in Letters* 409).

Two weeks before he died he wrote to Zelda, 'everything is my novel now – it has become of absorbing interest. I hope I'll be able to finish it by February' (*Life in Letters* 474). Despite sickness, it is clear that at the end of his life Fitzgerald was engaged thoroughly in his art and, being so engaged, whatever internal contradictions his final work of imagination confronted him with would surely have been resolved most stylishly. It was not only Zelda who, after his death, in a moving letter to Gerald and Sara Murphy, showed the kind of special discrimination that artists treasure, telling them, 'I grieve for his brilliant talent ... his devotion to those ... he felt were contributing to the aesthetic and spiritual purposes of his life' (*Sara and Gerald* 150); Raymond Chandler also recognised that he had 'one of the rarest qualities in all literature ... a kind of subdued magic, controlled and exquisite' (MacShane 239). With that exquisite control to guide him, Scott Fitzgerald would surely have completed *The Last Tycoon*, and found its perfect form.

7 Conclusion

Writing to Zelda in March 1940, Fitzgerald knew the balance sheet made bleak reading: 'Nothing has developed here. I write these "Pat Hobby" stories – and wait. I have a new idea now – a comedy series which will get me back into the big magazines – but my God I am a forgotten man'. Gatsby had to be taken out of the Modern Library because it didn't sell, which was a blow' (*Life in Letters* 439). With 'absolutely no offers in many months' (*Life in Letters* 441) from the Hollywood studios, his letters to Zelda in his last year of life are often heartbreaking studies in attrition, as, weakened by illness and continuing financial distress, he brooded over how writing stories and film scripts would make ends meet for himself, his wife, and daughter Scottie, then a student at Vassar College. The fiscal logic was stark. As he wrote to Zelda, 'The main thing is not to run up bills or wire me for extra funds. There simply aren't any and as you can imagine I am deeply in debt to the government and everyone else' (*Life in Letters* 442). Zelda's sad supplications from her sanatorium in Asheville, North Carolina – 'Would you be upset if I asked you for $15 and just left? ... Wont [*sic*] you send me $5 as soon as you can' (Bryer and Barks 332–3) – were voiced in full recognition of a more thorough bankruptcy when she told him, 'the resources that were once at our disposition are dissipated by Time' (Bryer and Barks 332). His mood was not curable by observation of the larger picture, which seemed leached of any uplift in what he called 'this dark and bloody world' (*Life in Letters* 442). The local context may have been the golden state, but its lustre had increasingly faded for Fitzgerald, who wrote, 'I have grown to hate California and would give my life for three years in France' (*Life in Letters* 442).

Exigency, economy, expenditure: remembrance of the past may have turned him towards France and youthful profligacy, but in life as in art, he was yet driven increasingly to appreciate the leaner virtues. After he died, Zelda's long view over his life saw him 'as exponent of the school of bitter necessities that followed the last world war' (Donnelly 150). Although renowned as the chronicler of opulent wealth, its personifications, gestures, signs and ruinations,

Fitzgerald's imagining of that world was often clarified in starkly oppositional terms: the Gatsby mansion, for instance, could not be so blatantly ascendant without the Valley of Ashes, the one being a meditation on the other. In his *Notebooks* he wrote that 'the cleverly expressed opposite of any generally accepted human idea is worth a fortune' (310);' Fitzgerald's knowledge and experience of that was not only indispensable to his art, but his increasing exposure to 'the school of bitter necessities' in an inter-war culture meant that the necessity of turning limited human and material resources to account in his last years gave rise to new possibilities. He believed that 'until the heart has run its entire race' (*Life in Letters* 466), the prize was worth the further effort to manage its dwindling resources. He knew the costs as well, and wrote to Zelda, 'extra waste of energy has to be paid for at a double price' (*Life in Letters* 466).

As he aged, Fitzgerald's aesthetic itself began to assert the benefits of 'less is more'. In that context, from California in 1937 he sent Thomas Wolfe a crucial advisory, perhaps the most succinct statement of his mature aesthetic that we have. It recommends the artist as a winnower of his own talent, and acknowledges the 'necessity to cultivate an alter ego, a more conscious artist', so that 'the more that the stronger man's inner tendencies are defined ... the more necessity to rarefy them, to use them sparingly'. Such frugality is definitive, hence 'the great writer ... will say only the things that he alone sees[s]'. It is this rigorous selective discipline that gives some purchase upon an art that survives, 'So Mme Bovary becomes eternal while Zola already rocks with age':

> Repression itself has a value, as with a poet who struggles for a nessessary ryme [*sic*] achieves accidentally a new word association that would not have come by any mental or even flow-of-consciousness process. The Nightingale is full of that.
>
> To a talent like mine of narrow scope there is not that problem. I must put everything in to have enough + even then I often haven't got enough. (*Life in Letters* 332)

Fitzgerald's modest self-appraisal here is, of course, impossible to endorse. If the door was narrow, it opened out onto enduring vistas. In much of his fiction his talent was rich, and in *The Great Gatsby* and *Tender is the Night*, assuredly much more than enough to gain admission, along with *Madame Bovary* and the 'Ode to a Nightingale', to the slopes of Parnassus.

Notes

INTRODUCTION

1. The phrase is Thom Gunn's, from his poem, 'My Sad Captains'.

INSIDE THE HYENA CAGE: *THE GREAT GATSBY* (1925)

2. The word 'ectoplasm' (26), and others like it from the contemporary scientific lexicon such as 'spectroscopic' (37), are used in the novel, showing Fitzgerald's willingness to apply the terms of a scientific world that reflect modernist mutations of perception; in these and other related contexts Ronald Berman's study, *The Great Gatsby and Modern Times* (1995), is indispensable reading.
3. Keats is, of course, much more explicitly referenced in *Tender is the Night*, the title and epigraph of which were drawn from his 'Ode to a Nightingale'. See Philip McGowan, 'Reading Fitzgerald Reading Keats'.

THE TRAGIC POWER: SELECTED SHORT STORIES AND *TENDER IS THE NIGHT* (1934)

4. Cf. André Le Vot: 'Gerald-Scott, Sara-Zelda, Scott-Sara in juxtaposition, permutation, fascination with themselves and each other. The identification would be complete in the various phases of *Tender is the Night* ... seen through the worshiping eyes of Rosemary against a background of sea and sun, Dick Diver in the opening chapters is Gerald, serene and magnanimous, ready to dare anything and do anything' (Le Vot 208). The admiration was reciprocal. According to Le Vot, 'Gerald wrote a kind of love letter to the Fitzgeralds on September 19, 1925 ... he described exactly that process of symbiosis that would form the composite character of the Divers in *Tender is the Night*. "We four communicate by our presence ... so that where we meet and when will never count. Currents run between us regardless: Scott will uncover values for me in Sara, just as Sara has known them in Zelda through her affection for Scott"' (Le Vot 209).
5. 'This was the period when Baoth, the sturdiest of the Murphy children, died of meningitis at school before his parents could reach him [1935]. Patrick was to die two years later' (Le Vot 261).
6. The famous phrase was used in a letter Hemingway sent to Fitzgerald from Paris in April 1926: 'Was not referring to guts but to something else. Grace under pressure. Guts never made any money for anybody except violin string manufacturers' (Baker 200).

7. James R. Mellow used the phrase for the title of his 1984 biography *Invented Lives: F. Scott and Zelda Fitzgerald*.
8. James's term denotes the dwindling of American roots in conditions of exile, and in 1898 he wrote with extraordinary prescience of the emergence and effect of forces responsible for what would now be referred to as globalism: 'Who shall say, at the rate things are going, what is to be 'near' home in the future and what is to be far from it? ... The globe is shrinking, for the imagination, to the size of an orange that can be played with' (cited by Weintraub, *The London Yankees* 380).
9. 'The tragic power of charm had been the book's main theme ever since he had first conceived of it in the Murphys' garden at Antibes back in 1925' (Piper 228).
10. Nicole Diver, too, is associated with repose: 'she liked to be active, though at times she gave an impression of repose that was at once static and evocative' (26).
11. This critique seems aimed especially at American men. One of the 'well-dressed American' men who nevertheless shows clear signs of uneasy comportment and 'spasmodic' mannerisms, 'had come in with two women who swooped and fluttered unself-consciously around a table' (51). Although these women are not identified explicitly as American, their relaxed occupation of this public space does suggest that in this scene Fitzgerald may have intended a gendered contrast at least.
12. 'The Riviera! The names of its resorts, Cannes, Nice, Monte Carlo, call up the memory of a hundred kings and princes who have lost their thrones and come here to die, of mysterious rajahs and boys flinging blue diamonds to English dancing girls, of Russian millionaires tossing away fortunes at roulette in the lost caviar days before the war'. 'How to Live on Practically Nothing a Year', *Saturday Evening Post*, 20 September 1924. Reprinted in *Afternoon of an Author*, 104.
13. Unlike Nicole, whose breeding ensures that the decline of old European aristocratic manners will be countered genetically by the ascendant American pluto-democracy: 'Nicole was the grand-daughter of a self-made American capitalist and the grand-daughter of a Count of the House of Lippe Weissenfeld' (53).
14. Arthur Adamov was a Russian émigré who had arrived in Paris in 1924, where he edited an avant-garde periodical, *Discontinuité*, and associated himself with the nonconformity of early modernism. His autobiography *L'Aveu* [*The Confession*] is a classic statement of the metaphysics of exile. There he diagnoses the postwar epoch as one sickening due to the loss of any sense of the sacred, peopled by neurotics who are afflicted by the disappearance of ultimate meaning in the world.
15. In this regard, it may be significant that as Dick fades from Nicole's view in the novel's last chapter, his final notes to her are from the small towns of upstate New York. Perhaps the implication is that American repatriation has provided him not with the spiritual integrity or reconstitution of homecoming, but rather with fragmentation of self. Identity is again associated with place, though here it is scattered, and as we are told in the novel's final words, Dick is also scattered, dispersed 'in one town or another' (315).

16. Fitzgerald told Laura Guthrie 'I am really a lone wolf. ... Everyone is lonely – the artist especially, it goes with creation. I create a world for others' (Turnbull, *Scott Fitzgerald* 265).

THE HEART OF HOLLYWOOD: *THE LAST TYCOON* (1941)

17. For an authoritative assessment of Fitzgerald's attitude towards Hollywood during the final four years of his life, see Michael Nowlin, '"A Gentile's Tragedy": Bearing the Word about Hollywood in *The Love of the Last Tycoon*'. *F. Scott Fitzgerald Review* 2 (2003): 156–85.
18. Breen's commanding presence is alluded to in *Tycoon*; in a conversation regarding script changes with director John Broaca and screenwriter Wylie White, Stahr demands that one of the main characters 'hit the priest'. When White protests that were that to happen they'd 'have the Catholics on our neck', Stahr replies: 'I've talked to Joe Breen. Priests have been hit. It doesn't reflect on them' (46–7).
19. Written in collaboration with Gerold Frank, this memoir of 1958 was hailed by Edmund Wilson in his long review of it in the *New Yorker* as 'the very best portrait of Fitzgerald that has yet been put into print' (24 January 1959, 34:115).

Bibliography

PRIMARY TEXTS, CORRESPONDENCE AND INTERVIEWS

Baker, Carlos, ed. *Ernest Hemingway: Selected Letters 1917–1961.* Frogmore, St Albans: Granada, 1981.

Bruccoli, Matthew J., ed. *F. Scott Fitzgerald: A Life in Letters.* New York: Scribner's, 1994.

Bryer, Jackson R. and Cathy W. Barks, eds. *Dear Scott, Dearest Zelda: The Love Letters of F. Scott and Zelda Fitzgerald.* New York: St. Martin's Griffin, 2002.

Bryer, Jackson R. and Judith S. Baughman, eds. *Conversations with F. Scott Fitzgerald.* Jackson: University Press of Mississippi, 2004.

Deffaa, Chip, ed. *F. Scott Fitzgerald: The Princeton Years. Selected Writings, 1914–1920.* Fort Bragg, California: Cypress House Press, 1996.

Fitzgerald, F. Scott. 'Absolution'. *The Collected Short Stories of F. Scott Fitzgerald.* London: Penguin, 1988. 398–412.

——. *Afternoon of an Author: A Selection of Uncollected Stories and Essays.* Ed. Arthur Mizener. New York: Scribner's, 1957.

——. *As Ever, Scott Fitz–: Letters Between F. Scott Fitzgerald and His Literary Agent Harold Ober 1919–1940.* Ed. Matthew J. Bruccoli. Philadelphia and New York: J.B. Lippincott, 1972.

——. 'Babylon Revisited'. *The Stories of F. Scott Fitzgerald. Vol. 2: The Crack-Up with Other Pieces and Stories.* Harmondsworth, Middlesex: Penguin, 1971. 110–34.

——. *The Beautiful and Damned.* Harmondsworth, Middlesex: Penguin, 1972.

——. *The Beautiful and Damned.* Ed. James L.W. West III. Cambridge: Cambridge University Press, 2008.

'"Cellar Door? Ugh!" Quoth Baltimore Writers'. Baltimore Post, 13 December 1932: 2.

——. *Correspondence of F. Scott Fitzgerald.* Ed. Matthew J. Bruccoli and Margaret M. Duggan. New York: Random House, 1980.

——. 'The Crack-Up'. *The Stories of F. Scott Fitzgerald. Vol. 2: The Crack-Up with Other Pieces and Stories.* Harmondsworth, Middlesex: Penguin, 1971. 39–56.

——. *The Crack-Up with Other Pieces and Stories.* London: Penguin, 1988.

——. 'Early Success'. *The Stories of F. Scott Fitzgerald. Vol. 2: The Crack-Up with Other Pieces and Stories.* Harmondsworth, Middlesex: Penguin, 1971. 57–63.

——. 'Echoes of the Jazz Age'. *The Stories of F. Scott Fitzgerald. Vol. 2: The Crack-Up with Other Pieces and Stories.* Harmondsworth, Middlesex: Penguin, 1971. 9–19.

——. *F. Scott Fitzgerald in His Own Time: A Miscellany.* Ed. Matthew J. Bruccoli and Jackson R. Bryer. New York: Popular Library, 1971.

——. *F. Scott Fitzgerald's Ledger (A Facsimile).* Ed. Matthew J. Bruccoli. Washington, DC: Bruccoli Clark/NCR Microcard Editions, 1972.
——. *The Great Gatsby.* Ed. Matthew J. Bruccoli. Cambridge: Cambridge University Press, 1991.
——. *The Great Gatsby.* Ed. Ruth Prigozy. Oxford: Oxford University Press, 1998.
——. 'Jacob's Ladder'. *Bits of Paradise: Twenty-one Uncollected Stories by F. Scott & Zelda Fitzgerald.* Harmondsworth, Middlesex: Penguin, 1976. 145–70.
——. *The Last Tycoon: An Unfinished Novel.* Ed. Edmund Wilson. New York: Scribner's, 1941.
——. *The Love of the Last Tycoon: A Western.* Ed. Matthew J. Bruccoli. London: Little, Brown, 1994.
——. 'Magnetism'. *The Collected Short Stories of F. Scott Fitzgerald.* London: Penguin, 1988. 443–63.
——. 'My Lost City'. *The Stories of F. Scott Fitzgerald. Vol. 2: The Crack-Up with Other Pieces and Stories.* Harmondsworth, Middlesex: Penguin, 1971. 20–31.
——. *The Notebooks of F. Scott Fitzgerald.* Ed. Matthew J. Bruccoli. New York and London: Harcourt Brace Jovanovich/Bruccoli Clark, 1978.
——. 'One Hundred False Starts'. *Afternoon of an Author.* New York: Scribner's, 1957. 127–36.
——. 'A Patriotic Short'. *The Collected Short Stories of F. Scott Fitzgerald.* London: Penguin, 1988. 312–15.
——. *The Princeton Years. Selected Writings 1914–1920.* Ed. Chip Deffaa. Fort Bragg: Cypress House Press, 1996.
——. 'A Short Trip Home'. *The Collected Short Stories of F. Scott Fitzgerald.* London: Penguin, 1988. 424–42.
——. 'The Swimmers'. *Bits of Paradise: Twenty-one Uncollected Stories by F. Scott & Zelda Fitzgerald.* Harmondsworth, Middlesex: Penguin, 1976. 171–91.
——. *Tender is the Night.* New York: Scribner's, 1934.
——. *Tender is the Night.* Norwalk: The Easton Press, 1991.
—— *Tender is the Night: A Romance.* London: Folio Society, 1987.
——. *Tender is the Night: A Romance.* Ed. Matthew J. Bruccoli. London: Everyman, 1996.
——. *Tender is the Night: A Romance.* Ware, Hertfordshire: Wordsworth, 2004.
——. *This Side of Paradise.* Ed. James L. W. West III. Cambridge: Cambridge University Press, 1995.
Fitzgerald, Zelda. *Save Me the Waltz.* London: Cape, 1968.
Gauss, Christian. *The Papers of Christian Gauss.* Ed. Katherine Gauss Jackson and Hiram Haydn. New York: Random House, 1957.
Gunn, Thom. *My Sad Captains.* London: Faber, 1961.
James, Henry. *Roderick Hudson.* London: Rupert Hart-Davis, 1961.
Lowell, Robert. *For the Union Dead.* London: Faber, 1966.
McBride, Mary Margaret. 'Looking at Youth'. *New York World-Telegram,* 4 June 1934: 21. *Conversations with F. Scott Fitzgerald.* Ed. Matthew J. Bruccoli and Judith S. Baughman. Jackson: University Press of Mississippi, 2004. 111–13.

MacShane, Frank, ed. *Selected Letters of Raymond Chandler.* New York: Columbia University Press, 1981.
Mok, Michel. *Great interviews of the 20th century: F Scott Fitzgerald.* Guardian News & Media, 2007.
Mosher, John Chapin. 'That Sad Young Man'. *Conversations with F. Scott Fitzgerald.* Ed. Matthew J. Bruccoli and Judith S. Baughman. Jackson: University Press of Mississippi, 2004. 77–80.
Pearce, Robert, ed. *The Sayings of F. Scott Fitzgerald.* London: Duckworth, 1995.
Tarr, Rodger L., ed. *Max and Marjorie: The Correspondence between Maxwell E. Perkins and Marjorie Kinnan Rawlins.* Gainesville: University Press of Florida, 1999.
Turnbull, Andrew, ed. *The Letters of F. Scott Fitzgerald.* Harmondsworth, Middlesex: Penguin, 1968.
Wilson, Edmund. *Letters on Literature and Politics 1912–1972.* Ed. Elena Wilson. New York: Farrar, Straus & Giroux, 1977.

BIOGRAPHIES AND MEMOIRS

Berg, A. Scott. *Max Perkins: Editor of Genius.* London: Hamish Hamilton, 1979.
Bruccoli, Matthew J. *Scott and Ernest: The Authority of Failure and the Authority of Success.* London: Bodley Head, 1978.
——. *Some Sort of Epic Grandeur: The Life of F. Scott Fitzgerald.* London: Hodder & Stoughton, 1981.
Buttitta, Tony. *The Lost Summer: A Personal Memoir of F. Scott Fitzgerald.* London: Sceptre, 1988.
Callaghan, Morley. *That Summer in Paris.* London: MacGibbon & Kee, 1963.
Donnelly, Honoria Murphy. *Sara & Gerald: Villa America and After.* New York: Holt, Rinehart & Winston, 1984.
Donaldson, Scott. *Fool for Love: A Biography of F. Scott Fitzgerald.* New York: Delta, 1983.
Graham, Sheilah. *College of One.* Harmondsworth, Middlesex: Penguin, 1969.
——. *The Real F. Scott Fitzgerald: Thirty-Five Years Later.* London: W.H. Allen, 1976.
——, and Gerold Frank. *Beloved Infidel: The Education of a Woman.* New York: Henry Holt, 1958.
Hemingway, Ernest. *A Moveable Feast.* London: Cape, 1964.
Hook, Andrew. *F. Scott Fitzgerald: A Literary Life.* Basingstoke: Palgrave Macmillan, 2002.
Kazin, Alfred. *Writing Was Everything.* Cambridge and London: Harvard University Press, 1999.
Kroll Ring, Frances. *Against the Current: As I Remember F. Scott Fitzgerald.* San Francisco: Donald S. Ellis, 1985.
Le Vot, André. *F. Scott Fitzgerald: A Biography.* Trans. William Byron. Garden City, New York: Doubleday, 1983.
Mellow, James R. *Invented Lives: F. Scott and Zelda Fitzgerald.* Boston: Houghton Mifflin, 1984.
Meyers, Jeffrey. *Scott Fitzgerald: A Biography.* New York: Cooper Square Press, 2000.

Milford, Nancy. *Zelda Fitzgerald*. Harmondsworth, Middlesex: Penguin, 1970.
Mizener, Arthur. *Scott Fitzgerald and His World*. London: Thames & Hudson, 1972.
——. *The Far Side of Paradise: A Biography of F. Scott Fitzgerald*. Boston: Houghton Mifflin, 1951.
Piper, Henry Dan. *F. Scott Fitzgerald: A Critical Portrait*. New York, Chicago and San Francisco: Holt, Rinehart & Winston, 1965.
Prigozy, Ruth. *F. Scott Fitzgerald*. London: Penguin, 2001.
Reilly, Edward J. *F. Scott Fitzgerald: A Biography*. Westport, CT: Greenwood, 2005.
Ross, Lillian. *Portrait of Hemingway*. Harmondsworth, Middlesex: Penguin, 1962.
Stein, Gertrude. *Paris France*. New York, Scribner's, 1940.
Taylor, Kendall. *Sometimes Madness is Wisdom: Zelda and Scott Fitzgerald: A Marriage*. New York: Ballantine, 2001.
Tomkins, Calvin. *Living Well Is the Best Revenge: Two Americans in Paris 1921 1933*. London: André Deutsch, 1972.
Turnbull, Andrew. *Scott Fitzgerald*. Harmondsworth, Middlesex: Penguin 1970.
Vaill, Amanda. *Everybody Was So Young: Gerald and Sara Murphy – A Lost Generation Love Story*. London: Warner Books, 1999.
Wilson, Edmund. 'A Weekend at Ellerslie'. *The Shores of Light: A Literary Chronicle of the Twenties and Thirties*. New York: Farrar, Straus & Young, 1952. 373–83.
——. 'F. Scott Fitzgerald'. *The Shores of Light: A Literary Chronicle of the Twenties and Thirties*. New York: Farrar, Straus & Young, 1952. 27–35.

BOOKS

Adamov, Arthur. *L'Aveu*. Paris: Sagittaire, 1946.
Allen, Joan M. *Candles and Carnival Lights: The Catholic Sensibility of F. Scott Fitzgerald*. New York: New York University Press, 1978.
Antolin-Pirès, Pascale. *L'Objet et ses doubles. Une relecture de Fitzgerald*. Bordeaux: Presses Universitaires de Bordeaux, 2000.
Assadi, Jamal and William Freedman, eds. *A Distant Drummer: Foreign Perspectives on F. Scott Fitzgerald*. New York: Lang, 2007.
Bellow, Saul. *Humboldt's Gift*. London: Secker & Warburg, 1975.
——. *The Victim*. Harmondsworth, Middlesex: Penguin, 1977.
Berman, Ronald. *Fitzgerald, Hemingway and the Twenties*. Tuscaloosa: University of Alabama Press, 2002.
——. *Fitzgerald–Wilson–Hemingway: Language and Experience*. Tuscaloosa: University of Alabama Press, 2003.
——. *The Great Gatsby and Fitzgerald's World of Ideas*. Tuscaloosa: University of Alabama Press, 1997.
——. *The Great Gatsby and Modern Times*. Urbana and Chicago: University of Illinois Press, 1994.
——. *Modernity and Progress: Fitzgerald, Hemingway, Orwell*. Tuscaloosa: University of Alabama Press, 2005.
Blackmur, R.P. *The Lion and the Honeycomb: Essays in Solicitude and Critique*. London: Methuen, 1956.

Blazek, William and Laura Rattray, eds. *Twenty-First-Century Readings of* Tender is the Night. Liverpool: Liverpool University Press, 2007.
Bloom, Harold. *F. Scott Fitzgerald*. New York: Chelsea House, 1985.
Bloom, Harold, ed. *F. Scott Fitzgerald*. Philadelphia: Chelsea House, 1999.
Bouzonvillers, Elisabeth. *Francis Scott Fitzgerald: écrivain du déséquilibre*. Paris: Belin, 2000.
Bradbury, Malcolm. *Dangerous Pilgrimages: Trans-Atlantic Mythologies & the Novel*. London: Secker & Warburg, 1995.
——, and McFarlane, J., eds. *Modernism: 1890–1930*. Harmondsworth, Middlesex: Penguin, 1981.
Brookeman, Christopher. *American Culture and Society since the 1930s*. London and Basingstoke: Macmillan, 1984.
Bruccoli, Matthew J. with Judith S. Baughman. *Reader's Companion to F. Scott Fitzgerald's* Tender is the Night. Columbia: University of South Carolina Press, 1996.
Bryer, Jackson R., ed. *The Short Stories of F. Scott Fitzgerald: New Approaches in Criticism*. Madison: University of Wisconsin Press, 1982.
——, ed. *New Essays on F. Scott Fitzgerald's Neglected Stories*. Columbia: University of Missouri Press, 1996.
——, Alan Margolies and Ruth Prigozy, eds. *F. Scott Fitzgerald: New Perspectives*. Athens and London: University of Georgia Press, 2000.
——, Ruth Prigozy and Milton R. Stern, eds. *F. Scott Fitzgerald in the Twenty-first Century: Centennial Essays*. Tuscaloosa and London: University of Alabama Press, 2003.
Callahan, John F. *The Illusions of a Nation: Myth and History in the Novels of F. Scott Fitzgerald*. Urbana, Chicago and London: University of Illinois Press, 1972.
Canterbury, E. Ray and Thomas Birch. *F. Scott Fitzgerald: Under the Influence*. New York: Paragon House, 2006.
Chambers, John B. *The Novels of F. Scott Fitzgerald*. New York: St. Martin's Press, 1989.
Claridge, Henry, ed. *F. Scott Fitzgerald: Critical Assessments*. 4 vols. Robertsbridge: Helm, 1992.
Cowley, Malcolm. *Exile's Return: A Literary Odyssey of the 1920's*. London: Bodley Head, 1961.
Cowley, Malcolm. *A Second Flowering: Works and Days of the Lost Generation*. London: André Deutsch, 1973.
Cross, K.G.W. *Scott Fitzgerald*. Edinburgh: Oliver & Boyd, 1964.
Curnutt, Kirk, ed. *A Historical Guide to F. Scott Fitzgerald*. New York: Oxford University Press, 2004.
Curnutt, Kirk. *The Cambridge Introduction to F. Scott Fitzgerald*. Cambridge: Cambridge University Press, 2007.
Dardis, Tom. *Some Time in the Sun: The Hollywood Years of Fitzgerald, Faulkner, Nathanael West, Aldous Huxley and James Agee*. New York: Scribner's, 1976.
Eble, Kenneth E., ed. *F. Scott Fitzgerald: A Collection of Criticism*. New York and London: McGraw-Hill, 1973.
Fisher, Philip. *Still the New World: American Literature in a Culture of Creative Destruction*. Cambridge and London: Harvard University Press, 1999.
Gay, Marie-Agnès. *Epiphanie et Fracture: l'évolution du point de vue narratif dans les romans de F. Scott Fitzgerald*. Paris : Didier érudition, 2000.

Hall, Donald. *The Oxford Book of American Literary Anecdotes.* New York: Oxford University Press, 1981.

Hemingway, Ernest *Fiesta.* London: Cape, 1959.

Hook, Andrew. *F. Scott Fitzgerald.* London and New York: Edward Arnold, 1992.

Kazin, Alfred, ed. *F. Scott Fitzgerald: The Man and His Work.* Cleveland and New York: World Publishing Company, 1951.

Kennedy, J. Gerald. *Imagining Paris: Exile, Writing and American Identity.* New Haven, CT and London: Yale University Press, 1993.

——, and Jackson R. Bryer, eds. *French Connections: Hemingway and Fitzgerald Abroad.* New York: St. Martin's Press, 1998.

Kuehl, John. *F. Scott Fitzgerald: A Study of the Short Fiction.* Boston: Twayne, 1991.

Kundu, Gautam. *Fitzgerald and the Influence of Film: The Language of Cinema in the Novels.* Jefferson, NC: McFarland, 2008.

Latham, Aaron. *Crazy Sundays: F. Scott Fitzgerald in Hollywood.* New York: Viking Press, 1971.

Lee, A. Robert, ed. *Scott Fitzgerald: The Promises of Life.* London: Vision Press, 1989.

Leff, Leonard J. and Gerald Simmons. *The Dame in the Kimono: Hollywood, Censorship and the Production Code.* Lexington: University of Kentucky Press, 2001.

Lehan, Richard D. *F. Scott Fitzgerald and the Craft of Fiction.* Carbondale and Edwardsville: Southern Illinois University Press, 1966.

Lewis, R.W.B. *Dante.* London: Weidenfeld & Nicolson, 2001.

Litz, A. Walton, ed. *Modern American Fiction: Essays in Criticism.* Oxford: Oxford University Press, 1983.

Mandal, Somdatta. *Reflections, Refractions, and Rejections: Three American Writers and the Celluloid World.* Leeds: Wisdom House, 2004.

Mangum, Bryant. *A Fortune Yet: Money in the Art of F. Scott Fitzgerald's Short Stories.* New York: Garland, 1991.

McCormick, John. *American Literature 1919–1932: A Comparative History.* London: Routledge & Kegan Paul, 1971.

Meredith, James H. *Understanding the Literature of World War I: A Student Casebook to Issues, Sources, and Historical Documents.* Westport, CT and London: Greenwood Press, 2004.

Moore, Benita A. *Escape into a Labyrinth: F. Scott Fitzgerald, Catholic Sensibility, and the American Way.* New York: Garland, 1988.

Nowlin, Michael. *F. Scott Fitzgerald's Racial Angles and the Business of Literary Greatness.* Basingstoke: Palgrave Macmillan, 2007.

Perosa, Sergio. *The Art of F. Scott Fitzgerald.* Ann Arbor: University of Michigan Press, 1965.

Prigozy, Ruth, ed. *The Cambridge Companion to F. Scott Fitzgerald.* Cambridge and New York: Cambridge University Press, 2002.

Ray, Robert B. *A Certain Tendency of the Hollywood Cinema, 1930–1980.* Princeton, NJ: Princeton University Press, 1985.

Rosten, Leo C. *Hollywood: The Movie Colony, the Movie Makers.* New York: Harcourt Brace, 1941.

Schiff, Jonathan. *Ashes to Ashes: Mourning and Social Difference in F. Scott Fitzgerald's Fiction.* Selinsgrove: Susquehanna University Press and London: Associated University Presses, 2001.

Sklar, Robert. *F. Scott Fitzgerald: The Last Laocoön*. Oxford and New York: Oxford University Press, 1969.

Stanley, Linda C. *The Foreign Critical Reception of F. Scott Fitzgerald: An Analysis and Annotated Bibliography*. Westport, CT: Greenwood Press, 1980.

Stanley, Linda C. *The Foreign Critical Reputation of F. Scott Fitzgerald: 1980–2000*. Westport, CT: Greenwood Press, 2004.

Steiner, George. *Extraterritorial: Papers on Literature and the Language Revolution*. New York: Atheneum, 1971.

——. *In Bluebeard's Castle: Some Notes Towards the Redefinition of Culture*. New Haven and London: Yale University Press, 1971.

——. *On Difficulty and Other Essays*. Oxford: Oxford University Press, 1978.

——. *Real Presences*. University of Chicago Press, 1989.

Stern, Milton R. *The Golden Moment: The Novels of F. Scott Fitzgerald*. Urbana, Chicago and London: University of Illinois Press, 1970.

Tredell, Nicolas, ed. *F. Scott Fitzgerald:* The Great Gatsby. Cambridge: Icon Books, 1997.

Walker, Marshall. *The Literature of the United States of America*. London: Macmillan, 1983.

Way, Brian. *F. Scott Fitzgerald and the Art of Social Fiction*. New York: St. Martin's Press, 1980.

Weintraub, Stanley. *The London Yankees: Portraits of American Writers and Artists in England 1894–1914*. London: W.H. Allen, 1979.

Williams, William Carlos. *In the American Grain*. London: MacGibbon & Kee, 1966.

Wilson, Edmund. *Axel's Castle: A Study in the Imaginative Literature of 1870–1930*. New York: Scribner's, 1969.

Yeats, W.B. *The Collected Poems of W. B. Yeats*. London: Macmillan, 1973.

ESSAYS AND REVIEWS

Antolin, Pascal. 'New York in *The Beautiful and Damned*: "A City of Words" '. *F. Scott Fitzgerald Review* 7 (2009): 113–25.

Barks, Cathy W. 'Collecting Fitzgerald'. *F. Scott Fitzgerald Review* 7 (2009): 182–5.

Berthoff, Warner. ' "The Flight of the Rocket" and "The Last Good Country": Fitzgerald and Hemingway in the 1920s'. *American Literature,* Vol. 9 of *The New Pelican Guide to English Literature*. Ed. Boris Ford. London: Penguin, 1988. 419–34.

Beston, Henry. '*The Beautiful and Damned*'. *F. Scott Fitzgerald in His Own Time: A Miscellany*. Ed. Matthew J. Bruccoli and Jackson R. Bryer. New York: Popular Library, 1971. 336–7.

Bewley, Marius. 'Scott Fitzgerald and the Collapse of the American Dream'. *The Eccentric Design: Form in the Classic American Novel*. London: Chatto & Windus, 1959. 259–87.

Bigsby, C.W.E. 'The Two Identities of F. Scott Fitzgerald'. *The American Novel and the Nineteen Twenties*. Ed. Malcolm Bradbury and David Palmer. London: Edward Arnold, 1971. 129–49.

Blazek, William. 'F. Scott Fitzgerald'. *A Companion to Twentieth-Century United States Fiction*. Ed. David Seed. Chichester, West Sussex: Wiley-Blackwell, 2010. 271–81.

Bogarde, Dirk. 'Paying the Cruel Price of Careless Happiness'. *Daily Telegraph* 8 November 1998: 8.

Brodwin, Stanley. 'F. Scott Fitzgerald and Willa Cather: A New Study'. *F. Scott Fitzgerald in the Twenty-first Century*. Ed. Jackson R. Bryer, Ruth Prigozy and Milton R. Stern. Tuscaloosa and London: University of Alabama Press, 2003. 173–89.

Bryer, Jackson R. 'F. Scott Fitzgerald'. *Sixteen Modern American Authors. Volume 2: A Survey of Research and Criticism since 1972*. Ed. Jackson R. Bryer. Durham and London: Duke University Press, 1989. 301–59.

Chase, Richard. '*The Great Gatsby*'. *Modern American Fiction: Essays in Criticism*. Ed. A. Walton Litz. Oxford: Oxford University Press, 1963. 127–31.

Cochoy, Nathalie. 'New York as a "Passing Stranger" in *The Beautiful and Damned*'. *F. Scott Fitzgerald Review* 4 (2005): 65–83.

Cowley, Malcolm. 'Third Act and Epilogue'. *F. Scott Fitzgerald: The Man and His Work*. Ed. Alfred Kazin. Cleveland and New York: World Publishing Company, 1951. 146–53.

Cowley, Malcolm. 'Fitzgerald: The Romance of Money'. *A Second Flowering: Works and Days of the Lost Generation*. London: André Deutsch, 1973. 19–47.

Curnutt, Kirk. 'F. Scott Fitzgerald, Age Consciousness, and the Rise of American Youth Culture'. *The Cambridge Companion to F. Scott Fitzgerald*. Ed. Ruth Prigozy. Cambridge: Cambridge University Press, 2002. 28–47.

DeVinney, Helen. 'Evidence of a Previously Unknown Fitzgerald Nurse: Correspondence from F. Scott Fitzgerald to Pauline Brownell'. *F. Scott Fitzgerald Review* 4 (2005): 190–6.

Donaldson, Scott. 'A Fitzgerald Autobiography'. *F. Scott Fitzgerald Review* 1 (2002): 143–57.

Friedman, Melvin J. '"The Swimmers": Paris and Virginia Reconciled'. *The Short Stories of F. Scott Fitzgerald: New Approaches in Criticism*. Ed. Jackson R. Bryer. Madison: University of Wisconsin Press, 1982. 251–60.

Frye, Steven. 'Fitzgerald's Catholicism Revisited: The Eucharistic Element in *The Beautiful and Damned*'. *F. Scott Fitzgerald: New Perspectives*. Ed. Jackson R. Bryer, Alan Margolies and Ruth Prigozy. Athens and London: University of Georgia Press, 2000. 63–77.

Giles, Paul. 'Conformity and Parody: Scott Fitzgerald and *The Great Gatsby*'. *American Catholic Arts and Fictions: Culture, Ideology, Aesthetics*. Cambridge and New York: Cambridge University Press, 1992. 169–87.

Glenday, Michael K. 'American Riviera: Style and Expatriation in *Tender is the Night*'. *Twenty-First-Century Readings of* Tender is the Night. Ed. William Blazek and Laura Rattray. Liverpool: Liverpool University Press, 2007. 143–59.

Hattersley, Roy. 'This is the myth that Gatsby built'. *Guardian* 15 May 2000: 14.

Häusermann, H.W. 'Fitzgerald's Religious Sense: Note and Query'. *Modern Fiction Studies* 2 (1956): 81–2.

Kahn, Sy. '*This Side of Paradise*: The Pageantry of Disillusion'. *F. Scott Fitzgerald: A Collection of Criticism*. New York and London: McGraw-Hill, 1973.

Kennedy, J. Gerald. 'Figuring the Damage: Fitzgerald's "Babylon Revisited" and Hemingway's "The Snows of Kilimanjaro"'. *French Connections: Hemingway and Fitzgerald Abroad*. Ed. J. Gerald Kennedy and Jackson R. Bryer. New York: St. Martin's Press, 1999. 317–43.

Kruse, Horst. '*The Great Gatsby*: A View from Kant's Window – Transatlantic Crosscurrents'. *F. Scott Fitzgerald Review* 2 (2003): 72–84.

——. 'The Real Jay Gatsby: Max von Gerlach, F. Scott Fitzgerald, and the Compositional History of *The Great Gatsby*'. *F. Scott Fitzgerald Review* 1 (2002): 45–83.

Kunce, Catherine and Paul M. Levitt. 'The Structure of *Gatsby*: A Vaudeville Show, Featuring Buffalo Bill and a Cast of Dozens'. *F. Scott Fitzgerald Review* 4 (2005): 101–28.

Lehan, Richard. 'The Romantic Self and the Uses of Place in the Stories of F. Scott Fitzgerald'. *The Short Stories of F. Scott Fitzgerald: New Approaches in Criticism*. Ed. Jackson R. Bryer. Madison: University of Wisconsin Press, 1982. 3–21.

Mangum, Bryant. 'The Short Stories of F. Scott Fitzgerald'. *The Cambridge Companion to F. Scott Fitzgerald*. Ed. Ruth Prigozy. Cambridge and New York: Cambridge University Press, 2002. 57–78.

Margolies, Alan. 'Fitzgerald and Hollywood'. *The Cambridge Companion to F. Scott Fitzgerald*. Ed. Ruth Prigozy. Cambridge and New York: Cambridge University Press, 2002. 189–208.

Massa, Ann. 'F. Scott Fitzgerald'. *American Literature in Context IV: 1900–1930*. London and New York: Methuen, 1982. 144–54.

McGowan, Philip. 'Reading Fitzgerald Reading Keats'. *Twenty-First-Century Readings of* Tender is the Night. Ed. William Blazek and Laura Rattray. Liverpool: Liverpool University Press, 2007. 204–20.

McMullen, Bonnie Shannon. '"Can't We Put it in Writing?": Some Short Precursors to *Tender is the Night*'. *Twenty-First-Century Readings of* Tender is the Night. Ed. William Blazek and Laura Rattray. Liverpool: Liverpool University Press, 2007. 16–33.

Miller, Linda Patterson. 'Fanny and Honoria Remember: September 1994'. *F. Scott Fitzgerald Review* 8 (2010): 3–22.

Mizener, Arthur. 'The Maturity of F. Scott Fitzgerald'. *Modern American Fiction: Essays in Criticism*. Ed. A. Walton Litz. London, Oxford and New York: Oxford University Press, 1963. 113–26.

——. 'The Poet of Borrowed Time'. *F. Scott Fitzgerald: The Man and His Work*. Ed. Alfred Kazin. Cleveland and New York: World Publishing Company, 1951. 23–45.

Monk, Donald. 'Fitzgerald: The Tissue of Style'. *Journal of American Studies* 17.1 (April 1983): 77–94.

Moore, Harry T. 'Preface' to *Save Me the Waltz* by Zelda Fitzgerald. London: Cape, 1969. vii–xi.

Nowlin, Michael. '"A Gentile's Tragedy": Bearing the Word about Hollywood in *The Love of the Last Tycoon*'. *F. Scott Fitzgerald Review* 2 (2003): 156–85.

Piper, Henry Dan. 'Social Criticism in the American Novel of the Nineteen Twenties'. *The American Novel and the Nineteen Twenties*. Ed. Malcolm Bradbury and David Palmer. London: Edward Arnold, 1971. 59–84.

Prigozy, Ruth. 'Fitzgerald's Short Stories and the Depression: An Artistic Crisis'. *F. Scott Fitzgerald in the Twenty-first Century*. Ed. Jackson R. Bryer, Ruth Prigozy and Milton R. Stern. Tuscaloosa and London: University of Alabama Press, 2003. 111–26.

Rascoe, Burton. '*This Side of Paradise*: A Youth in the Saddle'. *F. Scott Fitzgerald in His Own Time: A Miscellany*. Ed. Matthew J. Bruccoli and Jackson R. Bryer. New York: Popular Library, 1971. 305–6.

Raubicheck, Walter. 'The Catholic Romanticism of *This Side of Paradise*'. *F. Scott Fitzgerald in the Twenty-first Century*. Ed. Jackson R. Bryer, Ruth Prigozy and Milton R. Stern. Tuscaloosa and London: University of Alabama Press, 2003. 54–65.

Ring, Frances Kroll. 'Dinner with Jeremy, etc.' *F. Scott Fitzgerald Review 3* (2004): 3–14.

Rosenfeld, Paul. 'Fitzgerald before *The Great Gatsby*'. *F. Scott Fitzgerald: The Man and His Work*. Ed. Alfred Kazin. Cleveland and New York: World Publishing Company, 1951. 72–7.

Seed, David. 'Party-going: The Jazz Age Novels of Evelyn Waugh, Wyndham Lewis, F. Scott Fitzgerald and Carl Van Vechten'. *Forked Tongues?: Comparing Twentieth-Century British and American Literature*. Ed. Ann Massa and Alistair Stead. London and New York: Longman, 1994. 117–34.

Seldes, Gilbert. '*The Beautiful and Damned*: This Side of Innocence'. *F. Scott Fitzgerald in His Own Time: A Miscellany*. Ed. Matthew J. Bruccoli and Jackson R. Bryer. New York: Popular Library, 1971. 329–31.

Shain, Charles E. 'F. Scott Fitzgerald'. *Seven Modern American Novelists: An Introduction*. Ed. William Van O'Connor. Minneapolis: University of Minnesota Press and London: Oxford University Press, 1964. 81–117.

Tanner, Stephen L. 'The Devil and F. Scott Fitzgerald'. *F. Scott Fitzgerald in the Twenty-first Century: Centennial Essays*. Ed. Ruth Prigozy and Milton R. Stern. Tuscaloosa and London: University of Alabama Press, 2003. 66–78.

Tavernier-Courbin, Jacqueline. 'The Influence of France on Nicole Diver's Recovery in *Tender is the Night*'. *French Connections: Hemingway and Fitzgerald Abroad*. Ed. J. Gerald Kennedy and Jackson R. Bryer. New York: St. Martin's Press, 1998. 215–32.

Trilling, Lionel. 'F. Scott Fitzgerald'. *The Liberal Imagination: Essays on Literature and Society*. London: Mercury Books, 1961. 243–54.

Troy, William. 'Scott Fitzgerald – the Authority of Failure'. *F. Scott Fitzgerald: The Man and His Work*. Ed. Alfred Kazin. Cleveland and New York: World Publishing Company, 1951. 187–93.

Wescott, Glenway. 'The Moral of F. Scott Fitzgerald'. *F. Scott Fitzgerald: The Man and His Work*. Ed. Alfred Kazin. Cleveland and New York: World Publishing Company, 1951. 116–129.

West, James L.W. III. 'The Question of Vocation in *This Side of Paradise and The Beautiful and the Damned*'. *The Cambridge Companion to F. Scott Fitzgerald*. Ed. Ruth Prigozy. Cambridge and New York: Cambridge University Press, 2002. 48-56.

West, James L.W. III. 'Tender is the Night, "Jazzmania", and the Ellingson Matricide'. *Twenty-First-Century Readings of* Tender is the Night. Ed. William Blazek and Laura Rattray. Liverpool: Liverpool University Press, 2007. 34–49.

Index